W9-BLD-304

Where the Wind Blows

Where the Wind Blows

A Prairie Hearts Novel

Caroline Fyffe

Montlake
Romance

The characters and events portrayed in this book are fictitious. Any similarity to real persons, living or dead, is coincidental and not intended by the author.

First edition © 2009

Montlake edition © 2012

All rights reserved.

Printed in the United States of America.

No part of this book may be reproduced, or stored in a retrieval system, or transmitted in any form or by any means, electronic, mechanical, photo-copying, recording, or otherwise, without express written permission of the publisher.

Published by Montlake Romance
P.O. Box 400818
Las Vegas, NV 89140

ISBN-13: 9781612187129
ISBN-10: 1612187129

Dedicated to my Mother and Father—with love

CHAPTER ONE

Wyoming Territory, 1878

Chase Logan removed his hat and ran his hand through his hair, feeling it fall against the collar of his leather coat. How the heck was he going to break the news to Mrs. Strong? What if she swooned, or worse yet, started crying? He had little experience with women. Decent ones, anyway. Resting his arms on the smooth leather saddle horn, he gazed at his destination in the valley below. If not for the smoke curling from its chimney, he might think the cabin abandoned.

Agreeing to this was the stupidest thing he'd ever done. How on earth had he been talked into it? At the time, delivering the news to Nathan's wife hadn't seemed like much. He was heading to Cheyenne anyway. The cabin wasn't far out of the way. But now that he was here...

No use stalling, he thought, shaking his head. Best to just get it over with and be on his way.

He nudged his mount down the slope of the hill as the sun disappeared behind a craggy black mountain. Streams of golden light reflected off the open expanse of low-hanging clouds, painting the gray sky with swirls of pink and yellow, bringing to mind a freshly spun spiderweb. Chase drew his heavy collar around his neck and hunched his shoulders against the blustery October weather. It would be a cold one tonight.

Chase lingered at his mount's side longer than needed. Then he walked through the barnyard to the door and knocked. The low, metallic click of a gun being cocked resounded through the door.

"Who's there?" a female voice asked uneasily.

"My name's Chase Logan. I have a message for Mrs. Strong. Would that be you?"

"Yes," she answered after three beats of his heart.

Anxiety clenched Chase's chest. He wasn't sure if it was the woman's he was feeling, or his own.

"Say what you came to say, mister."

"I rode with Nathan at the Bar T," he said, still looking at the weathered boards in front of his face. "It'd be easier if we could speak without this door between us." He waited as the cold nipped at his ears.

She didn't respond. Chase glanced around the deserted yard, giving her as much time as she needed. Moments crept by. Finally, the door was unbarred and creaked open slowly, just wide enough to accommodate the tip of a shotgun barrel.

"Think you could put the gun down, ma'am, and open the door? I don't mean any harm. I'm a friend of your husband."

It felt like ages before the gun barrel gradually disappeared. The door protested loudly as it swung open to reveal a room that held several wooden chairs and a table. A rocker rested on a faded rag rug in front of the fireplace, and a cupboard sat forlornly next to the wall. Wood smoke and the wonderful aroma of freshly baked bread wafted on the air, making the room feel warm and homey. His stomach rumbled.

"I suppose it's all right if you come in, being you're an acquaintance of Nathan's," Mrs. Strong said as she stepped out from behind the door.

Chase drew his gaze from the potbelly stove, where something was simmering, to the girl—no, woman—who stood before him. She was young, as though she should still be home with her ma and pa, tending to younger sisters and brothers. Not here alone, being a wife to Nathan, a man surely over twice her age. And pretty too, with hair as pale as corn silk falling thick down her back. Her eyes, bluer than any Wyoming sky, seemed to already know his news; they were fathomless and sad.

"You're Nathan's wife?" he asked, arching an eyebrow.

"That's who you asked for, isn't it?" A small smile pulled at the corners of her mouth.

"Yes, ma'am. Just expected someone a bit more…mature."

Mrs. Strong's chin edged up. "Have a seat at the table, Mr. Logan. A cup of coffee will warm your insides."

Chase shifted his weight from one leg to the other. Turning his hat in his hands, it slipped from his fingers and dropped to the floor. He quickly picked it up. Sweat beaded on his brow despite the coolness of the evening.

The woman poured two cups of coffee from a chipped enamel coffeepot. Her hands trembled lightly. "You have a message from Nathan?"

Chase swallowed. Best just to spit it out fast. "Yes, ma'am. I'm sorry to be the one to tell you, surely I am, but…" He swallowed a second time. "Nathan is dead."

Mrs. Strong stood across from him, motionless but for the rise and fall of her chest. Chase wished he were anywhere but here.

"How?" she whispered.

"Well…" Chase mumbled, assessing the situation. Her serious eyes were searching his. Although he believed he was a pretty honest fellow, at least compared to the next, there was no way he was going to tell her Nathan was killed in a barroom brawl, shot over a game of poker with a saloon girl sitting on his lap. No, he just couldn't do it.

Stalling for time, he took the forgotten cups from her hands and set them on the table. He pulled out a chair and gestured for her to sit. He did the same, his mind galloping all the while.

"What happened was, uh…Nathan had the night watch and rode out around ten. It was stormy. Cattle were edgy. There was thunder and lightnin' and…uh…well, ma'am, no one really knows exactly what happened, but he was dead when we found him in the morning."

He jerked his gaze up to see what effect his story was having. He figured that if you had to die, that was a pretty honest way to go.

She sat motionless. Her knuckles whitened as she gripped the edge of the stained wood tabletop. Slowly, she lifted her gaze to his.

"Thank you for your trouble, Mr. Logan. Riding all this way to bring me this news. I'm sure it wasn't an easy task." She paused a moment. "I have beans simmering on the stove and a loaf of fresh bread. It's not fancy, but it'll fill your belly."

Chase was puzzled. He'd expected tears, or even fainting. Not this cool, almost indifferent calmness. He didn't know what to make of it.

"You don't have to go to the trouble of feeding me. There's plenty more on your mind about now." But his stomach rioted at his words. Nothing would be better than a thick slice of fresh bread. He envisioned a huge bowl of beans, steaming and hot. The image persisted, making his mouth water.

"Nonsense. You must be famished." She rose and took a bowl from the sideboard. Easing the hot lid from the cast-iron pot, she set it aside and then scooped heaping ladlefuls of beans into the bowl.

She was slender and straight, without many curves. Nothing like the saloon girls he was used to. They were well rounded everywhere a man could appreciate. By contrast, Mrs. Strong reminded him of a finely bred filly, young and fresh, willowy.

As she set the bowl before him, Chase cleared his throat, abashed by his wandering thoughts. She'd just lost her husband, for God's sake, and here he was comparing her with sporting women. "Thank you."

"I'm sorry I don't have any butter for the bread, but at least it's warm." She put the lid back on the pot and folded the dish towel. "I do have a bit of brown sugar, though, if you'd like some on your beans. Gives 'em a real fine flavor, if you have a sweet tooth."

"No sugar, thanks," he said, unable to bring himself to use any of her precious supply. He'd had some once when he was a boy. Couldn't quite remember where, but the taste still lingered in his memory.

He shoveled an enormous spoonful of beans into his mouth, savoring their tangy flavor. "Ma'am, these are the finest—" Looking up, he stopped midsentence. Mrs. Strong was hunched over the dry sink. Her shoulders shook, but she wasn't making a sound.

Swallowing hastily, he wiped his hands on his pants and stood, knocking the chair over with a bang. In two strides he was at her back.

CHAPTER TWO

Chase raised his hands to put them on Mrs. Strong's shoulders, then dropped them back down to his sides.

"Don't cry, ma'am." The downy hair at the nape of her neck appeared like that of a tiny duckling, but looked even softer. "Things will work out." Was it proper for him to comfort her like this? "What's your given name?" he asked gently.

"Jessie. My name's Jessie," she murmured, her tears changing her voice to a husky softness.

"Ah, Jessie. That's real pretty. Would you mind if I called you that?"

She shook her head.

A warm feeling took him by surprise, making him yearn for things he'd never had. Imagined feelings whispered through his mind, making his heart tighten up. "Come over here and sit by the fire. I've dealt you a healthy shock."

He rested a palm on the small of her back and guided her over to a chair by the hearth and sat her down.

After adding a log to the fire, Chase went to the sideboard. Women liked tea when they were feeling poorly. At least, that's what he'd heard. He rummaged around until he came upon some sassafras leaves. He dipped the small black kettle into the water bucket and set it on the stove to boil. He waited.

His bowl of beans was calling to him from his place at the table, but he doubted it would be mannerly to sit down and finish his meal. Instead, he helped himself to another cup of coffee and then leaned against the cupboard and contemplated the kettle.

She was a proud little thing, this Jessie, trying to keep her grief to herself. How had she managed out here all alone on her own? And now with winter approaching, what would she do without Nathan?

He prepared a cup of tea, carried it over to where she sat, and lightly touched her shoulder. When she didn't respond right away, he cleared his throat softly. "Jessie, try some of this."

Her startled gaze fixed on him. "Thank you."

She took the cup, but it rattled so violently, he feared it would end up in her lap. He reached out, covering her hands with his own, and steadied it until she had it under control. Her cheeks, now the color of summer roses, vied for his attention.

"I'll be fine now that I'm over the first shock," she said, avoiding his gaze. She blew on the hot tea before taking a sip.

"Do you have a friend or family member around I could notify for you?"

"Please don't worry, Mr. Logan. I can take care of myself. The only difference is, I won't be waiting for Nathan now. He'll never be coming home again."

Her words struck a chord. Whether it was the way she said it or the words themselves, he didn't know. But he knew exactly what she was feeling inside. Alone, small, and unworthy of someone's concern. Well, he wasn't going to leave her alone tonight; that was the final thing he could do for Nathan.

"Would you mind if I bedded down in your barn for the night? My horse is worn out, and it's getting late. I could just throw my bedroll on some straw and catch a good night's sleep." He gave his most hopeful look.

She smiled at that, bringing light back into her eyes. "I'm afraid the barn won't be much protection for you. It was Nathan's intention to fix the roof as soon as he came home this fall. But you're welcome to stay, if you'd like."

Surprised at the feeling her response brought, he smiled back. "Cody will appreciate some time in a stall, dry or not. I know I will too." With that, he glanced over at the table. And his bowl of beans.

"Just be careful. The other day I had the keenest feeling of being watched. Most likely it was just a coyote. Nathan said wolves don't come this close to settlements."

Jessie stood and crossed to the table. She lifted his bowl and scraped his beans back into the pot. Chase swallowed once. Twice.

Her lips curved up slightly. "Just heating them up a bit. Can't let you stay out in the barn without something hot in your belly to keep you from freezing, can I?"

The warm feeling was back, tightening his chest and warming his cheeks. He tried to hold on to it. Savor it. "No, ma'am, I don't suppose you could."

With the cowhand bedded down in the barn, Jessie struggled with the reality of his news. Panic gripped her, turning her insides cold. Nathan was dead. He wasn't coming home ever again. It was so sad, him dying like that. It must have been a horribly painful death. She didn't even get the chance to tell him good-bye on his last trip. He'd been a good man, taking her in.

Did this mean she'd lose Sarah too?

She reached for the tiny woolen bootie lying on the mantel as unshed tears stung the backs of her eyes. The stitching was uneven, the knots loose. But she'd knitted it with love and had dressed Sarah with it and its mate every day. She held it to her nose, breathing deeply.

Nothing. Not even a hint of Sarah's precious scent remained. With it pressed to her cheek, she rocked back and forth, picturing her face. Sarah had been only a toddler the last time she'd seen her at the orphanage. By now, she must be around four years old.

Jessie's heart pounded in her ears as she paced the floor, searching for answers. How could this happen now? Just when things were finally working out.

Wrapping her arms tightly around her middle, she doubled over in anguish. The tears finally came, running down her face like a stream after the first spring thaw. Angrily, she brushed them away.

She took a deep, calming breath and slowly sank into her rocker. Her mind drifted to the day her mother had walked away without explanation, leaving her frightened and alone on the doorstep of the orphanage where she'd spent year after year waiting for her return. Ten years was a very long time. Hunger and fear made very poor playmates.

"You said you'd come back for me," she whispered into the silence of the room. "Mothers aren't supposed to leave their little girls behind." A familiar knot lodged painfully in her chest.

Still, all was not hopeless. She released her breath with a shudder, unaware that she'd been holding it. Nathan was gone, yes, but she was alive and strong, and, God willing, she would work through this. She couldn't see how yet, but there had to be a way.

Chase groomed his horse in silence. The gelding stood quietly, his head hung low, his breathing even, as Chase went over him with a soft-bristled brush. "It'll be a cold day in July before I volunteer for the likes of that again, Cody." Unimpressed, the big bay stomped his hind hoof, as if to say, "Keep brushing."

"Sure is a sweet thing, though. Real pretty, too." Leaning across Cody's warm flank, Chase recalled the way she'd looked reaching up to get the bowl off the shelf. He shook his head and tucked the brush away in his saddlebag. He laid out his bedroll on some hay.

Relaxed on his back, he listened to Cody's melodious munching as the horse ate his supper. The rustling of something small burrowing in a corner drew his attention, but his mind kept circling back to Nathan's widow.

How'd she come to be married to Nathan in the first place? The old weather-beaten cowhand and the young fresh-faced girl... It was an odd combination.

But then, lots of people got thrown together in strange ways. Besides, it wasn't his place to worry about her.

He had to hit the trail. That job up in Miles City wouldn't wait forever. The Rocking Crown's sizable herd needed to be driven to Kansas City for shipping. After that, he'd head south for the winter months, then hire back on with the Double Sixes Ranch for the spring roundup. It was the same routine he'd been following for the past three years. The same routine that had been driving him hard ever since Molly...

Drawing a hand slowly across his face, Chase stared into the dimness of the barn's interior. How long had it been since he'd thought of her? A month? Maybe longer? Used to be that an hour didn't go by without the burning sting of guilt and anger riding him hard. Now it was more like a dull ache lodged somewhere in the chasm where his heart used to be.

Didn't matter that he'd been gone the day the bank was robbed and she'd disappeared. That fact didn't lessen his penitence in the least. He should have been there for her! She would have been there for him, no matter what. Would he run into her someday walking down a boardwalk? Would she fall into his arms, and would they marry? Or was she lying dead in a ravine, her sun-bleached bones as white as clay, the only testament to her life? Would he ever really know? After years of fruitless searching, he'd finally given up.

Chase shoved away the hurtful memory. Stretching his legs, he locked his fingers behind his head. He was a loner. Nothin' wrong with that. No one to answer to and no one to let down. Free as a clear mountain stream. He rolled over and closed his eyes.

CHAPTER THREE

$\mathcal{J}$essie, wrapped in her thick quilt, stepped out into the chilly night air. She couldn't sleep. The cabin walls were closing in around her, making it impossible for her to stay in bed a moment longer. Sighing, she plunked herself on the porch step and gazed wistfully into the darkness.

Poor Nathan. He'd always tried to do his best. He'd been kind to her and a good provider. Perhaps affectionate gratitude wasn't the kind of feeling a wife should have for her husband, but theirs had been an unusual marriage.

"Mind if I join you?"

Jessie startled at the sound of the deep voice. "Not at all," she finally replied, her heart pounding at Mr. Logan's sudden appearance.

His large form emerged out of the darkness. To Jessie's relief, he sat on the corner of the wood bin, some ten feet away. Silence encompassed the two.

"Couldn't sleep," he said finally. "Mouse kept waking me." His boots scraped across the ground as he stretched out his legs.

Jessie was grateful her puffy face was hidden by the darkness. "I needed a little air too." She drew her gaze away from the bulky outline of his coat and looked up into the velvety night sky. A star streaked brightly across the starry canopy spanning the horizon, sparkling as it went. She sucked in a breath. "Did you see that?"

"Yes."

"It was so beautiful."

"Um."

Jessie's mood lightened. It'd been so long since she'd had any company at all, even the unsettling presence of Mr. Logan was welcome. "Sometimes I pretend all those stars are angels watching over me. Do you suppose there're that many in heaven?"

A moment passed. He shifted his weight. She pictured his warm brown eyes looking her way.

"Don't rightly know, Mrs. Strong," he finally replied. "Don't believe too much in heaven or hell."

His melancholy tone gave her pause. "You don't believe in God?"

"Not since I was a little boy."

A crisp breeze brushed across her face and she huddled deeper into the quilt. "What do you think happens then...when we die?" She'd always believed in God, no matter how bad things got.

"You die, that's all. Dust to dust, as they say."

Jessie didn't respond. Clearly this stranger had heartaches of his own. He was tough and callused from life. A nomad on all accounts.

Mr. Logan stood. "You best get some rest."

He was so tall that from where Jessie sat, he looked as if he could pluck one of those stars right out of the sky.

"You're right," she said softly. "Tomorrow's sorrows will be here soon enough. Good night, Mr. Logan."

A knock on the door startled Jessie out of her sleep. The tapping came again, this time followed by Mr. Logan's deep voice.

"Mrs. Strong, you awake?"

In a sleepy panic, Jessie rolled from her fluffy mattress and grabbed the dress she'd worn the day before. She pulled it over her head and then fumbled with the long row of tiny buttons running from her chin to her waist. Realization of who was out there, and why, dawned on her, and a wave of sorrow filled her.

She ran her fingers once through her hair, trying to tame its wildness. After splashing water on her face, she glanced at her reflection in the mirror. Puffy, red eyes gazed back.

Mr. Logan's footsteps moved away as she hurried to open the door. He turned and faced her.

"Sorry, I should've realized you might want to sleep in after the night you had," he apologized.

"Have to face the day sooner or later." Jessie took a good long look. Just the sight of him standing in the morning light seemed to put things to right. A soft coating of trail dust covered his broadcloth shirt, but his face and hair were damp from a morning washing. Warm brown eyes, the ones she'd imagined last night, made her insides feel feathery.

"I'm going to pass through town on my way north." His hat dangled from his fingertips. "I can deliver a message if you'd like. Anyone you want me to notify?"

"No one."

"Don't worry, Jessie. Things have a way of working out." He clutched his hat to his chest and looked hesitant. "If I get a fire going, any chance you could make us a pot of coffee?"

Jessie held his gaze for a span of one heartbeat, and then turned and stepped toward the stove, leaving the door open for him to enter.

With steaming cups of coffee and a plate full of hot biscuits, they sat without talking. A light sprinkling of raindrops on the old shingle roof mingled with the crackling of the fire. The smell of wet earth drifted inside.

If she didn't want to talk, that was fine with him. The men he rode with were a quiet lot. He was accustomed to the silence. Still, her nearness was slightly unsettling in a pleasant sort of way. As much as he'd wanted a cup of coffee before riding out, maybe it hadn't been a good idea to come back to the cabin.

She wiped her mouth with her napkin and set it back in her lap. "Where are you from, Mr. Logan?"

"Nowhere in particular. Never knew my parents, or where I was born. Guess you'd call me a drifter of sorts."

She was looking at him in expectation. She tipped her head thoughtfully. Why he felt compelled to tell her more was a mystery. "I tried once. Settling down, that is. I saved until I had enough to buy a small spread. Just large enough to run fifty head or so."

The memory of Molly and the plans they'd made together hurt. He looked away. "Ranching lost its appeal. So I started riding for other outfits. I still own it, but it's run-down and vacant. Sure to be overgrown in thistle by now."

"I see."

She sipped her coffee. Chase thought she was going to go on. He hoped she would. He liked the sound of her voice, soft and feminine.

When he was ten, there'd been a schoolteacher who'd wanted him to come to her class. She'd hunt him down each day and try to coax him into the schoolhouse. He never went. All the same, Jessie's voice reminded him of that same woman who'd showed him concern as a boy.

"And you?" he asked. Her eyes were remarkable. Their particular shade of blue was one he'd never before seen. Amazingly, they sparkled in the morning light. "Are you from around here?"

"New Mexico Territory. Like you, I too was an orphan. I grew up in an orphanage there." Pausing, she fiddled with the biscuit on her plate as if gathering her courage. "I've a delivery coming soon. Probably next week. It's very important." Her brows knit together thoughtfully. "Nathan's death could change everything in my life.

And not the way you think." She searched his face unabashedly as if she'd find her answers hidden there.

From her tone it was obvious this was a very important matter. He didn't quite know how to respond. "Well…" he began.

She watched him intently as if waiting for his answer to materialize out of thin air.

He straightened. "Some folks look at their common sense through a magnifying glass, second-guessing themselves all the time. Now, to me, you seem like the clever sort of woman who could figure out most anything."

"Not this," she confessed. "When we married, Nathan promised me we could adopt Sarah, a little girl who lived in the orphanage with me. Before his last trip, he finally gave his permission to write asking for her. I did right away. They are bringing her out now."

He nodded, listening. He took another biscuit, broke it open, and watched steam curl to the ceiling like morning mist off a watering hole.

"Surely they won't let me keep her if Nathan is dead…Will they?"

"Next week, you say?"

"I'm not exactly sure. I don't know the day they left."

"Truthfully, Jessie, I don't know about adoption and the rules of such, but I truly believe honesty is always the best policy. Just tell them what happened, and most likely everything will be fine." That was hogwash, but what else could he say?

She considered him silently for a moment, as if mulling over what he'd just said, and then glanced at his cup. "More coffee?"

"No, thank you. I'd best be going."

Chase took the final bite of his biscuit. He dusted the crumbs from his fingers over his plate and placed his napkin on the blue-and-white-checkered tablecloth. Standing, he reached for his hat. "Much obliged for the meal."

The rumbling of wagon wheels could be heard outside. Jessie sprang to her feet. Chase turned. His gun hand eased down into position.

"Hello in the cabin," called a voice from outside. "Anyone home?"

"Mr. Hobbs!" Without hesitation Jessie rushed to the door and flung it open.

Out in the wagon, huddled in blankets, sat three forms, two large and one very small—all drenched to the skin from the morning rain.

"It's them!" she cried breathlessly. "Oh, my stars—they're early."

"Your delivery?"

"Y-yes."

As she stepped onto the porch, she glanced over her shoulder to Chase, who was close behind. He reached out and gently tipped her chin up so he could look into her eyes.

"Everything will work out. Don't put your umbrella up 'fore it rains." She gave him a tremulous smile, appreciative of his confidence, before hurrying out to the yard.

The occupants of the wagon looked around. She recognized Mr. Hobbs. The little bundle in the middle was Sarah. A young man of about thirteen or so was unfamiliar.

The lad hopped to the ground and began unloading baggage. Jessie hurried out to the wagon and lifted Sarah from the seat, hugging her to her breast. The child pushed her fists against Jessie's shoulders, craning her neck to find Mr. Hobbs. Her face turned cherry red as she started to cry.

"She's not used to you no more, Jess," Mr. Hobbs said apologetically. He gently lifted the child from her arms.

"But—but—" Jessie stammered, hurt. "I'm not a stranger."

"Of course not. Just give her a little time to get reacquainted."

Jessie was crushed. Sarah was only a toddler when Jessie left the orphanage, but she hadn't thought the child would be so young that she wouldn't remember her at all. The little girl had been the center of her every thought. She tried not to show her disappointment as Mr. Hobbs beamed with pleasure at their reunion.

"Jessie, it's wonderful to see you. You've grown into a beautiful woman, but then, I always knew you would." He gave her an affectionate squeeze. "This is Gabe Garrison. He's only been with us a short time, but since he's older, I asked him to make the trip with me. An extra pair of hands is always useful on the trail."

The young man turned a weary face to Jessie. He was a handsome boy with thick chestnut hair, a few strands of which fell down into clear green eyes. With an unsure smile, he brushed at his travel-stained clothes and stuck out his hand. "Howdy, ma'am."

"Welcome," Jessie replied, smiling.

Chase watched curiously from the porch. The older man was obviously very fond of Jessie, like an uncle or father, he supposed. As if feeling the scrutiny from Chase, the man glanced up at the porch and approached him eagerly with an outstretched hand. He grasped Chase's hand and shook it.

"Nathan Strong, good to finally meet you. I'm glad to see Jessie has married such a strapping young man." He smiled and winked at Jessie. "Handsome, too. Does this old man's heart good to know you and Sarah finally have a home of your own."

CHAPTER FOUR

$\mathcal{C}$hase glanced at Jessie and felt his face go hot. Jessie hesitated, and then stepped up to his side and threaded her arm through his. She smiled up at him lightly, but her eyes were pleading.

His eyes narrowed as he turned back to Mr. Hobbs. A moment passed in complete silence. Mr. Hobbs tilted his head questioningly.

"Pleased to make your acquaintance. Any friend of Jessie's is...a friend of mine."

As the group shuffled into the cabin noisily and settled in, Chase brooded in the doorway. One minute he was Chase Logan, getting ready to ride out. The next he was Nathan Strong—with a wife and family.

"I'm going," he said suddenly. "Don't wait supper." Turning, he seized his coat from the wall peg and stomped out the door.

He crossed the yard quickly, ignoring the puddles of mud he was traipsing through. Why the heck had he volunteered to ride out here in the first place? That was mistake number one. His second was coming in this morning for a cup of coffee. Couldn't a man have a little hot sustenance to make it through the day? At the bar in town is where he ought to be right now, by golly. At the bar!

Halfway to the barn Jessie caught him.

"Mr. Logan, wait." She threw herself against him in an effort to halt his progress. She grabbed his arm and pulled, setting her heels in the mud. Chase strode on as if she were no bigger than a speck in a sandstorm.

"I'm sorry, honestly," she panted, struggling to keep hold of him. "I never meant for that to happen. It just did, and then I didn't know what to do."

Her hair tumbled across her face, and her rain-dampened skirt caught between her legs, almost tripping her. Chase stopped abruptly, sending her twirling like a top. He snatched her by the back of the collar moments before she landed on the ground. They were both spattered in mud and soaked with rain. If he weren't so darn mad, he'd have laughed.

"What I did was outlandish. I know. But I had to. The thought of Sarah going back to that awful, cold, scary place is…unthinkable. But if you could stay for one day, just one more, it would mean the world to me. And her. *And* Nathan." Her hands gripped his shirt frantically.

Chase looked away, avoiding her pleading face. Still, in her disheveled, rain-soaked dress, she was beautiful. He'd already helped her get her precious delivery, right? Now he'd just be on his way. No sense getting tangled any tighter in this sticky web.

He glanced down into her face, where a mixture of emotions clouded her eyes. He brushed a strand of hair from her rain-dampened cheek. "Good luck, Jessie," he said softly, his anger put on hold for the moment. He turned to leave.

"Don't go. You're him. My guardian angel. The one my mother told me about before she left me. I realized it back there on the porch. I need your help."

That was a low blow Chase hadn't been expecting. Guardian angel! Why didn't she go and ask Molly about that? Some protection he'd been for her.

Jessie's hands fell to her sides when he pulled out of her grasp and walked away. Inside the barn he quickly saddled Cody, mounted up, and ducked through the door, finding her still standing where he'd left her. He loped up the hill and didn't look back.

Jessie made her way back to the cabin. Inside, she tried to smile at Sarah's worried expression but felt the corners of her lips wobble uncontrollably. So much was at stake. "Oh, that silly Nathan going hunting now. Whatever will I do with him?" She winked at Sarah and gestured to the soiled dress that clung to her legs like a sack. "I'll only take a quick moment to change and then we'll get you all settled in." Before anyone could respond, Jessie hurried into her bedroom and closed the door, slumping against it.

She squeezed her eyes shut, forcing back the tears threatening to spill. She would drive that man from her mind. She had to. Sarah was scared, tired, and hungry. She needed some love and attention.

As she unbuttoned her wet dress, Mrs. Hobbs's words echoed from her past. *"You're plain, Jessie McGentry. Can't make a silk purse out of a sow's ear. But take heart, lots of men value a strong back over beauty—regardless of scars."* For the thousandth time in her life Jessie wondered how sweet, caring Mr. Hobbs had been yoked to such a malicious woman.

As was her habit, Jessie reached around and touched one of the red welts that covered the majority of her back. Physically, she was healed, and they never hurt. As long as she didn't look at them, she could forget about their grotesque presence. But like it or not, they *were* there, with their semblance of disgrace tenaciously trying to undermine her confidence.

She tossed the dress into the corner and donned her other. Her scars had given her a strength she hadn't had before, she reminded herself. *Everything* happened for a reason. Even horrible things. One just had to look hard enough to see what that reason was.

Jessie splashed her face with water and combed her hair, then braided it down her back. She squared her shoulders and forced a smile to her lips. She was strong—and alive. She'd get through this predicament and keep Sarah too. But the deception was hard.

It went against everything she believed in. And especially since it was dear Mr. Hobbs she was lying to. She must get him on his way back to the orphanage as soon as possible, before he had a chance to discover the truth about Nathan.

Reentering the room, Jessie looked about. Gabe sat in front of the fire with Sarah perched on his knee. When the child saw Jessie, however, her smile disappeared.

Jessie's soft voice grew gentler still. "Sarah, honey, don't you remember me?"

Sarah stared, motionless. It was as if she hadn't heard a word. Jessie turned questioningly to Mr. Hobbs.

"No worries. She can hear all right," he said. "And she understands everything. But she rarely speaks. Every once in a while she surprises us, though. Don't you, Sarah?"

Sarah's somber gaze tracked slowly from Jessie to Mr. Hobbs and back again.

"Quiet is fine with me." Jessie ran a finger lightly down Sarah's cheek.

"Amen," Mr. Hobbs agreed, chuckling. Gentle warmth shone in his eyes. "Just between you and me, I'll take the quiet ones any day."

Gabe snorted in disbelief. "Well, she wasn't very shy this morning. When I opened my eyes, there was Sarah, grinnin' like the skunk that got the last egg. She'd gotten into the honey and had it smeared all over." Shaking his head, he gazed fondly at the child.

"How long will Mr. Strong be gone?" Mr. Hobbs asked.

"I'm not sure." She looked away quickly, cringing inside for lying so easily. "What are your plans?" she asked, changing the subject. "How long can you stay?"

"Not too long. We're shorthanded back home. I wish I could stay a few days and visit with you a spell. It's been a time since you left the orphanage," he replied with an apologetic look.

Jessie's guilt thickened at her feeling of relief.

"Tonight will have to suffice—if the weather doesn't get any worse, that is. Oh, I almost forgot," he added, rummaging around in his satchel, pulling out a tattered piece of paper.

"I'll need to get both of your signatures on the adoption papers."

Wind blasted through the trees, causing pine boughs to bob and wave in the air. The storm had grown increasingly stronger, and now powerful gusts bent saplings precariously close to the ground. Gray and black thunderheads tumbled furiously across the sky, mirroring Chase's rumbling frustration.

He sulked silently as he rode, brooding. The stormy weather, with the promise of snow, added to his black mood. Normally he found Cody's easy stride relaxing and enjoyable, but now it did little to ease his mind.

If she were looking for husband number two, she'd picked the wrong man. He'd always known he had too much tumbleweed in his blood to ever settle anywhere. Besides, after Molly, he'd vowed he'd never be responsible for anyone ever again.

With an exaggerated grunt, he pulled his hat lower on his head, sending a rivulet of water gushing onto his saddle horn, over his leather chap, and down to the wet earth. Son of a gun! The storm was building, and so was his mood. He clamped his legs around his gelding a bit too hard, and in return, the horse pinned his ears irritably.

As a boy, and homeless, he'd been a target for bullies and even a few mean-spirited men. Jessie's deception stirred up an anthill of anger inside he hadn't felt in a very long time. He'd worked darn hard to forget all that—to get past it. He didn't appreciate being reminded. Still, he'd sure felt funny when she'd threaded her arm through his, claiming him as her own.

Well, he wasn't a boy anymore, and he'd stopped taking what was being dished out long ago. Despite the meager food sustaining him, when he'd hit puberty, he'd grown tall and muscular. He'd learned how to fend for himself, and although he didn't go looking for trouble, he didn't back down from it either. Men walked a wide circle around him.

Spotting a sheer wall, he headed in its direction. "Whoa, Cody." He beat his gloved hands together and reached back into his saddlebag for the small flask of brandy he carried for cold days like this.

He rummaged around, identifying each article by feel. Cody's brush. Pocket watch. Pouch of jerky. Harmonica. His hand stilled. Something unfamiliar. He felt it again.

Stunning realization hit him like a bullet between the eyes. He cursed a blue streak through clenched teeth and pounding heart.

Feeling Chase's agitation, Cody tossed his head several times and snorted loudly. Chomping on the curb bit, he pranced in place and pinned his ears.

Nathan's bankroll! He'd forgotten the most important reason he'd made the trip out to Jessie's place. First, he'd been distracted by her blue eyes and pretty smile. Then in his anger, he'd ridden off without even giving it a thought.

"We have to go back. Six hundred and ninety-eight dollars is a heck of a lot of money." He brought the leather pouch around to the front of the saddle and looked inside.

There was a roll of greenbacks Nathan had won in the poker game the night he was killed. A banknote from his last job. A few loose coins and a golden heart-shaped locket on a tarnished silver chain. On the back, the name *Jessie* was inscribed.

"She'll think I did this on purpose. That I wanted to come back. She'll be dancing the Texas two-step when she sees me," he bit out crossly. He stuffed the pouch back into his saddlebag and sat in silence. Long minutes passed. He stared across the blustery landscape. His Stetson took a beating as he leaned into the wind's anger. Slowly, he felt an old familiar grin creep across his face. Satisfaction spread through his bones.

"Well, Cody, maybe at first she'll be happy to see me, but then…Guardian angel, huh? She'll be wishing for one when I teach her a little lesson. We can spare a few days, let this storm blow over. The ranch in Miles City isn't expecting me for another three weeks. Besides, she *is* Nathan's widow, after all," he enlightened the edgy horse.

Chase dismounted and gazed across the landscape back toward his new destination. He slapped the reins methodically over and over onto his glove-covered palm. "I felt a might guilty riding off with her so unprepared for winter. I most certainly did."

He exhaled with satisfaction, sending a cloud of vapor billowing from his mouth. "I can't wait to see her face when she sees I've decided to come back and play 'husband' after all."

CHAPTER FIVE

*J*essie was figuring out sleeping arrangements when she heard a peculiar sound above the howling of the storm. Was that…*whistling*? Concentrating, she listened. There it was again.

Whistling, definitely. In moments, boot steps sounded on the porch, and the door opened. Startled, she swung around.

Chase Logan stood in the doorway. His hat was tipped back and he had a most mischievous look in his eyes.

"Evenin', sweetheart. Save me any supper? I'm so hungry I could eat a horse, hooves and all. Sorry, Cody," he chuckled, nodding in the direction of the barn.

Activity in the small cabin ceased. Sarah scurried behind Gabe's legs, wrapping one of her arms around each and peeking between the two.

"You—you're back!" Jessie managed at last. "I wasn't expecting you home so soon." Her heart thudded and she wondered, was it possible to be pleased and frightened at the same time?

Chase tossed his saddlebags into the corner and hung his coat on a peg. He sauntered into the room like a man staking a claim. He stopped just short of Jessie.

Bending low, he whispered into to her ear, "Did you miss me?" He straightened and looked her full in the face. His whiskey-colored eyes searched hers. Her face grew warm, and she dropped her gaze.

A feather's width away, she breathed in his scent: peppermint, crispness of outdoors, and—man. Chase arched an eyebrow and turned to the others.

"I've surprised my little wife speechless," he quipped. "Guess I'll just warm up a bit before this cold turns into frostbite. Don't let me interrupt you all." With that said, he stepped to the fire and spread his hands before it.

Jessie hurried to the stove and began gathering biscuits and beans and a few leftover slices of the ham Mr. Hobbs had brought. She warmed the coffee and set him a place at the table, using the one tan earthen plate that wasn't chipped. As she worked she studied Chase surreptitiously.

He stood by the fire, periodically stamping his feet. His face, chapped and red, was fascinating. He was, in fact, the finest looking man she'd ever seen. Heat prickled her cheeks again. She tried to draw her gaze away from his profile, but couldn't.

His forehead was rimmed with damp, wavy brown hair, creased from his hat. His eyebrows were dark and his lashes abundant. But it was his lips that caught and held Jessie's attention. Rough from the weather, they were drawn up at the corners in a mysterious smile.

Apparently feeling her stare, he turned. When he held her gaze in his, he nodded slowly, knowingly. Jessie snapped her attention back to the table and the supper she had set there. Her cheeks burned.

Why in the world had he returned?

"Your supper's ready. Come and eat. I'll pour your coffee." Her gaze skittered whenever he looked her way, yet she could feel his stare almost as truly as if he'd reached out and touched her.

While Chase ate, Jessie readied Sarah for bed. She washed the little girl's face with a warm, moist cloth, then brushed and braided her hair. Sarah didn't complain, but neither did she seem to be enjoying it much either. As Jessie slipped the soft nightgown over Sarah's head, she noticed the small, butterfly-looking birthmark on the child's left shoulder blade. Jessie's heart warmed. After all this time her little butterfly was finally home.

With that done, Jessie put the tiny bed Nathan had built for Sarah by the fire. She tucked Sarah in and kissed the child on the cheek. "Don't be scared now, Sarah, honey," Jessie whispered. "Gabe is going to be sleeping right here beside you. Isn't that right, Gabe?"

"You betcha." Gabe gave Sarah a wink. "Let's hope she don't keep me up with all her chatter."

Sarah's solemn gaze moved around the room until it rested on Mr. Logan. The child studied the big cowboy as he hunched over his meal. Before Sarah's eyelids fluttered closed, Jessie leaned forward and kissed her cheek. "Sleep well, my precious."

Jessie turned to find Mr. Logan staring again. What was he up to, anyway? He was making her jumpier than a hen in a yard full of roosters.

He, on the other hand, seemed the picture of calm. He'd pushed his chair back from the table and was sipping contentedly from his cup. Catching her gaze once again, he winked and smiled suggestively—much like a husband waiting for the young'uns to fall asleep. The heat radiating from her face was almost unbearable. She reflexively smoothed the front of her apron and hurried to the sink.

The interplay went unnoticed by the travelers. Wearied by their trip, Mr. Hobbs and Gabe lay on their bedrolls by the fire next to Sarah's bed. Their eyes were closed, but Jessie knew it was too soon for them to be fully asleep.

When she went to fetch the broom, Chase caught her hand and placed it on his shoulder. "I've had a catch in my shoulder all day, darlin'. Would you mind rubbin' it?"

Jessie jumped back as if scalded.

Chase chuckled. "Don't go gettin' riled. The way I see it, a man has a right to ask his wife for a little back rub now and then."

Jessie's pulse thrummed through her veins. Chase had her over a barrel, and she knew it. What scared her was that he knew it too. Biting her lower lip, she stepped behind him and placed her hands on his shoulders.

"That's my girl."

He blew out a long breath and she felt him relax. With determination, Jessie leaned into her hands, squeezing his shoulders with all her might.

Chase lunged out of his chair. "Why, you—! I ought to turn you over my knee this instant!" His voice rumbled ominously as he rubbed the offended spot.

"Wh—what's the matter?" Mr. Hobbs sat up, trying to focus his eyes.

"Nothing. Nothing. I was just trying to rub a kink out of… of…his neck." She smiled sweetly. "You can go on back to sleep."

She glared at Chase. He glared at her. Neither of them wanted the other to get the upper hand. Then Jessie remembered the saying about catching more flies with honey than with vinegar. Smiling sweetly, she nodded toward the chair. Chase sat back down, slowly, and she massaged his large shoulders in earnest, her heart firmly lodged in her throat.

"Thank you, Jessie." He drawled out her name. "That feels real nice."

She heard the lazy way he used her name. The tenderness he'd shown her yesterday when he'd first consoled her about Nathan's death was gone.

Jessie turned, her gaze resting for a moment on her bedroom door. My word, what was she going to do now? He plainly meant to sleep with her and act the part of her husband. And there was absolutely nothing she could do to stop him, unless she revealed the truth. But that would mean losing Sarah.

Moments passed like steps toward a hangman's scaffold, each bringing her closer to disaster. "Would you care for anything else?" she asked, her voice soft and solicitous.

Chase's eyes narrowed as he gave her a long look. Finally, he held up his cup.

Jessie took it to the stove, refilled it, and handed it back to him. "There you are. Take your time. I'll just be getting ready for bed."

The voice was sweet. Too sweet. Chase took a sip of the lukewarm brew, contemplating this puzzling switch. All of a sudden she seemed almost eager to turn in for the night. Maybe she wasn't missing her dead husband as much as he'd thought. He took another sip.

Wasn't *he* the one who was supposed to be making *her* nervous? Not the other way around. Actually, he had no intention of bedding Nathan's widow. He'd…been teasing, to teach her a lesson.

He drained his cup and clumsily plopped it back in its saucer with a clink. Slowly his eyelids drifted down to half-mast. The cold weather must've taken more out of him than he'd realized. Resting his head in the palm of his hands, he closed his eyes.

Just for a moment. I'm so exhausted.

From the bedroom, Jessie peeked out the door. He was still sitting at the table, but his head was propped in his hands—a good sign.

With luck, Mr. Hobbs would be on his way home in the morning. Right now, though, she had to figure out a way to get Mr. Logan into this bedroom.

Jessie fretted at how small the bed looked. It was definitely too small for his large frame, but she'd just have to manage somehow.

Tiptoeing, she blew out the lanterns, leaving only the one on her dresser burning. Returning to Chase, she bent close and whispered, "Psst, Mr. Logan…You awake?"

No answer.

She gave his shoulder a little shake.

"Huh-uh."

"Get on up now and follow me." Trying not to wake him too much, she took him by the shirtfront and pulled.

Nothing happened.

Shaking him a bit harder, she breathed into his ear, "Mr. Logan, please. I have a nice soft bed waiting for you. Think how good it'll feel. Just a few steps away."

A tiny smile curved the corners of his lips. He struggled to open his eyes.

With effort, she pulled him to his feet, slinging his arm over her shoulder. His weight almost toppled her. When she slid her other arm around his waist, he mumbled something and tried to snuggle her closer. Determinedly, she shepherded him into the bedroom.

With her door closed, she turned him around and gave a push. He sat with a plop on the end of her bed and fell back. His head glanced off the bedpost before landing on the pillow, but he didn't seem to notice.

"Serves you right." She lifted a boot to remove it. She pulled. It didn't budge. She tried again with the same results. "Dad-blasted old boot!"

"Turn around and straddle me, darlin'," Chase mumbled groggily.

"What!"

"Go on now." His words were slurred. "I won't bite."

Mortified, she hiked up her skirt and stepped over his leg, taking hold of his boot. She sucked in her breath and leaned forward. Her face flushed with the effort, but nothing happened.

Chase lifted his leg and rested his boot firmly on her backside. He gave a push.

The boot came off with a whoosh, landing Jessie on her knees. She repeated the process for the other boot, blushing in the dim light at the feel of his stocking foot on her bottom. She straightened his legs out on the bed, checked to see that he had fallen back asleep, and blew out the lantern.

In the dark room, she sat in her rocker and pulled her quilt around her shoulders. Chase's breathing was the only sound.

What in land's sake had she gotten herself into? She hadn't known how much laudanum it would take to knock someone of his size unconscious—so she'd been extra generous. One thing was certain. He was going to be one hungover, angry cowboy in the morning.

CHAPTER SIX

A whisper of sound stirred Chase out of his sleep. His temples reverberated painfully, a result of little hammers banging away in his head. Light pierced through to his brain as he dragged his eyes open. Immediately, he slammed them closed.

Feeling the bed move slightly, Chase peeked through his lashes at the foot of the bed. There sat the little girl, the special delivery, snuggled in a blanket and playing quietly with something.

As if feeling his gaze, Sarah's head popped up and she stared at him, startled. Chase groaned at the gentle sway of the bed, and her eyes widened even farther.

"Mornin'." His attempt at soft came out gravelly and cross.

She watched him curiously for a moment, and then ever so slightly elevated the sock-like doll she held in her hands. He looked at it and then nodded his appreciation.

No mistaking Sarah understood his admiration, for she proceeded playing happily as if he weren't there.

Chase rubbed his hand across his throbbing eyes and tried to settle his rolling stomach. Whatever Jessie had slipped him last night had knocked him out good. He hadn't been this sick in years.

Jessie stood close to the slightly ajar bedroom door, listening. The murmur of voices drifted out. Mr. Logan must be awake now, and talking with Sarah. A niggle of fear stirred inside her stomach as she tried to hear what he said. She was tempted to peek in to see if any color had returned to his deathly white face, but resisted.

Earlier she'd started a fire and put on a fresh pot of coffee. Propelled by nervous energy, she'd busied herself getting the cabin warmed up before everyone was awake and wanting breakfast. When Sarah had begun to stir, in an attempt to give Mr. Hobbs and Gabe as much rest as possible, she'd bundled the child up and placed her at the foot of her bed in hopes she would sleep until the chill was off the cabin. At that time, Mr. Logan was still sleeping heavily, his breath coming out in long, labored whooshes.

Jessie had hardly slept a wink. She'd passed the night in her rocker, between the bed and the door, checking the cowboy each time he made a strange noise. Late in the night she'd awakened to find her feet frozen with chilblains and her bottom painfully asleep.

Sarah came running out of the bedroom. Jessie scooped her up and gave her a gentle hug.

"Good morning, Sarah." Oh, the weight of the girl in her arms felt more wonderful than anything Jessie could remember. "Did you sleep well?"

Sarah popped two fingers into her mouth. Amazed at the happiness in the little girl's eyes, Jessie carried her over to the fire. She sat with Sarah on her lap and pointed down at Gabe.

"Look at that sleepyhead. Will he ever wake up?" Jessie rubbed Sarah's back slowly.

Sarah looked down at Gabe, then up into Jessie's face, and smiled sweetly, displaying two beautiful dimples. It was the prettiest sight Jessie had ever seen. Emotion squeezed her chest and a biscuit-sized lump threatened to close her throat. She had waited for this moment for an eternity. It was a dream come true.

"Seepin'." The child pointed a wet finger at him.

Jessie was so surprised at the sound of the raspy little voice she nearly fell off her chair. "Yes. Yes, sweetheart, Gabe is sleeping. But I think it's about time you woke him up, don't you?"

Knowing that Sarah felt the most comfortable with the boy, Jessie placed her down beside him and let her cuddle up. Sarah squirmed into Gabe's embrace and closed her eyes.

Jessie marveled at the closeness of the two. It would be nice if she could ask Gabe to stay on also. It would mean the world to Sarah, and he could be a big help to her around the farm. But another mouth to feed would be next to impossible. She was just scraping by as it was now. She knew from the orphanage that growing boys ate a whole lot of food.

The nape of Jessie's neck prickled. Turning, she was startled to see Mr. Logan leaning against the doorjamb, the intensity of his stare chilling. How long had he been there? His stockinged feet now brought excruciatingly humiliating memories to mind. He didn't seem to notice her discomfort and ran his hand through his disheveled hair.

"Mornin'." His voice was hard. His pasty-white face contrasted with his dangerously bloodshot eyes. To say he didn't look as if he felt very well would have been an understatement.

"Seems as if I had some help falling asleep last night. You wouldn't happen to know anything about that, would you?"

When she didn't answer, he moved slowly to the table, gingerly pulled out a chair, and sat down as if on eggshells.

"Out with it, Jessie. I feel like hell, and I think you know the reason. What did you dose my coffee with?"

Hearing activity by the fire, Jessie panicked. She hurried over and sat by his side until her face was just inches from his. "Laudanum. Please, Mr. Logan, I'm begging you not to say anything to Mr. Hobbs about that or who you really are. I know you have every right to, especially after everything I've done, but if you ever thought of Nathan as your friend, I beg you not to."

"Exactly what is it you want me to do?" She was taken aback when he reached over and took her hand in his.

"Well…" she began, her voice wobbling softly. She glanced briefly at the intimate pose of their hands and then back into his eyes. "I want you to keep up your pretense of being Nathan until Mr. Hobbs leaves."

"How long might that be?"

Hoping he wouldn't notice, Jessie discreetly extracted her hand from the warmth of his, while leaning in even closer. It was hard getting her thoughts together with him only a snail's breath away.

"I'm not exactly sure. Most likely only one more day."

A lopsided grin slowly formed on his face. Without a doubt he was enjoying this very much. She didn't care. She'd beg if she had to. She'd do anything to keep Sarah.

"And"—he paused for five or six seconds, his form of torture, she was sure—"what would the job entail?"

"Just husbandly things. Work around the barn, hunt, chop wood…"

"What's in it for me besides this hellish headache breaking in my skull?"

She cleared her throat gently, collecting her thoughts. "Hot meals. Clean laundry. Back rubs now and then." She gestured around the room. "A warm cabin and…soft bed."

He raised his eyebrows suggestively. She could hardly believe this was the same kindhearted, thoughtful cowboy who'd brought her the news about Nathan.

"And…" She faltered. "And everything—except that."

"Except what?"

His overly innocent tone made her want to shout. "You know exactly what I'm talking about, Chase Logan," Jessie whispered tensely.

"Nope, I don't. I've never had the pleasure of being married. I'm just an ignorant ole bachelor."

"The stuff that happens behind closed doors."

"Oh, now I'm starting to understand." His head was propped in his hands as if he didn't have the strength to hold it up on his own. Amusement shone in his eyes. "What about all the other things that happen outside the bedroom? Are they acceptable?"

Gabe sat up and stretched. "Mornin'."

Jessie turned her startled eyes back to Chase, who looked about as pleased as a man could get. She snatched up his hand and held it between her own. "Yes, everything is acceptable, everything except that. Will you do it?"

"Under one condition," he said, all playfulness gone. "I'm running things around here. I'm the point, and you're the drag. Understand?"

Jessie nodded. Was that some cowboy reference? Oh well. At least he'd agreed.

"Oh, just one more thing."

Jessie was rising when Chase brought her back down by a gentle tug on her hand. He looked directly into her eyes. "You best start calling me Nathan."

CHAPTER SEVEN

*A*round the table, the morning meal of oatmeal and biscuits was concluding. Exceedingly cramped, the three adults, Gabe, and Sarah all competed for space.

For a moment, Jessie was lost in thought, her chair wedged close to Mr. Logan's. Their arms brushed intimately from time to time, sending an intense surge of confusion with each encounter. Her make-believe spouse, agreeable and at ease, eating and chatting with Mr. Hobbs, was the picture of husbandly consideration. The meal progressed without blunder on either her or Mr. Logan's part, and his presence had actually been a pleasure. She was relieved.

Chase was excusing himself when Mr. Hobbs, with a gleam in his withered, old eyes asked, "So, Nathan, how did you find our Jess? Where did the two of you meet? I never did get the full story."

Chase wiped his mouth slowly. "We met…" He cleared his throat and glanced at Jessie. "We met…"

Jessie rested her hand on Chase's forearm. "I met Nathan…in a town where I finally secured employment," she said softly.

"Yes," Chase interrupted, "she was inquiring about work at the mercantile. She was so slender and beautiful." He drew out each flattering word as if it were honey on his lips. "I just *had* to introduce myself. Whoever could forget those beautiful blue eyes?" Turning, he smiled into her face. "I couldn't even look away. I was smitten."

Jessie forced herself to gaze lovingly back at Chase, hoping she didn't look as foolish as she felt. His eyes twinkled with such merriment, she wanted to stomp on his foot, but instead she picked up his plate and took it to the sink.

"I was buying supplies that day," he went on. "It was a very fast courtship." He laughed, a rich, deep sound, bringing with it a ripple of pleasure. "I wasn't letting that one get away."

Mr. Hobbs's eyes were brimming with tenderness. His lips tipped in a smile, and he nodded.

Jessie went back and forth clearing the table. His version of the story was much prettier than the truth. Much sweeter than a handful of desperate women perched on a platform in front of a roomful of men. Less hurtful than the sight of everyone averting their gaze when they were shown a portion of her ugly, scarred back. Much less humiliating than being the only one left, standing there alone. That is, until Nathan Strong stepped forward to offer her his hand.

Yes. She liked Chase's version much better.

Chase stood and excused himself and went into the bedroom.

"Full, Sarah?" Jessie inquired, changing the subject. Her peaceful bubble had burst. Agitation from the horribly dishonest situation she'd gotten herself into enveloped her. Her insides knotted up, tight and unsettling.

The little girl nodded, and then turned her attention to Gabe, sticking her spoon into his bowl.

"I'm trying to get her to mind her manners, ma'am, but she won't. She's real perky today." The boy removed her spoon from his empty bowl and placed it back into her own.

"Well, we're packed and ready to go," Mr. Hobbs announced. "I hope you will forgive me, Jessie, for the short stay, but I don't want to wait. If we do, we may get snowed in." He paused, looking doubtful. "There's something I would like to discuss with you and Mr. Strong."

"I'm here," said Chase as he came through the bedroom door. He had his saddlebags slung over his shoulder and rifle in hand.

"Gabe, take my bag out to the wagon, please," Mr. Hobbs said. When the boy was gone, he continued. "I'm not trying to force you into any quick decisions, but I really brought Gabe out in hopes you might be able to take him in too. He's almost to the age where he'll be going off on his own, so he wouldn't be a hardship for long. Actually, I think he could be a big help to you." Mr. Hobbs ran his handkerchief across his forehead. "He can hunt and track. He's capable and handy—and a good boy."

Turning to Jessie, Mr. Hobbs beseeched her. "I'm sorry to be putting you on the spot like this, but there's really no room for him at the orphanage. We're overcrowded. If you don't take him in, I'll be forced to find him a job in some town." His face was solemn. "And as you know, that's a pig in a poke."

Mr. Hobbs took a breath and went on quickly. "I'm sure I don't have to remind you how attached he is to Sarah. Thinks of her as his sister. He had one, but on the wagon train west the cholera took her, along with his parents. He's had a lot of heartache for one so young."

Chase thought about Gabe. How old was he? Thirteen? That was considered a man in the West. He'd be a huge help to Jessie when it was time for Chase to leave.

"The boy can stay," Chase said, and looked down at Jessie to see if she was going to argue with him. He slid his arm around her waist and pulled her close.

She hesitated slightly before she relaxed and leaned into his side. "Yes, we'd be happy to have him."

Gabe returned just then from the wagon, and Jessie walked over to him and placed her hand on his shoulder. "We'd be proud to have you join our family. It won't be easy living out here, but you seem like the type who'd take to it well."

"Thank you, ma'am," Gabe said somberly. "I promise you won't be sorry."

"I will if you keep calling me 'ma'am,'" she said playfully. "It's Jessie. I insist."

Mr. Hobbs was all smiles. "Marvelous! Now that that's taken care of, let's get the papers signed so I can be on my way." Mr. Hobbs rummaged through his things until he drew out a handful of crumpled papers.

Chase's palms began to sweat. Jessie would think him a simpleton for sure. Just because he couldn't read or write didn't mean he was ignorant. He just never had the same chances other children did. He'd spent all his time surviving.

Mr. Hobbs laid the papers on the table and dipped his pen into his capsule of ink. "Just sign here at the bottom."

Chase looked down at the papers as if he was reading them over, a skill he'd perfected over the years. He looked to Jessie and then to Mr. Hobbs.

"Ladies first."

Jessie took the pen. She placed it on the second line and slowly scrolled a series of elegant, curving letters. Her penmanship was an art. She probably wrote her full name too—too bad he couldn't read it. He might have liked to know her middle name.

"Your turn," she said, and handed the pen to Chase. Taking it without hesitation, he dipped into the ink and scratched out an X on the top line above her name. Without another word, he turned, took the food Jessie had wrapped up for him, and nodded to the group.

"He's going hunting," Jessie said, filling in the embarrassing gap. "Again." She followed Chase to the door. A blast of north wind blew in, bringing with it the cold, crisp scent of winter.

"Well, I'm off too," Mr. Hobbs said. "Take good care of Sarah, and, Gabe, you help Jessie and Mr. Strong. Mind your manners."

They embraced for long moments and Jessie couldn't hold back her tears. "Tell everyone I said hello."

"I will, sweetheart." He kissed her forehead then set her away from him and brushed her tears away with his thumb. "I'm just so thankful to see how wonderful everything has turned out for you. Take good care."

The cabin seemed very quiet now without the two men. Several hours passed in conversation and games with Sarah. Jessie busied herself making bread. She kneaded dough until she thought her arms would fall off, and then set the pans by the fire to rise.

"I'm going to fetch some water. Will you keep your eye on Sarah, make sure she stays far away from the fire?" She buttoned up her coat and pulled on some mittens.

Gabe stood immediately and looked over at the pump in the kitchen, confused. "Water?"

"That only gives me a trickle. When I have washing, I go to the creek."

"I'll go. Just point me in the right direction."

"Thanks, but I really need to get outside for a little while. I've been inside so long I'm about to go stir crazy. Fresh air will do me good." She appreciated his willingness to help. "Be back in a jiffy."

Bundled up, with bucket in hand, Jessie made her way along the narrow path behind the cabin. It meandered some twenty feet and then disappeared into a grove of trees. Ducking under the moistened limbs she let her eyes adjust to the darkened woodland and then carefully descended the short decline. It was icy. Time and again she forced her thoughts away from Mr. Logan.

Why couldn't she stop thinking about Chase? And why had he returned in the first place? Just to help her? That had to be it. He'd had a change of heart after seeing Sarah. Why else?

The rushing water lapped along its banks, splashing and looking for an escape. The narrow beach, scattered with rocks of all sizes and shades, gave her immense pleasure. Nathan had told her that this exact spot had moved him so much, he had leased the cabin immediately and settled here. She came here often when she felt lonely, and it always lifted her spirits. It was beautiful beyond compare.

Taking care not to get the hem of her dress wet, Jessie knelt on her usual rock and hefted the wooden bucket by its rope handle, dipping it in the water. The bucket caught with force as water splashed over her arms, nearly pulling it from her grasp.

As she struggled to hold on, a movement on the opposite bank made her look up. Jessie's heart stopped. The bucket dropped from her fingers and careened away.

Not thirty feet away sat three Indians on their horses.

CHAPTER EIGHT

*J*essie scrambled backward. As she did, her dress tangled in her boots, and she landed hard on the sand. Her gut reaction was to turn and run, but she remembered what Nathan had told her the first time he had left her here alone.

"If you see an Indian, try not to show any fear. Don't scream or run. Most are curious about white women is all, and just want a look."

Ignoring the pain radiating through her body, Jessie slowly picked herself up and started cautiously backing away.

Two were magnificent-looking men in their buckskins and feathers. Their cloaks were made of an animal skin of some kind, which still had a head attached and dangling off to the side. The Indians' faces revealed not the slightest expression as Jessie stared into their eyes.

The third Indian was a youth, probably around Gabe's age. He held the reins of a riderless horse that danced around nervously, snorting and pawing the ground. When the horse turned, the saddle and saddlebags on the horse were familiar.

"Oh no," Jessie whispered under her breath. "Chase." Summoning her courage, she forced her legs to move, to climb up the bank. Backing slowly all the way to the edge of the trees, she then turned and ran to the cabin.

"Gabe!" She pounded the door with her frozen fists. "Open up!"

The door flew open, and Jessie bolted inside. She slammed it with both hands and dropped the bar. She struggled to catch her breath.

"What's wrong?"

"Indians. Three by the creek. They have Chase's horse."

"Who's Chase?" he asked, confused.

"Nathan!" She cursed her forgetfulness. "Chase is his nickname and what I call him most."

"You're sure it was his? Lots of horses look the same."

"I'm sure. I need to look for him. If he's still alive—oh God, let him be alive—" she panted. "I'll bring him home."

"I'm the one who should go," Gabe protested. "If you find him, you won't be able to lift him or nothing. How will you get him back here?"

Desperation burned inside Jessie. She wouldn't think about that now. She worked quickly to put on more layers of clothing. That was a bridge she'd cross when she found him. Sarah, frightened from all the turmoil, started crying.

Gabe took Jessie by the shoulders. "Stop. I'll find him. I promise. If you go, you'll just end up freezing to death, and then Sarah will be an orphan again. Do you want her to go back to the orphanage?"

Jessie strengthened her resolve. Gabe was right. He was stronger. He knew how to track.

How long had Chase been gone? Four hours? How long before a man froze to death in this weather? A million and one questions exploded in her mind.

"I'll need some food. No telling how long this'll take." Reaching into his pack, Gabe pulled out a revolver. He spun the chamber, then started loading it.

"You know how to use that?"

"I'm a deadeye. I hunted for the wagon train all the time."

"Have you ever shot a man?"

"No. But if it comes down to that…"

Jessie stepped close. "I hope it won't, Gabe. Please be careful. Come back, and bring Cha...Nathan. God go with you."

Jessie stuffed a small blanket and some bread into Gabe's pack as he put on his heavy coat. She picked up Sarah and held her so she could give Gabe a kiss good-bye. Silently Jessie prayed that she was doing the right thing in sending Gabe to find Chase. Or was she condemning the boy to his *own* death?

Chase lay facedown on the frozen ground. The arm trapped beneath his body throbbed, but he couldn't muster the strength to roll over. Pain unlike any he'd ever experienced pressed his skull with unbelievable force. The damp, debris-strewn forest floor was hard as stone, and every inch of his body ached.

What had happened? He remembered taking aim on the deer he'd been tracking. The next thing he knew, he was kissing the cold, hard ground in this uncomfortable position.

Blood.

He could smell it but didn't know where it was coming from. His mind strained to put the pieces together. His thoughts were like little silverfish, darting around. Try as he might, he was unable to grasp a single one.

Focusing on a leaf lying close to his nose, Chase struggled to stay awake. His last thought before losing consciousness was of a pretty young girl with shining hair the color of the sun. Had he actually held her hand, her warmth mingling with his own? Or had it all been a dream? As he faded into darkness, he held fast to the memory as long as he could.

Mr. Strong's trail was easy to find. Gabe kept his body low to the ground and moved quickly. Back in Virginia, his father had taught him early how to survive in the woods. His father had taken pride in his only son.

"Pa, I sure miss you, and boy, could I use your help right about now. This isn't a game today. A man's life is at stake."

Gabe scanned the clearing and found the deer tracks Mr. Strong had been following. Moving too quickly when tracking could be a deadly mistake. Pausing, he studied his back trail for any signs of movement.

The woodland was eerie. Quiet. Nothing but him and the crunch of the frozen ground. He didn't want to think about what he would do if he came face-to-face with the Indians Jessie had seen. Stories of what they did to their white captives had abounded on the wagon train. They were too gruesome to think about now.

Behind, something rolled down the ravine. Gabe whirled, heart pounding, and drew his gun at the…pinecone. It wobbled a couple times, then stilled. It took a few moments for Gabe's heart to stop breaking through his chest. He smiled his relief and went on.

Rounding the bend, he spotted Mr. Strong sprawled out face-down on the ground. Not one hundred feet away lay a deer, dead, a clean shot through the heart.

His heart beating like a tom-tom, Gabe forced himself to advance slowly. Rolling Mr. Strong over took some effort. A crease on his forehead oozed blood, which trickled over his face and down his neck. Gabe put his ear to Mr. Strong's mouth to listen for any sign of life.

It was difficult for Gabe to hear anything over the pounding of the blood rushing through his own veins. After a moment, Mr. Strong's breath came soft as a whisper, and relief washed over the boy. Taking his blanket out of his pack, Gabe quickly covered him, tucking it in tight.

"I don't want to leave the deer you risked your life for, so I'm going to take a few minutes to string it up and gut it, right quick. Meat's too hard to come by to be wasted."

While he worked, Gabe pondered how he'd get Mr. Strong back to the cabin. When he was done with the deer, he swiftly hacked down two young birch trees. He took the blanket off Chase and tied it to the makeshift poles with twine he'd brought along, creating a travois.

"This should hold to get you back." Gabe struggled to scoot Mr. Strong onto the makeshift contraption.

"What took you so long?"

Gabe jumped at the sound of the hoarse voice.

"Easy," Mr. Strong soothed. "It's just you and me, and right now I'm feeling about next to nothin'. Where's my horse?"

"Indians have him. There were three of them by the creek when Jessie went to get water. The fourth riderless horse she recognized as yours. That's when she sent me out to find you."

Gabe picked up the ends of the travois. "Hang on. Pulling you over these hills will be like trying to pick fly dung outta the pepper pot."

CHAPTER NINE

$\mathcal{J}$essie paced before the hearth, her hands twisting restlessly, her eyebrows drawn downward in a V. The fire's soothing glow did nothing to thaw the ice coursing through her veins. What if Chase were dead, and now Gabe as well?

As the hours passed and Gabe failed to return, Sarah grew fitful. She cried disconsolately until Jessie had no choice but to put her in her bed, patting her back until the little girl fell asleep.

"I'm sorry, Sarah, for having gotten you into this mess," Jessie said softly. "I only wanted to spare you the nightmares I lived through growing up in the orphanage. I wanted you to have a real home, with a mama and a papa. Perhaps brothers and sisters someday. Now Nathan's dead, and maybe Chase *and* Gabe as well. It's my fault for not telling the truth right from the beginning. This is all a result of one small lie."

Limp from worry, she felt like crying, but she didn't. Instead, she stared into the fire imagining all the things that could be happening out there in the dark.

Sounds from outside caught Jessie's attention. She tiptoed over and put her ear next to the door.

"We made it, Mr. Strong. We're here."

Gabe! Jessie threw the bar up and swung the door open wide.

"You're home!" she sobbed, rushing to help Gabe pull the travois inside onto the rug.

Jessie fell to her knees beside Chase's limp body. His face was ashen and blood was everywhere. She cradled his frozen cheek in the palm of her hand. "How is he?" was all she could squeak past the egg-sized lump in her throat.

"He's been shot. The bullet grazed his head. He spoke a few words to me at first, but that was hours ago. He's lost a lot more blood since then. I'll admit, I'm worried." Gabe's brow wrinkled in thought. "There was a buck he or someone had shot too. It's all quite strange."

Jessie looked at the gash, which still oozed blood. "Help me get him into bed." The two struggled to get the travois through the room and into the bedroom.

"We can get him up on the bed, if we both lift," Jessie said.

"Careful, he's awful heavy," Gabe answered. "I'll take his shoulders, you take his legs. On the count of three."

Sarah stood drowsily in the bedroom doorway. Her tousled hair stuck out from her head, and her little brow was furrowed with worry. "Pee-pee."

"One, two, *three...*"

Jessie heaved for all she was worth. Chase landed on the edge of the bed, a weak moan escaping his lips. Sliding him over, Jessie set to work on his boots, which were just as stubborn now as they'd been the night before.

"Here, let me." Gabe's voice was tinged with exhaustion.

Sarah began to whine.

"What's the matter?" Jessie asked, going to her and picking her up. "He'll be all right. He just has a little cut on the side of his head." Jessie prayed it was the truth.

"Pee-pee."

"Oh. You're a very good girl." She kissed Sarah, then smiled into her worried face. "Come on, let's find the chamber pot."

When Jessie returned she handed Sarah off to Gabe. The boy had removed Chase's shirt and unfastened the six buttons of his undershirt that began at his neck. The worn cotton was neatly folded back and revealed a well-muscled chest that was lightly sprinkled with dark, wavy hair. His abdomen, almost visible through the thinness of the fabric, rippled as he breathed and reminded her of a bull, lean and powerful. Here was the kind of man the girls used to whisper about at the orphanage. The stories brought heat to Jessie's face even now. She pulled her gaze from Chase's body and contemplated his handsome, sleeping face. He was such a good man. Her heart tightened up at the thought of the pain he must be in, and hurried to get the things she needed to tend his wound. She set the kettle to boil and ripped several clean dishcloths into rags.

Jessie washed the blood from Chase's face and neck quickly, and wrapped him in a warm blanket. He slept, his head bandaged with the white strips of cloth. The hours passed, but Chase didn't regain consciousness.

Jessie was slicing bread when Gabe came in from the barn, his face grave.

"What is it?"

"Mr. Strong's horse is back, but he's cut up some."

"Will he be all right?"

"Yes, I think it was the Indians who returned him, because the wounds are cleaned and dressed with poultices. I don't think we have to worry about them anymore. If they hadn't come to warn us, Mr. Strong may have died out there."

Chase moaned, drawing their attention. Jessie hurried to his bedside, placing her hand on his forehead. He was much hotter than he'd been an hour ago, fairly sizzling at her touch.

Jessie took the blanket off and gently pulled his undershirt over his head. She bathed his face and chest with water from her porcelain pitcher. Again and again, she ran the cool cotton cloth across his hot forehead and down his chest and arms. Though she worked quickly, he seemed to get more agitated by the minute. He thrashed about, mumbling incoherently.

Sarah, distressed by his actions, began to whimper.

"It's all right, honey, don't worry." Gabe lifted the child, hugging her close. She curled up against his chest and popped her fingers into her mouth. "I'll get her some of the bread you were slicing. Are you hungry, Jessie?"

"No. My stomach feels like it's full of horseshoes. But you two go ahead and eat something."

He nodded and carried Sarah into the other room. "In the morning, I think I should take the horse and fetch the buck I told you about," he called softly.

Jessie paused, her hand lingering on Chase's shoulder, the heat of his feverish body radiating up through her fingertips.

"We don't know who tried to kill Chase, or whether the perpetrator is still around. You don't think it was the Indians?"

"I don't." Gabe was back in the doorway, Sarah still in his arms. "Why would they come and warn us? Or for that matter, why return Mr. Strong's horse? If I ride I can be there and back in two hours. Shouldn't be too dangerous then."

When she didn't answer right away, Gabe continued. "It's settled. I'll leave at dawn and be back in time for breakfast."

When Sarah and Gabe were asleep for the night, Jessie returned to sit with Chase. Her cheek on his forehead told her his fever was far worse. He thrashed about so much Jessie worried he might actually fall from the bed.

"Molly?"

"Shhh," Jessie whispered, stroking his head with the cool rag.

"Molly," he sighed again.

His voice held such anguish. Whatever he was reliving was terribly painful.

Chase loved a girl named Molly. That was clear by the tone of his voice. Jessie reminded herself sternly she had no reason to feel anything for Chase, except gratitude for his help. Besides, he was doing right by Nathan. But it was hard not to be drawn to him. If she had a lick of sense, she'd best remember that he was leaving. As soon as he was well, God willing, he'd be getting on with his life.

Jessie dipped the cloth in cool water and continued to bathe his face and shoulders. She wetted each arm and stopped at his fingertips. Gradually, Chase began to relax. His breathing evened out, and he seemed to be resting more easily. She took the opportunity to check his head wound. It had stopped bleeding, but the skin around the wound was red and puffy.

As the eldest of the girls in the orphanage, she'd been the one to do all the doctoring. She frequently had to look after the needs of the other children, especially since there were no funds for a physician.

Though she was used to patching people up, she was thankful the bullet had only grazed the skin. She didn't want to think about what it might have been like if she'd had to dig it out.

The night passed slowly. Chase didn't regain consciousness. He thrashed about, and once in his delirium he had taken her hand and held it to his lips.

"Sorry...Molly..." His voice cracked and Jessie feared he might even cry.

"Shhh. Everything's all right now. Just rest. I don't know what has you so sad, but you must remember that around every dark cloud is a silver lining. Sometimes it's hard to find, but it's there. You just have to look very closely."

His eyelids fluttered, and then Chase opened his eyes briefly, tried to focus, and then closed them again. He'd finally calmed in the early morning hours. Exhausted, Jessie sat sleeping by his side.

Gabe tapped her shoulder. "How is he?"

"Better, I think. Cooler. But he's still asleep and..." Jessie's voice broke and she looked away.

"He'll wake up any minute. He's just weak is all."

Jessie tried to smile. "Thank you, Gabe."

"Sarah's still asleep. I'm off to get the deer."

Jessie nodded. "Be careful."

"Wake up, Chase. Please…open your eyes."

There it was again. The voice of the angel. Chase had heard it on and off during the night. He'd tried to drag himself out of the black hole he found himself in, to follow it, but it was proving very difficult.

"You were so kind to come back and help me with Sarah. I can never repay you for that. You are sweet and caring. You did for us what only a father or husband would do. No—more than that, a hero. No, even more, a saint! And now, because of your generosity, you're hurt."

The angel's voice was sad. It tore at his insides. Maybe he was dying and she was here to take him to his just reward. Heaven or hell—it didn't matter as long as she'd be there with him. He struggled to open his eyes. He wanted to see her.

She sat close, only a boot length away. Her head was bent with her forehead cradled in one of her hands. With the back of the other she brushed away silent tears.

"Don't," he whispered. "Don't fret over a saddle bum like me."

CHAPTER TEN

*Y*ou're awake!"

Trying to focus, Chase stared at her trembling mouth. The angel turned out to be the slip of a girl he remembered from his dreams. She seemed to be happy he was awake. He managed a wobbly smile.

"Water."

"Yes. I have some right here."

She cradled his head gently and held a cup of cool water to his parched lips. She was gazing at him like a calf at its mother come feeding time. Fully conscious now, Chase realized he was bare chested, with only his long johns between him and the world. Worst of all, his head was trussed up like a churchgoing woman in her best Sunday hat.

"What…happened?"

"We don't know. You went out hunting and got shot. That was yesterday."

"And Cody?"

"Either he came back on his own or some Indians brought him. We aren't sure. Gabe took him this morning to get the deer you killed before you were ambushed. He'll be back anytime now."

Chase relaxed. "Good. You're going to need that meat."

The boy was already proving his worth. Bone tired, Chase sank farther into his pillow. It was like he hadn't slept in a month—no, a year. Maybe he'd close his eyes for just a moment...

With Chase conscious again, Jessie felt certain he'd taken a turn for the better, and was able to look to the future with a lighter heart. When he fell into a restful sleep, she took the opportunity to check on Sarah and tidy up the cabin.

The little girl was still sleeping in her bed, holding tight to her dolly. Her hair glistened in the morning light streaming through the windowpane.

Jessie carried a chair over to the china hutch. Climbing up, she pushed an old kerosene lamp carefully to the side and felt around the top of the cabinet until her fingers touched a rectangular tin can. She brought down the tobacco container, placed it on the table, and opened the lid.

A small daguerreotype of Nathan was there from when he'd served in the cavalry. Jessie picked it up and looked at his kind face. Sheepishly, she thought that with everything happening so fast the last two days, she'd not even mourned him for a moment. She didn't even know where he was buried.

"I'm sorry." She ran her finger across his image.

Placing it aside, she looked at Nathan's father's silver pocket watch. On the day they'd been married Nathan had given it to her and told her it was worth a good sum. He instructed her to put it away in hiding in case of emergencies. Now, she took out the money on the bottom of the tin and counted it carefully. Fourteen dollars and forty-six cents. Not much for the months to come, but enough—if she were prudent.

If possible, she'd buy some dried apples and make some pies to sell at Hollyhock's Mercantile. Mrs. Hollyhock had said she'd sell any baked goods Jessie brought in. Folks in town thought it a real treat to buy something already baked and ready to eat. She'd check to see if the store had any in stock the next time she went to town for supplies.

Chase glowered at Jessie when she entered the room and picked up the tray. "I've eaten so much, I feel like a poisoned pup. What is that concoction, anyway?"

She smiled. "Possum broth."

His stomach clenched. Rolling to his side, Chase felt his face turning three shades of green as his stomach tried to push it out. Jessie ran to the kitchen and came back with a pot. Holding it next to the bed, she stroked his forehead soothingly.

"It's all right. Just relax and let it come. You'll feel better if you do."

After a few moments he lay back into his pillow and slung his arm over his eyes. "It's passed."

"Fine, but I'm leaving the pot right here in case you need it later. Don't feel embarrassed. Queasiness is common with head injuries, and besides, I've tended lots of sick children at the orphanage. It doesn't bother me at all."

"I feel more helpless than a cow in quicksand."

Jessie laughed. "That's natural. Just rest. Your strength will come back faster if you do."

Chase chastised himself for watching her soft-looking lips every time she laughed. It was stupid. He felt sick. He shouldn't be daydreaming about kissing her. It'd been years since he'd gotten worked up over a woman, and he'd thought he might never again.

Molly had paid dearly for loving him. Since then, the blood in his veins ran cool.

He closed his eyes as she fussed here and there and was relieved when he heard her finally leave the room.

It wasn't long before Jessie was back, and this time she held a cloth and a basin of water. He eyed her suspiciously. He'd discovered how stubborn she could be when on a mission of mercy. But his head hurt, so he held his tongue.

She fluffed his pillows and arranged his blanket around his shoulders. He watched her silently all the while, never taking his gaze from her face.

The cool cloth glided across his brow and down one side of his face. He groaned.

"Did I hurt you?" she asked, anxiety in her voice.

"No." Chase hated himself for being so weak. *Send her away. Tell her to quit smothering me with all this attention.*

"I haven't thanked you properly for coming back that first night. For helping me to keep Sarah. That was very kind of you." She'd finished with his face and now pulled the blanket down to expose his chest and belly.

Chase yanked it back up.

"Don't be so shy, Chase," Jessie teased. "I've been taking care of you for the past day and a half. No need to fidget now. Just relax and enjoy a little pampering."

Oh, he was enjoying it all right. Better think about something else. A cold soak in a mountain stream.

Jessie dipped the cloth and wrung it out. "I don't know how I can ever repay you for what you did."

All right, a stream in late December, frozen by a blizzard.

"And for signing the adoption papers for Sarah," Jessie continued. "I know it's illegal to sign someone else's name to a legal document, and you could have refused to do it. It was clever to put an X—you can't get into trouble for forgery." She ran the cloth down his right arm. "Chase, are you listening to anything I've said?"

Desire racked his body. He clenched his teeth and nodded.

"I said that I hope someday I'll be able to repay you for what you did for me, for coming back because I needed you."

It took a second for Chase to digest her words. Something about the word *repay* had caught his attention. *Repay. Repay.* He had the nagging feeling there was something important he was supposed to tell her, or ask her. But he'd be darned if he could remember what it was. The harder he tried, the more his head hurt.

"Enough. I'm awake now and I can tend to myself." He grabbed the cloth from her hand and held it out of her reach. She came around the far side of the bed to get it, but he stuck it under the blanket.

Jessie conceded with a sigh. "All right, you win. Is there anything else you need?" She glanced over her shoulder at a sound in the doorway. There stood Sarah, swinging her doll from hand to hand.

"Come in, sweetheart. I'm all finished up, and Chase needs some company. Just don't jiggle the bed."

"Da better?" Sarah asked, a serious look on her face.

Startled, Chase looked to Jessie. Sarah was so young, he'd never expected her to make the connection between Jessie and him being her ma and pa so soon. Now, almost without fail, she was in for another heartbreak. "I'm not up to socializing," he grumbled and looked away, but not before he saw the hurt look on Jessie's face.

"Suit yourself," she replied, then turned to Sarah. "I need your help in the kitchen anyway. Let's leave this irritable ole bear alone."

He glanced back. Sarah regarded him with a wondering expression. He wished she'd hurry up and skedaddle. But she didn't. She climbed up onto the chair next to the bed and slowly, as if uncertain, leaned over and gave him a kiss on his bandaged head.

"Well, *I* think she's just what the doctor ordered." With that, Jessie scooped Sarah up and left the room.

Humming, Jessie busied herself making a stew out of the venison Gabe had brought home this morning. She happily threw out the possum broth she'd been feeding Chase, thankful they had fresh meat.

Gabe not only butchered the deer, cutting it into steaks and haunches, but also preserved it by wrapping the pieces in salted gunnysacks. He was now in the smokehouse getting some of the meat ready to be processed.

She had two potatoes and three turnips left in her vegetable drawer. With the venison and warm bread, tonight would be a feast.

Jessie wiped her hands and pushed a strand of hair out of her face. The stew simmered and the vegetables roasted alongside. She was exhausted. Between worrying over Chase and staying up all night nursing his fever, and sitting up the night before in the chair, she didn't have an ounce of energy left. Gabe's bedroll lay invitingly by the fire, and she couldn't resist. She'd only lie down for a moment. Then she'd get up and set the table. Sarah was napping in her bed and Gabe was still outside. No one would miss her for now.

CHAPTER ELEVEN

*T*he house was too quiet. Years of living on the trail had taught Chase to trust his gut instincts, and the silence in the other room didn't feel right.

Pulling back the blanket, he rose unsteadily and took his gun from the dresser drawer. He paused until the spinning in his head stopped and then checked the chambers. Empty. He then took two bullets from the drawer and slipped them silently into his pistol.

Dressed in his long johns, he made his way to the door. He peered around the doorframe. A pot on the stove was bubbling. The fire in the hearth was burning. Everything seemed in order, but there was no sign of the others.

Continuing into the room, he spotted Jessie lying on Gabe's bedroll, sleeping peacefully.

She was on her side with her hands tucked under her cheek. She'd taken her hair out of the braid, and it twisted and flowed around her shoulders, more beautiful than any silken shawl.

He was spellbound. Never had he seen a creature more alluring, all loveliness and innocence rolled into one. Her lashes fluttered on her cheek as she dreamed, and when she sighed, her mouth formed into a pout. Chase had the sudden urge to gather her into his arms and never let her go.

The door's opening startled him out of his daydream.

He quickly held a finger to his lips.

Gabe looked wide-eyed at him, then grinned mischievously. "You going to a parade?"

Chase gave him a look that said he wasn't in the mood for teasing.

"You look kinda peaked, actually," Gabe said, serious now. "You better get back to bed."

Chase knew he must look a sight, dressed in long johns, his gun drawn, and his head trussed up. "Don't you be giving me orders just because you went and saved my life. You're still wet behind the ears, and don't you forget it." He was feeling poorly again and didn't need any bossing.

"Yes, sir." Gabe chuckled softly as he went to the sink to wash.

"I want Jessie to rest," Chase said, again looking at her in wonder. "I'll grab my clothes, and you get supper on the table. Sarah must be about ready to wake up, and she'll be howling to fill her belly. We'll eat as quietly as possible."

The three ate silently at the table while Jessie slept on by the fire. The only sound was the clanking of the utensils and a slurp of coffee every now and then.

Every time Sarah started to make any noise, Chase would hold his finger to his lips, and Sarah would giggle as if they were playing a game. Copying him, she'd then put her own finger to her lips and shake her head at Gabe.

After supper Chase summoned the strength to carry Jessie to her room. He removed her shoes and woolen stockings. He stopped at the dress. She'd probably be mad as a scalded cat to wake up and find herself in her shift. On the other hand, she needed her rest, and she'd no doubt sleep better and longer without the constricting dress she had on now.

Cursing under his breath, he fumbled with the tiny buttons that ran down the front of her bodice, feeling like the worst sort of Peeping Tom. Whoever had designed such a fandangled piece of clothing should be tarred, feathered, and left for the coyotes.

Getting the yards of fabric over her head was no easy task. Jessie began to awaken.

"What is it?" she asked sleepily.

"I'm just tucking you in." He held his breath to see if she'd make a fuss, then pulled the blanket up under her chin softly. "You've been tendin' to me nonstop, and now you're dog tired. Don't make a scene, Jessie."

Her sleepy gaze caught his, and he felt it clear to his boots. In the next moment her eyelids closed and she snuggled into her pillow.

He couldn't help but wonder at her threadbare petticoat. She must have had this same one since she was a young girl. Its edges were frayed, and it was much too small. Any lace it might have had was long since gone.

After seeing this raggedy one, wouldn't a husband buy her a new one, for Pete's sake? The sight of her long legs, combined with the exertion, had him more light-headed than he'd already been. He needed to lay his aching head down soon too. He covered her with the blanket and left her to sleep.

Gabe was finished with the supper dishes when Chase entered the room. Sarah played with something by the fire and seemed content.

"Jessie still asleep?" Gabe asked, keeping his voice low.

"Yep, and I think she'll sleep right through the night. She's plumb wore out."

"I left her some supper on the stove, in case she wakes up hungry."

"That was thinking ahead." Chase lowered himself into a chair and rested his head in his hands.

"You don't look like you feel too good. If you want to turn in early, I'll watch Sarah and put her to bed in an hour or so when she gets sleepy." Gabe dried his hands and sat down at the table.

"Think I will. But first I'm going to check on my horse and take a look around outside. Whoever shot me could still be hanging around."

Chase struggled into his heavy coat with Gabe's help. He took his hat from the wall and put it on gingerly, feeling it squeeze his sore temple like a vise. Taking his rifle from the corner, he checked its chambers. "After I leave, drop the bar on the door."

It took longer for Chase to check the area than he expected. He had to stop several times and rest, closing his eyes to ease the pounding in his head. Lady Luck had been with him. Another quarter inch and he would've been dead, without a doubt.

He was no stranger to close calls. Four times he'd taken a bullet. Been stabbed twice. And once accused of stealing a horse. He would have hanged for that, if Molly hadn't spoken up. She gave him a truthful alibi, unmindful of what it did to her own reputation.

The memory burned. They'd been so young. So alone. He'd learned many things from Molly. What it felt like to belong somewhere, to someone. How it felt to build dreams. He'd learned the joy of loving a woman with Molly too.

He'd gladly give his own life to bring her back. "That was a lifetime ago," he muttered. "But it's something worth remembering when I get to thinking I could ever settle in somewhere. Build a life with someone new." Jessie's blue eyes shone vividly in his mind.

Upon his return, Chase found Sarah asleep and Gabe cleaning Jessie's shotgun. The firearm was apart on the table, and Gabe was oiling each part meticulously.

"Find anything?"

"No. But that's not to say someone's not watching us from up the ridge. I'll do a thorough search tomorrow." Chase stripped off his coat and hung it with his hat on a peg. "Did Jessie wake up?"

"Nope. It's been quiet. Sarah got sleepy and fell asleep early herself." Gabe snapped the shotgun back together and ran a soft cotton cloth over the barrel. The metal glistened in the lamplight, and Chase could remember the thrill of cleaning his very own gun for the first time.

"Made some coffee." Gabe rose and walked to the stove, refilling his cup. "Like some?"

"Sure. Anything to thaw out my insides."

Gabe placed both cups on the table and sat.

Chase glanced at Jessie's bedroom door. He was feeling particularly edgy tonight. He sipped his coffee slowly, watching Gabe take his pistol apart for cleaning. A half hour passed in silence.

"I'm turning in," Chase finally said. "Leave this lamp on the table burning low tonight. If there's trouble, I don't want to be fumbling around in the dark. Wake me if you hear anything unusual."

"Yes, sir."

At the hearth, Chase gazed at Sarah, asleep in her bed. An overwhelming urge to bend down and reciprocate the kiss she'd given him earlier caught him off guard. She certainly was a little magnet, but he knew better than to let himself be pulled in. Instead, he leaned over and blew out the lamp flickering dimly on the mantle.

"Good night...honey," he whispered, remembering tenderly again the kiss she'd placed on his beat-up ole head. She'd wanted to make him feel better and all he did now was feel worse.

Unexpectedly, her eyes opened. Shyly raising her arms to him, she waited. Emotions warred within Chase. He wanted to hold her. But it would only make it harder when he left. Wasn't it better to confuse her now than to break her heart later?

Grimly, he nodded to her as if she were just an acquaintance on the street.

Sarah studied him for a moment. Then, without a trace of emotion, she snuggled back into her blanket.

CHAPTER TWELVE

*H*e was stalling. Lying down next to Jessie was now seriously problematic. He desired her. He wouldn't be a man if he felt otherwise. But, on the other hand, he wasn't an animal either. He recognized goodness in this young woman. He'd never do anything to hurt her.

As he stripped off his shirt and tossed it onto the chair, Chase remembered a bit of wisdom he'd heard from a man he'd once ridden with. Mack, older and trail-wise, had taught him what it took to stay alive on a cattle drive. *"Remember, son," Mack had said, "if you ain't got a choice, be brave. Many a man has come through the worst of situations on heart alone."*

Quietly, Chase sat in Jessie's rocker and removed his boots. Easing down on the tiny bed, he grimaced as it creaked under his weight. He hesitated, watching to see if the movement would wake her.

Being gentle, he pushed her arm over to her body and tucked the blanket like a cocoon around her. She still didn't stir, so he lay back on top of the cover, stretching his legs out the best he could. With his fingers locked behind his head, he listened to the noises of the night.

The hoot of an owl somewhere far off.

The ticking of the clock over the fireplace mantel.

The breathing of Nathan's widow lying inches away...

Nathan! Chase almost sat up when he remembered Nathan's bankroll. That's what had been dogging his thoughts. He needed to give it to Jessie tomorrow, first thing. If she thought him a hound, so be it.

As the hour grew late, the temperature in the cabin dropped. Jessie's scent, soft and feminine, kept Chase in a constant state of awareness. Taking a deep breath, he released it slowly, trying to concentrate on anything but what was keeping him awake.

He thought of his past and some of the mistakes he'd made along the way. "Killing don't make a soft pillow at night," he whispered in the darkness. "Regardless of who draws first."

That was a mistake. Jessie mumbled something and snuggled in close to Chase's side. He rolled over to avoid her, but her arm slid up over his side.

She's testing my willpower and doesn't even know it.

He was leaving, his good sense reminded him. This was Nathan's widow. Even though she'd granted him some husbandly rights, physical closeness certainly wasn't one of them. Against his good sense, he rolled back. Jessie's face, close to his, was intoxicating.

"Jessie. Wake up."

She made a little sound.

That was enough invitation for Chase. Leaning forward, he gave in to the temptation that had been riding him hard and brushed her lips lightly with his. A second passed. "Mmm," he whispered. "You taste sweet like sugar plum pie."

Jessie's eyes opened. As comprehension dawned, she gasped, her hand covering her mouth.

Chase reached out to quiet her, to tell her absolutely nothing had happened. Well, almost nothing, but she struggled against his embrace and pushed against the restraining blanket. Chase drew back.

"It's all right, Jess. I'm sorry. It was all my doing. Please don't cry."

And he *was* sorry. She was the new widow of a trusting friend. *I'm a horse's ass.*

At that moment, Sarah cried out from the other room.

Jessie jumped up and Chase followed. Jessie gathered Sarah up, and rocked her in her arms. The commotion had Gabe sitting in his bedroll.

"What's wrong?" he asked, pushing his hair from his eyes.

"Sarah's having a nightmare," Jessie said. "You can go back to sleep. I'll take care of her."

Clasping Sarah to her breast, Jessie felt the wild beat of the girl's heart against her own. She smoothed the brown curls out of her face and stroked them down her back.

Chase hung back. He looked unsure. The next time Jessie glanced up he was gone, back into her room.

"Shhh...please don't cry," she crooned, echoing the words Chase had whispered to her just moments ago. "It's all right, sweetheart. It was just a bad dream."

"Dark, dark root," Sarah cried.

"No, no, there's no root cellar here, honey. You don't have to think about that anymore, ever again."

From out of the past, a montage of nightmares descended. Jessie remembered vividly her last day at the orphanage.

"What have we here? Only one shoe?" Mrs. Hobbs's voice fairly crackled as she advanced on Sarah. "Jessie, take her and put her in the root cellar until after breakfast. Children must learn responsibility."

Jessie had to control her rage. If she spoke out in Sarah's defense, as she had in the past, it would only make things worse for Sarah.

As she had hugged Sarah close, the other children regarded her with sympathy. None of them liked to be left in the root cellar. But Sarah, who was so afraid of the dark, was especially fearful.

"It'll be all right, sweetheart," whispered Jessie. *"I'll stay with you. Mrs. Hobbs—that old meanie—will never know."*

Sarah, who'd buried her head against Jessie's neck, nodded slightly. *"That's my girl."* Jessie knew from her own experiences what it meant to "go to the cellar." It was dark and cold there, and full of scary sounds. Whenever Mr. Hobbs was gone, his wife looked for opportunities to put children there. Jessie would take the switch gladly, before leaving Sarah alone.

As Jessie rocked Sarah, the memory was as vivid as if the incident had occurred yesterday. If it felt that real—that raw—to her, how much more had Sarah suffered being so young? What else might have happened after Jessie left the orphanage? She shuddered at the thought.

"Shhh…baby, it's all over now. I'm here, and I'll never let anyone scare you ever again."

"Mama, Mama," Sarah sobbed, holding tight to Jessie's neck.

Jessie passed the night with Sarah in her arms. She laid a blanket down beside Gabe and stayed there.

Near dawn, Jessie placed Sarah back in her bed, then stretched out her cramped, cold legs and arms. She quailed at the thought of seeing Chase this morning. He could be waking up any minute, and the thought sent her into a panic. She needed some time to herself to sort out her feelings, but in this little cabin, privacy was impossible.

I'll go into town! We need a few supplies, and the weather is mild enough, why there's barely a hint of frost in the air. If she left now, she could get everything she needed and be back in time to put on supper.

She quickly scribbled out a note explaining where she was and asked Gabe to take care of Sarah and Chase. The sun was just peeking over the mountain as she closed the door. A breeze played about her ankles, making the rain-soaked leaves dance and sway in her path.

How good it felt to be out of the cabin. With her head up and shoulders back, her cares and worries drifted away. The morning air was invigorating. Just one day at a time, she thought. *That's how I'll make it through.*

Inevitably, her thoughts drifted back to...Chase. *No! I won't think of him this morning!* Tingles, like a bellyful of bees, skittered around inside her.

What about Nathan? And all he'd done to help her? Shouldn't she be thinking of him, now gone to his grave? Shouldn't she be overcome with grief?

He was my lawfully wedded husband. What is wrong with me? I'm horrible!

Rounding the bend, Jessie got her first good look at Valley Springs in two long months. It wasn't much of a town, with its two streets and handful of houses. But it did have a dry goods store, a blacksmith's shop, and one restaurant, as well as a small building that served as a school during the week and a church on Sunday. Of course there was a saloon.

Jessie hurried, excited to see Mrs. Hollyhock. Her elderly friend had a talent for making her laugh. Since it was early, the town was still quiet, except for the ring of metal striking metal. Mr. Shepard, the blacksmith, was at work in his shop.

Garth Shepard had been the first person she'd met when Nathan brought her home to Valley Springs. Garth was a tall, strapping young man with arms the size of tree stumps. Fair-haired and brawny, he had sun-browned skin that never lacked the sheen that comes from working in the heat. Mr. Shepard was always locking his sights on her, no matter that she was a married woman.

Maybe, if she were careful, she could creep past his smithy without being noticed. His smile, disarmingly charming, melted even the coolest female heart, or so it seemed. Young girls—and all too many of the married ladies too—were constantly batting their lashes at him in hopes of drawing his attention.

Jessie released a sigh of relief. A few more steps and she'd be past his shop. But at the moment of that happy thought, a large form stepped onto the wooden boardwalk in the direct line of her path.

CHAPTER THIRTEEN

"How do, Jessie?" Garth said, as he wiped his hands on a rag looped over his belt. His eyes twinkled. "You're looking *mighty* pretty today."

"Hello, Garth." Jessie tipped her chin up, looking him in the face. "I'm just fine." She disliked how his powerful gaze always seemed to be dancing the two-step from the top of her head to her boot-clad feet. She felt like a prized steer at an auction. It was irritating.

"Where's Nathan? Is he in town with you today?" He stepped closer, bringing with him the sour odor of horse manure and sweat. Her senses twitched.

"No, he isn't," Jessie said evenly, a flash of anger threatening. She knew why he was asking about Nathan. Garth, in his ingratiating way, had several times voiced his disapproval of her walking into town alone. She dreaded having to tell him she was once again unescorted. But it was unavoidable—and none of his business anyway!

Garth looked as if he was mentally counting to ten. Then he extended his hands, palms up, in a silent plea. "Mrs. Strong... Jessie," he drawled. "It's *not safe* for you to venture this far alone. Why can't you get that through your pretty little head?"

"You've said that before, Mr. Shepard, and I thank you for your concern, but I'm not alone." She waved her arm dramatically.

"I know," Garth replied, backing down. "God's by your side."

"That's right. It's not that far, and when one lives alone, it can't be helped. Besides, I enjoy it. Winter won't wait forever, and sometimes there're things I need."

Jessie glanced about to see if they were drawing attention. With his reputation, she didn't want to start people talking. "Nice to see you, Mr. Shepard, but I must be on my way."

Disappointment clouded the blacksmith's face. "My buckboard is hitched. Let me know when you're done and I'll be happy to give you a ride home."

"That's very kind of you. But Mrs. Hollyhock sees to it that my purchases are delivered. Thank you all the same."

The bell above the door tinkled as Jessie stepped into the mercantile. Wonderful warm air enveloped her, and the tantalizing aromas of coffee, spice, and leather wafted about. Oh, it smelled so good. So much better than Garth! She took a deep breath and closed her eyes, savoring every sensation.

"Lord a'mighty, child, you're a sight for sore eyes!" Tiny Mrs. Hollyhock, clad from head to toe in brown and blue calico, came bustling over to Jessie and wrapped her in a bony embrace.

A lump formed in her throat as she basked in the attention. During the time she and Nathan had lived in Valley Springs, the little bird of a woman had come to mean a great deal to her.

"How are you, child? Is that husband of yours treating you good?" Mrs. Hollyhock's eyes twinkled and she glanced down at Jessie's tummy. "I'm trying to be patient." There was nothing in the world Mrs. Hollyhock loved more than babies.

Jessie laughed. "I'm just fine, Mrs. Hollyhock." The old woman took Jessie's hands in her own and held them wide, getting a good look at her. "It is so good to see you. I've missed you."

Mrs. Hollyhock's eyes narrowed, and her expression dropped. "I see that smile on your face, but it looks to me as if you've been worryin' yourself about somethin', girlie. Go on, out with it."

"Everything's fine. Really! I'm just here to say hello to my dear friend and to pick up some things I need at home. Here's my list." Jessie handed the paper to Mrs. Hollyhock with as much aplomb as she could muster.

Mrs. Hollyhock smiled, but concern shown in her eyes. "Not much on this list, honey, for as long as you've stayed away. Sure this is enough?"

Jessie nodded. It was all she could afford, with her dwindling resources.

"How 'bout a sassafras ta wet your throat? It's on the house."

"No, thank you."

"Well, I know ya like tea. Help yourself to a cup and some teacakes over on the confection counter. I'll only be a minute, and then we'll sit and have ourselves a good, long chat. If ya want ta read my Bible, it's where I always keep it. I know how ya like that."

Mrs. Hollyhock scurried about, plucking dried apples and other goods off the shelf, scooping flour, measuring a small amount of sugar, a small amount of coffee. Jessie saw her slip some sticks of candy, some peppermint balls, a handful of sours, and something else discreetly into her sack. It was a ritual she'd started the first time Jessie had come to town alone.

Sipping from her steaming cup, Jessie looked eagerly through the dry-goods section. She longed to buy some pretty material for Sarah. It'd be nice to stitch her up a new dress and perhaps a little nightshift too. She ran her fingers along a satin trimming that hung loosely from a high shelf cluttered with ribbons and bows.

After winter, she promised herself, if she had any money left, she'd buy a few things for the child. For now, though, she had to make her money stretch as far as possible. Food was her only concern.

She stopped, the ribbon held between her fingers and thumb. Was this how her mother had felt? Had she wanted nice things for her daughter, but was unable to provide them for her? With Sarah now depending on her, Jessie understood a little better the power of a mother's love. She knew she'd do anything for her.

The bell above the door sounded, and Jessie turned to see who was entering. Two men ambled in. They were filthy and had shifty eyes. Unease niggled inside her.

"Look who's here, Lonnie," one man said. His lecherous grin revealed several broken teeth.

The other man, who was looking at some traps, swung around. His oily black hair glistened on his scalp. "Why, Joe, I do believe it's Mrs. Strong."

How in the world do they know me! Rattled, Jessie ignored the comment and tried to go about her business as calmly as possible. She couldn't imagine how they knew her name. She set her tea-cup down and scooted around the corner of the aisle, picking up a copy of *Farmer's Home Journal.* She studied it intently as she walked slowly toward the shovels.

With her back to the men she never heard Lonnie approach until he swatted her bottom. "Hey, girl, we're talkin' to you."

Jessie whirled. Her arm came up defensively but he gripped it roughly, sending hot pain shooting down her arm. She struggled, trying desperately to get free.

"She's mad enough to chew splinters," he laughed and spittle hit her in the face. "I guess she figures I ain't good enough for her." Yanking her close, he leered unpleasantly. His rotten breath made her gag.

"Come on. Give me a kiss."

Mrs. Hollyhock hurried from the back room to Jessie's defense. "You sidewinder, get out of here!" She snatched the feather duster from her apron pocket and shook it in his face as if it were a dangerous steel blade.

"This store is for good, decent folk, not tramps like you," Mrs. Hollyhock spouted angrily, but Jessie could see the fear in her eyes.

The man named Lonnie lashed out. He hit Mrs. Hollyhock on the shoulder and knocked the duster from the old woman's grasp. A shriek ripped from her throat as she fell against the cracker barrel, and then crumpled to the floor. Her little round glasses bounced off her face, slid across the old pine floor, and wedged themselves into a crack in the wall.

CHAPTER FOURTEEN

*H*orrified at the sight of Mrs. Hollyhock motionless on the floor, Jessie balled her fist and punched her attacker in the face with every ounce of strength she possessed. Blood gushed from his nose. When his grip loosened, she wrenched her wrist free and ran to her friend.

Lonnie drew back, astounded, but only for a moment. He started forward, rage contorting his face. The palm of his hand covered one side of his face, and blood was everywhere.

"Cousin Virgil, quick!" Mrs. Hollyhock screamed. "Run down and get Garth. There's trouble in the store." The slam of the back door was followed by the sound of running feet.

"Come on, brother. Let's go," Joe said. He'd been watching the interchange with amusement. "I don't want to tangle with that bull of a blacksmith."

Lonnie stopped, but didn't leave until dragged by the other man through the store. "You ain't seen the last of me, sugar pie," he called out angrily.

When the door slammed, Jessie helped Mrs. Hollyhock over to a chair. She retrieved the old woman's glasses and gently slid them back into place.

"You've had a bad scare by them smelly, no-account curs," the old woman said shakily. "Why, I'd like to skin 'em alive, manhandling you that way." When Mrs. Hollyhock tried to stand, her arms and legs shook violently and she swayed precariously to one side.

"Don't you dare get up," Jessie scolded her gently, pressing her back into the seat. "How do you feel? Does anything hurt?"

Jessie pulled a chair close when her own legs began to wobble. She put her arms around the skinny old woman and held her close. "You sure you're OK?" she whispered close to her ear. Mrs. Hollyhock nodded but stayed in her embrace.

Jessie inhaled deeply, willing her heart to slow down. The thought of that horrid face so close to hers made her shudder. She scrubbed her cheek in disgust and closed her eyes, trying to force his image from her mind. His fetid breath seemed to linger in the air, coiling around her.

The door burst open forcefully, causing a picture to fall from the wall and crash to the floor, glass breaking everywhere. Garth rushed in, his shirt hanging open and a horseshoe still in his hand. He dropped to his knees in front of Jessie, his hands on both sides of the chair arms. Virgil hurried to Mrs. Hollyhock's side.

"Did they hurt you, Jessie?" His face was dark with anger and his voice trembled menacingly. "Because if they did, I'll hunt them down for the animals they are!"

"No, no, Garth. I'm all right. Just a little shaken up," Jessie replied. "But they did hurt Mrs. Hollyhock. Knocked her down. Can you take her up to her room?"

"Here, honey, I'm fine now. All I needed was a second to catch my breath," Mrs. Hollyhock said in a wobbly voice. She looked as if she'd aged twenty years in that few seconds.

Garth dropped his hands and stood, looking around the store. "They gone?"

Jessie nodded.

"Virgil, help me take Mrs. Hollyhock upstairs. "No arguments from you, Violet," he said when Mrs. Hollyhock started to protest. "Then get Jessie's things packed up. I'm taking her home."

Chase awoke by degrees, his hand testing the wound on his head. Sometime during the night the bandage had fallen off. No matter—he didn't need it anymore.

He'd lain awake worrying over Jessie and Sarah and the mess he'd created. Near dawn he'd finally fallen asleep, and now he was having difficulty coming out of it.

As he tucked in his rumpled, slept-in shirt, he noticed he wasn't dizzy anymore. After a strong cup of coffee, he'd face Jessie and apologize for the events of last night. He'd give her Nathan's pay and get ready to depart. Everything was taken care of with the adoption, and he felt a lot better now that Gabe was here. In his gut he didn't feel the Indians were a real threat, because Jessie had been out here long enough and they were used to having her around. Most likely, they were watching out for her. The big question remained: who'd shot him, and why?

Pouring a cup of coffee, Chase wondered where everyone was. He would've been more concerned had he not heard voices ten minutes earlier.

Gabe entered with Sarah held high on his shoulders. She had a tight hold on his hair, but the boy didn't seem to mind.

"Where've you been?" Chase asked from his chair at the table.

"Sarah needed a trip to the necessary, so I gave her a piggyback. Easier than putting her boots on."

"Where's Jessie?" Chase asked, trying to seem nonchalant.

"Didn't you see it?"

Like waking up nose to nose with a rattler, Chase was instantly alert. Chastising himself, he realized with dismay that he should've kept an eye on her, even if she didn't want him to.

He snatched up the scrap of paper lying on the table. It was impossible to make any sense whatsoever out of the little lines and dots going this way and that. As he concentrated on the letters, the note began to quiver.

Angrily he thrust the note at Gabe and jammed his fingers through his hair. "Well?" he almost shouted.

Gabe stared.

"What's it say?"

Gabe looked back at the note.

"It says Jessie went to town for supplies. Says not to worry, that she'll be back in time to fix supper."

"That it?"

Gabe cleared his throat. "It asks me to take care of you and Sarah."

"Why didn't you wake me up as soon as you read this?"

Flinching, the boy took a step back. "I thought you knew. That you two had talked about it before."

Chase reminded himself to go easy. It was his fault Jessie had left. Not the boy's.

"How long do you think she's been gone?" he asked more civilly.

Gabe shrugged. "She must've left around sunup, because I woke up not long after, and she was already gone."

Chase went quickly to the door and swung it open. The sun was nowhere to be seen as large, dark clouds covered the sky.

How in the world did I sleep so late?

He went straight to the barn, threw his saddle on his horse, and was mounted within minutes. Cody, fresh from no use for a few days, humped his back and pinned his ears.

"Quit it." Chase gave him a slight taste of his spur to get the gelding's attention. The horse humped up again, this time honestly trying to throw Chase off. Chase rode it out with practiced ease, then collected the animal while scanning the area.

Jessie's small, booted footprints in the dampened dirt of the road were easy to see. He started after her at a ground-covering trot.

After about a mile, Chase ventured off the road to the top of a knoll to survey the surrounding area. The jingling of a harness came from around the hill, where the road went next.

Turning, he loped his horse into some trees, and then peered through the brush, as a buckboard with two people approached. Well, he needn't have worried. There sat Jessie next to a stranger. She gazed at her escort as he said something to her.

She laughed.

Chase, too far away to make out any of the conversation, swore under his breath.

CHAPTER FIFTEEN

*C*hase knew he should be relieved at seeing her—just to know she wasn't lying dead somewhere, or abducted. But he wasn't. The sight of her made him angrier than he'd like to admit.

As they approached, the man placed his arm around the back of Jessie's seat. Leaning toward her, he pointed at something alongside the trail.

"Well, Cody, isn't *that* just the coziest picture you ever did see?" Jealousy gripped him like a vise. He waited until the wagon passed by, and then galloped ahead to another hidden vantage point. As the wagon approached again, he strained to catch their words.

"Jessie, I mean it. This only goes to prove…"

The wagon pulled away out of hearing range. Scowling, Chase turned Cody, and the horse bolted up the trail.

As the wagon approached a third time, Jessie finally turned her attention in his direction. It was the first time he'd seen her face since their encounter last night. Warmth flooded through him.

She looked up the embankment. Alarmed he'd get caught in the embarrassing act of eavesdropping, he held his breath and didn't move. Luckily, at that moment, a gust of wind picked up her skirt, billowing it around her knees. Hastily, she pushed it down, tucking it under her legs.

Chase couldn't miss the stranger boldly taking in the curve of her calf and delicate ankle. He fought the urge to ride down there forthwith and introduce this Casanova's teeth to the back of his throat. Instead he galloped ahead to another hideout.

"Is he home?"

Without a doubt, the man spoke with familiarity. And why did he want to know, anyway? Chase thumped his fist onto his thigh.

The buckboard stopped next to the barn and Jessie's escort passed the reins into his left hand. With his right he reached up, pushing a strand of hair from her face.

Chase watched with grim fascination. Could they be sweethearts? Jessie had been alone for long stretches at a time. It was possible.

Standing abruptly, Jessie turned to climb from the wagon. The man reached for her arm, pulling her back in. He flicked the reins over the horses' backs, starting the wagon rolling.

As the buckboard neared the cabin, Chase took the long way around the hill to the back of the homestead. He concealed Cody in the thicket by the stream and crept to the side of the cabin, where he had a view of the front—and could finally hear easily.

"I'm sorry! I didn't want to make you angry with me, Jessie. It's just...I had to let you know how I feel." The man pleaded, his face a mask of remorse.

Jessie studied him, and Chase wondered what she was thinking when she looked at him so.

"Thank you for coming to our aid today, Garth," she said. "I don't like to think of what might've happened if you hadn't been there."

Her aid?

"No need to thank me. You know I'm honored to help in any way I can. At any time." The man's voice was sincere.

Leaning his aching head against the rough-cut logs, Chase closed his eyes wearily. It was clear this man was interested in Jessie. What he didn't know was what she felt for him. Chase took a long breath, exhaling slowly. This web was getting stickier and more tangled by the hour. He clenched his fists. Somehow, against his will, and just as he'd feared, this slight woman had worked her way under his skin.

"Jessie, that you?" Gabe called through the door.

"Yes, you can open up."

The door swung wide, and Gabe stepped out, holding Sarah. Seeing the tall stranger standing next to Jessie, Sarah hugged Gabe tightly about the neck.

"It's all right, Sarah," Jessie explained. "This is Mr. Shepard. He's the blacksmith in town and a friend of mine. He was kind enough to give me and the supplies a ride home." She didn't want to alarm either of them with details of what had happened in the mercantile.

"Who do we have here?" Garth asked.

"This is my new family, Gabe Garrison and Sarah," Jessie said, taking Sarah from the boy. She smiled even though her stomach knotted painfully. Any moment Chase might come barging out of the cabin. How would she explain his presence? Especially if he was still in his long johns. If the news got out she had a man staying at her place while Nathan was away, it would be…bad. Very bad. Folks around here didn't take kindly to that kind of behavior.

"Here, sugar." Garth offered a piece of candy to Sarah, but she just looked at him, holding tighter to Jessie. "She sure is a pretty little thing. Where'd she come from?"

Jessie's irritation returned with a snap. She knew Garth only meant well, but honestly, he was making it difficult. It was none of his business. She was tired of his constant meddling.

"I have a busy day, Garth. Thank you very much again for the ride. And for all your concern. You did more than was called for, and I'm much obliged."

"And the boy's her brother?" Garth asked, as if he hadn't heard a word she said. He was watching Gabe unload the sacks off the back of the wagon. With his legs spread wide and his huge hands stuffed into the pockets of his homespun pants, Garth looked something of a boy himself.

"Now he is," Jessie replied, once more wishing he'd hurry up and be on his way. Chase was sure to hear them talking and come out. It was only a matter of seconds. That'd be a rock in a wasp's nest she didn't need.

"Is Nathan here?"

"Uh, no, *Nathan's not here.*" She intentionally raised her voice, trying to signal Chase to stay inside. Thank goodness Gabe was interested in the horses and wasn't paying any attention to them.

Garth gave her a strange look. "Hunting?"

She smiled.

"The wagon's unloaded," Gabe called, stroking the neck of one of the horses. "Want me to water your horses?"

"No, thanks," Garth answered. "Now, you two run along so I can have a word with your new ma."

Gabe's back stiffened at the dismissal, but lifted Sarah from Jessie's arms. "I'll be right inside," he said over his shoulder, stepping into the cabin.

"Well, he's protective of you, that's for sure," Garth said, smiling. "I'm glad to see you have some dependable help. At the first sign of trouble send him running to town, and I'll be back quick."

Stepping closer, he dropped his voice. "Is Mr. Strong really hunting, or you just saying that to get rid of me? He's not gone working somewhere far off again with winter coming on, has he? Because if he has, I have a mind to up and move you all into town where you'll be safe and people can keep an eye on you. Even with the boy, you're like a sitting duck out here alone, just asking for trouble."

He lifted her hand and held it between his own. "I wouldn't be surprised if those two drifters came out here later on with bad intent."

She pulled her hand from his. "Now, quit your fretting. We'll be just fine." With that, she stepped purposefully toward the cabin in an effort to send him on his way.

"Never met a more stubborn woman—or one with more grit," Garth announced, shaking his head ruefully. He climbed up onto the seat and picked up the reins. "You're one heck of a woman, Jessie Strong. Without a doubt. One of a kind."

CHAPTER SIXTEEN

*J*essie waited impatiently as Garth's buckboard rumbled down the trail. She wasn't taking any chances he might turn around and come back. She needed to know he was gone for good. Finally his wagon disappeared around the corner, and she went inside, relieved.

Shelving the supplies and preparing the evening meal, Jessie's thoughts went round and round. With quavering hands she placed the kettle on the stove to warm. She'd already covered the eggs she'd purchased at the mercantile with limewater to preserve them.

Nonchalance was hard when she asked Gabe about Chase's whereabouts. He'd whispered to her Chase had been quite angry when he found her missing and was out looking for her.

Her first reaction was concern over Chase's health—was he strong enough to be out riding so soon? Head wounds were nothing to take lightly. But soon she began to brood over the confrontation to come. Was he mad she'd walked into town without telling him? Or would he be more appalled at her wanton behavior last night?

Gabe looked confused with her quiet state. "Can I set the table?"

"Please." Jessie worked busily, absorbed in thought. Her movements were automatic as the apple slices caramelized in the pot she stirred. Mrs. Hollyhock had given her the pie recipe when Jessie had first come to town. She'd worked hard to get it right, trying to impress Nathan with her baking skills. After her first few disasters, he'd declared her pies the finest he'd ever tasted.

Pleasure warmed her as she remembered Nathan's face the day he'd contemplated her first perfect pie. *"Nothin' better to soothe a man's soul than a fresh-baked apple pie," he'd said, picking up a sweet bite and holding it to his nose. "Have I died and gone to heaven?"*

Poor Nathan. Barely passed and *still* she hadn't taken any time to mourn him. She hoped he would understand why. There just hadn't been one free second!

Jessie retreated to her room, seeking the comfort of solitude. She splashed cool water on her face and ran her brush through her hair and then let it fall loose down her back. She didn't have the will or the energy to fix it any other way.

Waiting for Chase's return was making her sick. She wished he'd hurry up so she could get it over with. Whatever his reaction was going to be, it would be easier to endure than this torture of facing the unknown.

Now isn't this just fine? she chastised herself, slipping on a clean apron and tying the sash behind her back. *You're worrying yourself sick, and he's not even your real husband. He can be as mad as he wants, and that's just too bad.*

A light tapping on her door made Jessie jump. It was Gabe. "Jessie, he's home. He's bedding down his horse."

When Chase stepped into the cabin, a sweet scent in the air caused his mouth to water. The warm aroma of cinnamon enveloped him, making his taste buds tingle.

Jessie, stirring something in a pot on the stove, glanced in his direction. Her face glowed from the heat; her glossy hair hung in loose locks down her back. Chase, reminding himself he was angry with her, looked away.

Gabe gave him a worried smile, and little Sarah scampered up and hugged his leg.

"How are you feeling?" Jessie asked.

Chase hesitated. The memory of her in that wagon still rankled. He decided to let her stew. Then, against his better judgment, he picked Sarah up, swinging her in the air.

"And how are you, little bit?" Taking one of Sarah's long brown curls, he tickled her nose. She giggled and squirmed in his embrace.

"Sure smells good, don't it, Chase?" Gabe went to the washbowl and scrubbed his face and hands. Slicking his hair back with his wet fingers, he took his seat.

"It's ready," Jessie said, placing a plate filled with biscuits in the middle of the table. "Sit before it gets cold."

When they were all settled, Jessie began, "Lord, we thank you kindly for this food."

Chase looked around, uncomfortable with the prayer. The children sat, heads bowed and eyes closed. He glanced down at his hands in his lap and shifted in his chair.

"Thank you for our family and the help you send our way."

A cautious glance found her looking at him from beneath her lashes.

"Thank you too," she continued, closing her eyes, "for the roof over our heads. May we always be thankful for all your blessings. Amen."

"Amen," the children chorused.

Chase looked up with relief.

"Pass me your plates and I'll dish up your supper," Jessie requested softly.

Chase ate in silence. Gabe shoveled as fast as he could, and Sarah pushed her food around her plate, never taking a bite.

It was one of the best suppers Chase could remember. After three huge helpings, complemented by four hot, flakey biscuits, he finally pushed his chair back.

"I hope you saved room for dessert." Jessie's voice was carefully neutral.

"I'll have to wait a while. Couldn't eat another bite even if I wanted to."

He took the last sip of his coffee from Jessie's tiny porcelain cup and set it carefully back in its saucer, trying not to feel silly. "That was one of the best meals I've ever had, Jessie," he said, rubbing his stomach. "Thank you."

Her face flushed prettily and her eyes darkened with pleasure. He could see how a man could find himself getting used to this kind of spoiling right quick. A little word of kindness was magic in itself.

The twilight hours passed. Gabe helped Jessie clean up while Chase sat by the fire, polishing his guns. With dessert eaten and everything put away proper, Jessie read to Sarah from a tattered little book she'd brought from her room. It was a story about a princess and a frog, and his occasional chuckle garnered him a smile from Jessie, with a look in her eyes he couldn't decipher, but which all the same made his insides feel warm. Finally, with Gabe in his bedroll by the fire and Sarah tucked away, there was nothing left to do but retire.

Jessie excused herself and went to her room, leaving Chase looking out the window.

There was no doubt they needed to talk.

May as well get it over with, he thought. He went to her door and tapped lightly. It swung open, and there she stood.

"Mind if I come in?" Chase kept his voice low.

Stepping back, Jessie gestured for him to enter.

As he did, he reminded himself he was still angry with her for her behavior this morning. It had been inconsiderate and foolish. He shouldn't let her off too easy. At the same time, the hearty supper and apple pie had mellowed him considerably, and if he wasn't careful, he would put the whole issue to bed without a word.

"I'm sorry if I made you mad," she started, looking into his eyes. The sincerity in her voice softened him further.

He sat on the edge of the bed. When she remained standing, he looked to the spot next to him, arching his brows in expectation. She resisted for a moment, and then took her place next to him.

He cleared his throat. "When I woke up this morning and you were gone, it gave me a scare. I didn't know why you'd run off, or if you were even coming back. For all I knew, you could've been on the next stage to who-knows-where, or maybe abducted by a band of Sioux."

He couldn't remember a sight as fetching as the way she looked at this moment. Her hair looked so enticing, falling around her shoulders in the soft candlelight. The vision would be one he'd hold forever, to take out and savor on cold, lonely nights. Nathan had been one lucky man.

"And also because you said I was in charge, and then you ran off without so much as a by-your-leave. I was planning to make that trip tomorrow and get you all stocked up for winter."

Jessie reached up gently to check his wound. Her chin tilted slightly as she regarded him. "You were hurt and needed to regain your strength," she countered stubbornly. "Besides, I've done it before. Lots of times."

Chase smiled to himself at her attempt to avoid the real reason for her trip into town. He wanted to have it out. Clear the air.

"I know why you went, Jessie, and it has nothin' to do with my injury or your needing supplies. I'm going to be honest, so you can put yourself at ease. What happened last night was a mistake. I should never have kissed you. It won't happen again."

Jessie looked surprised, as if she'd been expecting him to chastise her, or something else.

"It wasn't all your fault," she whispered. "I..."

"Shhh...it was. You were asleep. Dreaming. I took liberties that were not in our bargain. I'm sorry."

"Why're you being so nice?"

"Believe me, Jess, I'm not all sugar and nice. I just don't want you feeling bad about something you had no control over. Now tell me what happened in town today that has you spooked."

Jessie gave him a funny look. Chase knew she was trying to figure out how he'd learned of the confrontation.

"I was waiting for my supplies when two men entered the mercantile. One was being a nuisance, is all."

"Out with it," he persisted. "I know there's more to this story." Chase's gut was tightening.

"A man—I think his name was Lonnie—grabbed my arm and tried to kiss me." Jessie took a breath. "Mrs. Hollyhock got knocked to the floor when she came to my aid. I hit the man in the face."

"Do you know him? Seen him around town before?"

She stood and walked over by the window. "No. They ran away when they heard the blacksmith was coming to help."

"How'd you get home?"

Chase felt a momentary twinge of guilt asking a question he already knew the answer to, but he had to see what she'd say about the man.

"Mr. Shepard, the blacksmith, brought me home in his buckboard."

The thought of her being manhandled made his blood run hot. Not wanting to alarm her, he reined in his temper.

He stood too. "Well, that's exactly why I was worried when you took off. What would've happened if you'd run into these men out of town? There wouldn't have been the blacksmith or anyone else around to stop them." He shook his head. "I'm going to town tomorrow to buy you a horse. Leastwise you won't have to walk anymore. Can you ride?"

She turned around, surprised. "You can't. A horse costs money, a lot of it. I can't afford one." She planted her hands on her hips as if making her point known.

Now would be a good time to tell her about Nathan's pay tucked away in his saddlebag. Perfect way to broach the subject. But in truth, he knew the minute that he did, this tenuous rapport building between them would come crashing down. No doubt, she'd think him the lowest of low. He'd already decided he was going to buy her supplies and a horse out of his pay so she could put hers away to save for the future. He wanted to do something for her and Sarah before he left, and this just felt right. With that decision firmly reached, he resolved to keep the money secret a little longer and then surprise her with it when he was leaving.

"Chase, you've done way too much for us already. Your duty to your friend is fulfilled." She stomped her foot. "I mean it. You can leave with a clear conscience!"

Her feistiness made him laugh. "Booting me out so soon? I don't think I'm quite ready to leave…just yet. Have you fulfilled your end of the bargain?"

"My end?" There was a note of uncertainty in her voice.

"Fine time to forget." His gaze was drawn to her eyebrows and their expressive tilt of worry. "If I pretended to be Nathan for you, I could reap some husbandly benefits—not all of course, but some. Remember? Up until now, all I've gotten is shot in the head, some bruised ribs, and a heap of worry."

Chase didn't know why all of a sudden he had the urge to badger Jessie. Maybe it was the sight of her and the blacksmith cuddled together in the wagon.

"Now come here and tell me what kind of horse you'd like." He smiled mischievously and took her hand.

"No!" She tried to pull away, but he wouldn't let her.

"Good, mindful wives aren't supposed to say no to their husbands." Without warning, Chase gave a swift pull, and Jessie tumbled onto the bed. He grasped both her wrists in one hand and tickled her sides with the other.

She gasped in surprise and tried to twist away. "I take back every nice thing I've ever thought about you," she sputtered and laughed, the sound high-pitched and jaunty. "Y-You're a big," she gasped several times, "ox!" Amid their struggles her elbow caught Chase in the side. He gasped and then joined in laughing.

"Ouch! You're a lot stronger than you look."

"Nothing less than you deserve. You just said what happened last night wouldn't happen again, and now…and now you're attacking me."

"Attacking you?" Chase laughed again. He couldn't remember the last time he'd felt so good. His fingers ran down her arm and danced around her rib cage.

Jessie shrieked. She twisted from side to side, trying to escape his fingers.

"Please, oh please, stop, stop."

He did.

As Jessie quieted, Chase gazed down into her flushed face. She'd closed her eyes and thick lashes rested softly against her silky skin. *Kiss her.*

The lone candle on the dresser flickered. Silence embraced the two, and the whole world seemed to condense into this one little room. *Kiss her.*

What was he doing? Thinking about kissing her moments after he'd told her it had been a mistake. What was wrong with him anyway? But, her lips looked so soft.

Would it hurt? One night together.

Hell!

He wasn't thinking clearly. He was leaving. There was no justifying taking advantage of her vulnerability. Women took these things seriously, and, knowing Jessie, she would probably be eaten alive with regret and never forgive herself. Her best interest should be his only concern. But it was hard to stop when she seemed so willing.

After a moment, Jessie opened her eyes. Her smoky gaze was racked with desire. She pulled him down into her arms and nuzzled his throat. Her legs twined between his and she pulled him closer. Chase inhaled her sweet vanilla scent, struggling to remember why he was holding back.

"Don't play with me, Jessie."

"It's all right," she murmured. "I don't want to stop." She pressed her body to his.

The whispered announcement cut through the haze in Chase's head.

"You sure? I mean, it's not like I'm staying or anything."

Her eyes caressed his face tenderly. "You could if you wanted," she breathed. Her gaze lingered on his mouth.

He tore his gaze from her face and stared at the wall. "You know it's not in me to settle down. And even if I did try, I'd only end up hurting you, or breaking your heart." He looked down at her angrily. *Or something much worse could happen to you, or little Sarah.* "I'm just not the settling type!"

Chase saw her tremble and knew what her invitation must have cost her. He felt miserable. It was better if she found somebody else. Somebody dependable like the blacksmith, who could take care of her, give her the things she needed.

Chase pulled away.

"I understand," she responded softly.

He couldn't miss the hurt written all over her face.

"Chase," Jessie began."Sometimes things affect our lives so powerfully that we think only of the bad—I know I do. But in truth, it had to happen. I know it sounds strange. Whatever it is, there is good too. Look for it. You may be surprised."

He narrowed his eyes and looked at her for a long moment, then rolled off the bed and straightened his shirt. "I'll be leaving tomorrow. I'll ride into town and tell them about Nathan's death. Pick up more supplies and buy you a side of beef that'll last you till spring. I'll try to find you a suitable horse but if I can't do that, I'll leave you mine."

CHAPTER SEVENTEEN

*A*wake at sunrise, Chase eased himself out of the rocking chair, where he'd slept all night. Jessie had tossed and turned, eventually curling into a little ball before finally falling asleep. Her mumblings had awakened him, so he'd pulled the blankets up around her shoulders and tucked her in. It was the least he could do for her. She seemed to be sleeping soundly now. He tiptoed out to avoid waking her.

The cabin was quiet with the young'uns still asleep. Chase lit the stove and set the pot on for coffee.

His mind was made up. He wasn't changing it. Telling Gabe was going to be hard, though. Explaining that the last few days had all been make-believe, and now it was time for him to be heading out, would be tough. No matter how Chase circled it, Gabe was gonna think he was a cold-hearted skunk.

"Mornin'," Gabe mumbled from his bedroll. His disheveled hair shaded his eyes, and he yawned. "Didn't hear you get up. Where's Jessie?"

"Still sleeping."

Chase waited as Gabe got up and slung his blanket around his shoulders, a shield from the cold. When Gabe returned from the outhouse, Chase motioned for him to have a seat at the table. He kept his voice low so he wouldn't wake Sarah. "Got some things to explain and I'd like to get it done before the little one wakes up." Handing Gabe a cup of hot coffee, he drew up a chair.

Silence hung ominously in the room. By the size of the boy's eyes, Chase knew he must be thinking he'd stepped out of line.

"Nothing's wrong, Gabe, so don't worry. Well, something's wrong, but it doesn't involve you. You've been doing a fine job around here."

Chase held back a smile as he saw Gabe release the breath he'd been holding. They both took a sip from their cups, and their eyes met over the rims. Chase was first to speak.

"I don't know how to tell you this, so I'm just going to say it outright. I think you're man enough to understand."

He had Gabe's full attention.

"I'm not Nathan Strong. Been pretending. To help Jessie so she'd be able to adopt Sarah." Chase leaned back in his chair.

Color came up in Gabe's face and his eyes narrowed.

"Nathan was working for the same spread I was. Got himself killed. I brought Jessie the news the night before you arrived."

Gabe shot up. His chair twirled, almost falling over. With fists clenched he leaned toward Chase. "You sayin' you and her"—he motioned with his head to the bedroom—"*ain't married*?"

"That's what I'm saying."

Gabe was across the table in a heartbeat. Coffee mugs went flying, landing with a crash on the floor. Gabe had a death hold around Chase's neck, and it was all Chase could do not to fall to the ground.

"Stop it, Gabe! Let me explain," Chase gasped, prying the boy's fingers from around his neck. Gabe Garrison was wiry and strong. Chase hoped he could peel the boy from his throat without using force, but it didn't seem possible at this point.

As quick as he'd attacked, Gabe dropped his arms and turned from Chase, making for the door.

"Gabe! Hold on." Chase lunged for him and caught his arm.

"Let go," Gabe cried, choking on the words.

"Let me explain." Chase held him to the spot. "It's not what you're thinking."

Gabe's face glowered as he swallowed once. "Yeah? You tell me now, just what *am* I thinking?" The question was low, hurtful. "I know. It wasn't you, sleeping in there with Jessie the past few nights. Right?"

The boy had him there. Things looked bad from the kid's standpoint, and Chase didn't have any foolproof answers.

Gabe wrenched free the moment Jessie appeared in her bedroom doorway, a startled look on her face.

"What's going on?" she questioned, taking in the puddles of coffee on the floor and Gabe's hard, angry expression.

Chase was taken aback. Her face was pasty white, with lines around her eyes and mouth. She slumped on the doorframe, as if needing its support.

Taking advantage of the interruption, Gabe ripped his coat from the peg and ran out the door.

"Horse pucky," Chase uttered as the door banged closed. He'd made a mess of it now. He turned to Jessie. "You don't look well. Are you sick?"

"I'm fine. Just need to make a trip outside."

She didn't look fine. Last night she hadn't looked sick, but she'd been broody while asleep. Now she looked almost nervous, too. Chase watched as she disappeared through the door.

Five minutes…ten minutes…fifteen crept by.

Where in the devil was she? He'd have gone looking for her, but felt she needed her privacy. Women were fussy about that sort of thing.

Sarah, who'd somehow slept through all the commotion, was awake now and hungry as a bear cub after hibernation. Chase felt oddly helpless in the face of her need. He offered her a leathery piece of jerky from his saddlebag, but she rejected it, her face clouding with impending tears.

"Hungry," she whined.

"I know, I know. Jessie will be right back. She'll fix you something, all right?" As her tears began to fall, he stomped to the door. Sensibilities be danged!

At that moment, Jessie stepped in. She looked from Chase, to Sarah's wobbly frown, and back again. "What's wrong?"

Unnerved by his helplessness, he responded harshly. "Sarah's hungry, and I couldn't find anything she wanted." He strode over to the child, picked her up, and faced Jessie angrily, as if waiting for an answer.

Jessie was dumbfounded. What could she tell him? That her head was squeezing her eyes out of their sockets? That her cramped and bloated stomach felt as if it'd been pummeled in a fistfight? It was all she could do to not shout back at him.

Taking a deep breath she forced a smile. "Sorry," she replied evenly. "I just needed some morning air to clear my head. How about biscuits and gravy?"

Sarah stopped crying and wiggled out of Chase's embrace. She ran up to Jessie and held out her arms. Too weary to lift her, Jessie knelt down and kissed her tear-dampened cheek.

"One…two…three." With Sarah on a chair next to her, Jessie let the child scoop the heaping cups of flour and dump them into a clay mixing bowl. She showed her how to form a small well in the center and then carefully pour some water inside. Jessie took over mixing the powdery concoction slowly at first, and then with gusto.

Chase was leaving today.

Folding the dough over, she gave it a punch. That was just fine with her. They didn't need *him*. *She* certainly didn't. Actually, she was glad he was finally going. Things around here had gotten way too complicated.

"Breakfast is almost ready," she said over her shoulder to Chase as she stirred the gravy. "Call Gabe in from the barn."

"He's not in the barn. I'm not sure where he is. I told him about us this morning."

Jessie turned from her chore as his words sank in, the wooden spoon clattering to the floor. "*What* did you say?"

"I said, he's not in—"

"How could you?"she asked heatedly. "How could you go and do something like that without telling me first? I would have liked to explain things to him myself. I can't imagine what he's feeling right now."

Chase didn't respond, just pinned her in an icy stare.

"Well? How did he take it? You not being Nathan and all?"

"Not good."

He was lucky she wasn't holding the spoon any longer because she just might aim it at his head. "What did he say—exactly?" She was tired of dragging every word out of him. This was important. She wasn't in the mood to play cat and mouse.

"Didn't say much of anything. Just went for my throat when he found out we weren't married." Chase gingerly touched the red welts Gabe had left behind. "Defending your honor."

Jessie hurried to the door.

"Where do you think you're going?"

"To look for Gabe," Jessie shot back. "I need to explain…"

"Give him some time to work it out on his own. He's a smart kid." Chase picked up Sarah and put her on a chair at the table. "Don't you fall off now," he said as he pushed her up to the table. "Besides, this one's real hungry. We'll have another uprising on our hands if we don't get some grub into her."

After breakfast Jessie cleaned the kitchen and started a kettle of water boiling in the front yard for the laundry she did once a week. Her lower abdomen, racked with cramps, was all she could think about. If only she could lie down on her bed and die. Since Chase was set on leaving no matter what, she wished he'd just hurry up and go.

The object of her musings came outside and leaned against the porch post. Sarah followed and sat on the step. *Why is he hanging around? Hasn't he ever seen someone doing laundry before?* She pushed some towels under the bubbling water with her wooden paddle. Without warning, she swayed to one side, dangerously close to the hot water.

Chase sprang down the steps, gathering her in his arms. Limp as a rag doll, she leaned into him, drinking in his familiar scent, longing to say so many things.

"Jessie, what's wrong? I can tell you're not feeling well. What is it?" Chase's face was etched with concern.

"Just a bad stomachache. It'll pass," she said, making no attempt to leave his embrace.

"You're going to lie down for a bit." Chase stood back and looked into her face. "I won't take no for an answer."

He scooped her up, carried her into the cabin, and placed her on the bed.

"Nursing me has plumb wore you out. I'll watch Sarah till you're feeling better."

"Chase?" She closed her eyes and burrowed down into the soft mattress.

"Yes?"

"You won't leave without saying good-bye, will you?"

She felt him brush a strand of hair from her face and tuck it behind her ear. "No, I won't. Now get some rest."

CHAPTER EIGHTEEN

The wash was much harder than Chase had expected. He'd done his own laundry before, but the whole of that consisted of a shirt or two, a pair of long johns, and some socks. Washing for a family of three was quite another story.

His shirtsleeves rolled to his elbows, he plunged another pair of socks into the rinse bucket. By the time he'd finished scrubbing Jessie's dresses and Sarah's two small ones, he'd worked up a sheen on his face and rings of sweat under his arms.

Gabe's things were the last of it. He shoved them into the pot, giving them a good swish.

Sarah was happy as a tadpole. Her job was to fetch small logs from the woodpile whenever the fire grew low. She was to stop at the line he'd drawn in the dirt fifteen feet back. Now, she struggled with a piece of wood nearly as long as she was.

As Gabe's clothes boiled in the soapy water, Chase rinsed Jessie's and Sarah's things and spread them on bushes to dry. This chore would be easier if there was a clothesline. A clothesline…

Long strides took him to the barn, where he untied his lariat from his saddle. He strung the hard cord rope between two sturdy trees, then flopped the wet clothes across it to dry. At the rinse bucket he withdrew a worn chemise belonging to Jessie. She must've washed it and left it to soak before he took over the job. Dipping it several times, he wrung it carefully, being cautious not to rip the threadbare garment.

Sarah tugged his pant leg.

"Da, more wood," Sarah said, pointing proudly to the big log she'd finally managed to drag over to him. Accomplishment shone in her eyes. He didn't have the heart to scold her for coming too close to the fire. "Thanks...honey. You're sure a big help. Now stay back where I showed you."

Sarah beamed her pleasure, and then ran back to the woodpile to tackle another piece. Perhaps she was so young she wouldn't remember the brief role he'd played in her life and forget all about him after he left. Somehow, though, this thought didn't make him feel any better.

He finished with Gabe's clothes and was surprised to find his own dirty pants and extra shirt at the bottom of the bucket. Obviously Jessie meant to wash his clothes too.

With shooting pains up his back and aching arms, he rinsed the last pair of socks. Taking Sarah with him, Chase carried the rinse bucket to the back of the cabin and dumped the murky water on Jessie's small garden. Almost everything was dead now that winter was at hand, but a few pea vines seemed to be hanging on to the bitter end.

Footsteps crunched on the frozen ground. He turned in time to see Jessie scurrying to the outhouse. Whatever was wrong, she wasn't giving him the whole story. In a few moments, he saw her leave the outhouse and hurry toward the creek.

Chase doused the fire, lifted Sarah and followed behind Jessie. As they approached the stream, Jessie, crouched next to the water, looked as if she were rinsing something out.

If she had something to wash, why hadn't she done it in the kettle with everything else? Why hide it at the creek? She turned and made a wringing motion, then began to arrange what looked like strips of cloth over the rocks to dry.

Of course! He felt like a horse's behind for not figuring it out sooner. The facts of life didn't embarrass him. But they certainly would Jessie. He wished she wouldn't worry about hiding—it was natural, and nothing to be ashamed of. Was she sad? Sorry she wouldn't be having Nathan's child? Women seemed to set such stock in babies.

Chase quickly retraced his steps to the front porch. "Let's get this soapy water dumped 'fore your ma comes back. She'll be happy to see we finished all the washing," Chase said with a grin. Sarah clapped her hands with excitement.

Jessie rounded the corner of the cabin and stopped dead in her tracks. It did look odd—clothing of all shapes and sizes fluttering from the newly strung clothesline in the chilly breeze. Suddenly, he was mighty glad he'd made the effort to help.

"My goodness. You—you really shouldn't have," Jessie stammered. "I was planning on doing it right now."

"Sarah and I needed something to pass the time." Chase bent down and picked up Sarah.

Jessie dabbed at the corners of her eyes.

"Hey, don't cry," he said teasingly. "Next time we'll leave it all for you." Chase was trying to lighten the moment, but they both knew there wouldn't be a next time.

Jessie looked off to the woods. "Chase, I'm worried about Gabe. He's been gone several hours. What if he has run off for good? I wish I could've explained things to him myself."

Truth be known, Chase was worried too. He'd thought Gabe would've returned by now. These mountains were wild, untamed. An unarmed boy was easy pickings.

"Maybe he used his head and walked into town," he said, trying to sound casual. "He's probably having a grand time looking around as we speak." He didn't really think that. The way the boy had been feeling this morning, he'd probably run off not knowing where he was headed. "I'll saddle Cody and take a look around."

Jessie nodded, looking wan and tired.

Sarah, hearing Chase was leaving, hugged his neck with her strong little arms, burying her face into his windblown hair.

"Bye-bye, Da." She tilted her head, gazing into his eyes. Chase's throat closed.

He kissed her forehead and then set her on the ground. "Bye, Sarah. Take good care of your ma, you hear?"

Gabe wandered deeper into the forest, paying little attention to the distance he was traveling. How could they have lied to him like that? He was such a fool. Here he'd been admiring Mr. Strong—*Chase*, he thought bitterly—and wanting to be just like him when he was grown. And all the while, Chase'd been dallying with Jessie. He still couldn't believe it!

Should've bloodied his nose when I had the jump on him. Bloodied it good!

"I know what you always told me, Pa, that settling things with my fists ain't the best way. But it's just not right for him to be treating her like some common...common...well, you know what I mean." Gabe spoke to the sky as if he were directly addressing his father.

Gabe caught sight of Chase and Cody as they climbed up the steep trail he'd just covered. He stopped, waiting for the horse to approach.

"You all right?" Chase called, his voice harsh. "Jessie is worried sick about you."

Gabe nodded. He didn't feel like talking to the man.

Chase extended his arm. "Climb aboard." Finally, after several moments, Gabe grasped it and swung up behind Chase. They rode back down through the trees.

As they neared the homestead, Chase brought Cody to a halt, and Gabe swung off.

"Look, Gabe, I know you're disappointed in the way things have turned out." Chase looked down at him for a long moment, his mouth a straight, hard line. "I'm sure you know by now that life's not fair. Just when you think you've been dealt a winning hand, the devil will throw down an ace. That's a fact."

Gabe figured Chase was waiting for him to say something. Maybe tell him he understood. Well, he couldn't do that. Not only had Chase hurt Jessie's reputation, but he also planned to leave—breaking up what had seemed to Gabe to be a perfect family. A family he wanted to claim as his own.

"When I was fourteen, I had been on my own for four years," Chase continued. "Just a little older than you. What I'm trying to say is, you've got to be the man of the house now. Accept responsibilities. Jessie needs your help. She'll depend on it." Chase cleared his throat. "So when something gets you down, you can't just up and run off. Take it like a man, the good and the bad, and do what's right for you and your family."

Gabe stared at the ground. He'd been thinking Chase was doing what was right for the family too, before he learned the truth.

"I'm going into town," Chase went on. "I'll be looking for a horse for you and Jessie and pick up some supplies you'll need this winter. I'm sorry if things didn't work out like you wanted."

Chase whirled his horse around and galloped off in the opposite direction. Even after everything that'd happened today, after all his feelings of disappointment and anger toward Chase, no matter how hard he tried to hate him, he couldn't.

He loved him.

There was no denying it.

CHAPTER NINETEEN

Chase rode down the muddy street of Valley Springs, a small town that looked like any number of the small towns he'd traveled through over the years. Since it didn't claim a sheriff's office, he decided the next best place to deliver the news about Nathan would be the mercantile.

First, though, he'd stop at the saloon. Have a drink. It was a good way to get a feel for this sleepy little town and wet his dry throat.

As he tied Cody to the empty hitching rail, a man stepped out of an eatery from across the street. The man stood for a moment and stared boldly. Chase gave him a nod before stepping into the dark interior of the bar.

It took a few moments for his eyes to adjust to the dim light, and his sense of smell was bombarded with unpleasant odors. There'd been a time in his life when hanging around a bar, gambling, and plain cutting up had seemed enjoyable pursuits. But those days were long past. Whatever the attraction of those activities, he didn't feel it anymore and couldn't believe he ever had. Especially since spending the last few days with Jessie, where things were clean, sweet smelling, and homey. There had to be more to life than this. Now the reek of unwashed bodies and stale smoke turned his stomach.

"What can I do ya for, mister?" the barkeep asked.

"Whiskey." Placing two bits on the battered bar top, Chase looked into the mirror behind the bar and studied the room through its reflection. One man sat at a corner table, shuffling a deck of cards. He caught Chase's gaze in the mirror and held out the deck in silent invitation.

Without turning, Chase shook his head. "No, thanks." Lifting his whiskey, he took a drink.

"You new in town?" the bartender asked as he polished a clear glass tumbler. "Plannin' to stay?"

He was a short, stocky man with a shiny, bald head. A bushy, black handlebar mustache made up for the lack of hair on top.

Chase shrugged. He didn't give out information about himself—a survival tactic he'd learned long ago. "Maybe."

There was a sound from outside, and a youth came striding through the swinging doors. His scruffy, long hair was in need of a good scrubbing.

"Sorry I'm late, Pops, but Ma wouldn't let me out any sooner." He stood looking Chase up and down as he waited for the barkeep to answer.

"Oh, go on now and get your apron. If it's not one thing, it's surely another. Start with the sweeping and then empty the trash."

"Sure thing." The boy hurried into the back room, emerging with an apron in one hand and a broom in the other.

"This town have a place a man can get a bath and shave?" Chase asked as he watched the boy sweep. The lad reminded Chase of himself at that age. He'd had just such a job for a man named Rattlesnake. Meanest son of a cuss this side of the Mississippi. As soon shoot you as sell you a drink.

"Yeah. Across the street in the back of the eatery. Isaac Mahoney and his sister Megan have a tub they let out for fifty cents. If you want a haircut and shave, Megan'll do that for an extra two bits. Would you be wantin' it now?" he asked.

"The sooner, the better."

The barkeep turned to the boy. "Jake, run across the street and have Ike warm some water. And tell Megan to sharpen her razor. Don't want no dull blade, haw haw."

Chase didn't see the humor in the old man's remark but laughed anyway. "How 'bout a telegraph office?"

"Sure do. Just got a line in last year," the little man announced proudly. "It's down at the stage office on the north end of town."

Chase took a sip. "Don't suppose you've also got a smithy around here."

"Well, I'm sure surprised you didn't see the blacksmith shop as you rode in. Can't miss it, block down from Hollyhock's."

"Now that you mention it, I do remember seeing the place. He any good with horses?"

"About the best in the territory. Name's Garth Shepard. People think right highly of him around here."

I'll bet they do, Chase thought, tossing back the last of his drink.

"Another?"

"No, thanks."

The kid ambled back into the saloon humming a tune. "Water'll be hot in about fifteen minutes." Remnants of some kind of pastry clung to his mouth.

"Thanks." Chase dug into his pocket and flipped him a coin. Jake caught it midair.

"Thanks, mister. If you have need of anything else, let me know."

"Hey, you work for me. Remember?" the bartender said, wagging his finger at the boy.

"Sure, Pops, I know." Jake went back to his sweeping and humming.

"You know anyone by the name of Lonnie?" Chase asked.

"Can't rightly say I know him, but he's been in here a time or two. Said he's a prospector and has a claim upriver a ways. I think he's just some no-account, blowing smoke. I haven't seen him for a while. Heard he caused some trouble yesterday in the store," he said, pausing to wipe his bald head with the same cloth he'd been polishing the glasses with.

Chase looked down at his glass and frowned.

"Jake! You seen that gold digger Lonnie around lately?" the bartender called.

"Naw. Been nigh on a week since I seen him."

"If he happens in while I'm still in town," Chase said, "I'd appreciate you letting me know."

"What's your name, mister?" the barkeep asked. "Need to know who'm asking for."

"Chase Logan. Don't forget, now."

"Sure thing."

"Mr. Logan," Jake called from the back. "I'm Jake. If you need anything, don't forget to ask *me*." Hefting the trash barrel, he stepped out the back door.

"Little hustler," Chase said under his breath. The kid would do all right for himself if he stayed out of trouble.

Finished with his scrubbing, Chase luxuriated in the steaming hot water. It'd been a while since he'd actually washed in a tub, so he decided to soak as long as the water stayed hot.

The tub was large, but then, so was Chase. His shoulders weren't fully submerged, and his knees protruded out of the soapy bubbles like twin mountain peaks. Still, the hot water caressed his torso like a loving bride easing away the pain of his sore ribs. Leaning his head back against the wall, he closed his eyes.

Uninvited visions of Jessie in a tub of bubbles popped into his head. Her hair was swept up in an enticing fashion on top of her head, just begging for him to pull out a pin to set it free, and little beads of water slipped slowly down her neck, disappearing into the bubbles.

CHAPTER TWENTY

*A*h, hell."

"Did ya say somethin', Mr. Logan? 'Tis anythin' you be needin'?" Megan Mahoney's lilting Irish brogue made its way through the locked door.

Was her ear pressed to the door? "No, I'm fine." She'd almost insisted on helping him off with his clothes and into the tub. He'd finally succeeded in shooing her out and turning the lock.

"My razor's sharp, and I'm ready anytime. But don't let me rush ya, now. I know how delightful a hot, bubbly bath can be."

"Meg!" Ike's scolding voice rang sharp. "Leave Mr. Logan alone. How can he relax with you squawking like a jabber bird? Now, skedaddle from that door until he's ready to come out."

"I'm just trying to be friendly, Isaac," Megan said plaintively.

Chase reached for the large towel on the metal stand. Standing, he quickly rubbed himself dry and redressed in his clothes.

As promised, Megan was waiting for him on the other side of the door. She hadn't left, just stopped talking. She had her shaving kit all lined up, ready to give Chase a barbering.

"Now, just sit down and make yourself comfortable, Mr. Logan. Don't be worrying…I've done this many, many times," she said, smiling as he seated himself. She carefully placed a hot rag across his stubbled face, then whipped up a bowlful of lather.

Chase tried to relax, but Megan seemed awfully feather-brained to be trusted with a razor so close to his throat.

She began to scrape. The first few strokes were nerve-racking. But distracting noises floated in from the other room, where Megan's brother was serving meals, and soon Chase was relaxed and enjoying himself.

It was close to noon, and the hearty aromas of lunches being served next door wafted in to taunt his empty belly. His stomach rumbled.

"Oh," Megan said, and then giggled. She sat up and wiped the razor on a towel. "You're hungry. You must try some of Isaac's mutton pie. 'Tis as heavenly as hot cocoa for Christmas."

It occurred to Chase that as recently as a week ago he would have loved the attention he was receiving now. Welcomed her flirtatious ways and pretty face. Megan was the sort of female any man would find very attractive. But now all he could think about was tying up loose ends and getting back to the cabin to make sure everything was all right...with Jessie.

"Meg!" Ike called from the other room. "Are you almost finished with Mr. Logan? We're gettin' plenty busy out here. I need your help."

"I'm just about done." She mopped the remaining bits of lather from Chase's face and held up a mirror.

As Chase was leaving the building, he nearly ran into the blacksmith, who was entering the room at the same time. The door opening wouldn't accommodate both large men.

"Are you Mr. Shepard, the blacksmith?" Chase asked, stepping back to give him room to enter.

"That's me, all right. You need some work done?" Garth asked with a friendly smile. His gaze roamed the room until it landed on Megan, and he gave her a wink.

"I'm looking for a horse to buy. Has to be gentle."

"Have a couple down at my place I just traded for some work on a prairie schooner. You're welcome to come take a look."

"I'll do that when you're done with your meal."

Chase set out for the stage office and sent two telegrams: one to the Rocking Crown, informing them of a short delay in his arrival, and one to the First National Bank of Logan Meadows.

Chase made it a practice to wire the better part of his pay to his bank account every few months. He kept just the bare minimum to make it to the next job, with a little extra left over. His savings were something he took seriously, a nest egg for the future. This time he kept most back, planning on using it for Jessie's supplies. That way she could save Nathan's for the days ahead.

Back when he was eighteen, Chase had been as wild as they came, and after one particularly rowdy night he landed in jail for disturbing the peace. The town banker, Frank Lloyd, came and bailed him out. At the time it had been a mystery to Chase why he'd do such a thing. To pay off his debt to him, Frank had had Chase doing small jobs here and there, all the while instilling in him a curiosity for finance.

Frank Lloyd turned out to be the best thing that ever happened to Chase, teaching him the principles of saving and investments and such. Chase was a willing pupil, with a quick grasp for figures. The two made contact every few years, and Frank watched over Chase's money, making small investments for him now and then.

After wiring his money Chase entered the mercantile. The potbelly stove heated the room and tangy scents of spice and sugar made his mouth water.

The rustling of skirts drew his attention to the first aisle, where a small woman was dusting the shelves with a brown feather duster.

"Oh—may I help you?" She bustled over to him, dusting as she came.

"Yes, ma'am. I need a few supplies."

"Well, you've come to the right place, young man," she said, boldly looking him up and down. "Do you have a list of the things you need?"

"No, actually I don't. I want supplies sent out to Nathan Strong's place. Enough for passing the winter without having to scrimp." The second he'd mentioned Nathan Strong the woman nearly stood at attention. "Be sure to include coffee, tea, sugar, and flour. Throw in any canned goods you have and some candy. Some bolts of fabric would be good, and three blankets, if you have them."

"Mercy me, that's a large order." The quantity and variety of things he wanted seemed to surprise the wiry little woman. "You must be kin—a brother, maybe, of Mr. Strong's?" Curiosity burned in her intense blue eyes.

"No, actually I'm not." Chase was relieved the store was empty except for the two of them. "I'm an acquaintance of Mr. Strong's. I rode with him on his last job. He was killed, and I brought the news to his widow."

All color drained from her face. "Oh, my! Poor Jessie!" The woman was clucking her cheeks now, and Chase couldn't help but notice her resemblance to a chicken.

"Poor child. My, my, my. Have you told her yet?" The woman began fanning herself with the feather duster, and bits of fluff floated here and there.

"Yes. I just came from there." Chase spotted a rope coiled on the wall. "And throw in that rope," he said, pointing.

"Yes, yes." The old woman scurried here and there, piling things on the counter. "I'll ride out with Virgil when he delivers your things. I need to see how Jessie is takin' the news."

"Fine, but I have some other business I need to take care of first. I'll be back in about an hour, and then we'll go out together."

The blacksmith's shop was small, with corrals around the sides and out back. A small living area was built above the lower stable. Chase was struck by how neat and well kept everything was. A new coat of white paint made the building stand out in a town where everything else was in drastic need of repair.

The ring of metal on metal reverberated. Entering the smithy, he found Mr. Shepard bent over the hoof of a massive black horse.

"Howdy."

"Howdy, Mr. Logan," Garth said, straightening. He took his handkerchief from his pocket and wiped his face and the back of his neck. "Megan over at the eatery told me your name."

Chase, trying hard not to like this man, flexed his shoulders. He'd seen him yesterday enjoying Jessie's company entirely too much. But his sunny disposition and generous manner were hard to dismiss. Chase held out his hand, and Garth took it in his. The men shook while sizing each other up.

"I'd like to take a look at those horses you mentioned," Chase said after a pause. "I need something real gentle and broke solid."

"They're 'round back. Come on, I'll show you."

Chase peered into the corral at the motley group—three horses and a mule stood ankle deep in muck. Garth took a rope and, not giving notice to the mud he was trudging through, brought the first horse over for Chase to inspect.

When Chase stepped into the corral and approached, the gray pinned his ears. "Nope. Don't want him. The other two? Are they gentle?"

"Seem to be," Garth answered. "Haven't seen them bite, kick, or do anything dangerous."

They halted the two and brought them out. The little chestnut mare stood patiently, enjoying the attention. The paint, head hung low, ignored the men completely. After leading them around and picking up their feet, Chase rode each animal around the block.

"Great. How much?"

"Eighteen each. That includes the equipment."

Chase tied the horses in front of the mercantile and entered. The chicken-like storekeeper was busy helping a young lady who was straightening some bolts of fabric. Both women looked up as he approached.

"Looky who's here, Beth—the man I was telling you about," the storekeeper said, rushing forward to greet him.

He cringed inwardly. The last thing he wanted to do today was chitchat in the house-goods section with two women he didn't know. Mrs. Happyhill, or whatever her name was, took hold of his arm and towed him toward the young woman.

"Beth, this is Mr....uh..."

"Logan," Chase filled in for her.

"I'm pleased to make your acquaintance, Mr. Logan," she replied, her cheeks instantly darkening to crimson splotches.

"He's the one who worked with Mr. Strong and is sendin' all the food and such out to the Strongs' homestead," the storekeeper—Mrs. Hollyhock, that was her name, Chase remembered—said as she gazed up at Chase. "Don't he look just like my Tommy? The resemblance is strikin'."

Pausing, she took out a handkerchief and dabbed at the corners of her eyes. "I'm sorry, Mr. Logan, I didn't mean to go on like that. It's just been so long since my handsome boy rode away. I'm always hoping, waiting..."

"There, there," the young woman said a bit impatiently. "Don't cry, Violet."

"I'm set to go," Chase broke in. "Are the things I ordered ready?" The sooner he was out the door, the better. Females put him on edge, especially crying ones.

"Yes, they're 'round back on the buckboard, Mr. Logan. Just let me grab my shawl, and Virgil and I'll be ready too." Turning to the other woman, she asked, "Beth, would you mind closing up? I want to ride out with Mr. Logan and check on Jessie. I'm jist sure she's takin' the news real hard, poor little thing."

CHAPTER TWENTY-ONE

*A*s soon as the buckboard stopped, Mrs. Hollyhock climbed spryly from the wagon without assistance and rushed to the cabin door. Moments later, she enfolded Jessie in her embrace, and they rocked from side to side. Gabe and Sarah watched from the fireplace, not knowing who the stranger was. Virgil came in slowly, his bowler hat clutched in his fingers.

Mrs. Hollyhock pulled back and studied Jessie's face, then sucked in her breath.

"You're white as a sheet, girl. Come lie down before you fall over. I'll bet my bloomers you've not had a bite to eat all day."

Jessie glanced furtively out the door, searching for Chase. She hadn't seen him yet and was frantic with the thought he hadn't come back. Finally she spotted him as he tied his reins to the back of the wagon, alongside two other horses she'd never seen. Relief flooded her. He'd gotten a shave and bath, and looked exceptionally handsome. She caught his glance and searched his eyes, and suddenly she longed to feel his arms holding her tight. As if he had read her thoughts, he took a step in her direction, but before she could respond, Sarah came at him like a cat after a mouse.

"Da's back, Da's back," she sang, running down the stairs and vaulting into his embrace. Chase lifted her high. As he swung her down, Jessie heard him whisper into the child's ear.

"Shhh…Your ma's not feelin' well."

His voice, soft as worn leather, sent tingles dancing down her spine. She glanced at Mrs. Hollyhock to see if she'd heard what Sarah had called Chase. To her relief, the old woman was in her own world, fussing over Jessie as she hustled her toward her bedroom.

Secluded in the room, Mrs. Hollyhock insisted that Jessie remove her shoes and lie down. She propped her feet on a pillow and bustled about, fluffing blankets and opening the window.

"Oh, poor girl. It must've been a horrible shock to learn your man's passed on. Iffin' you'd like, I'll stay out here with ya till you're over the worst of it."

"That's very kind of you, Mrs. Hollyhock, but it's really not necessary," Jessie said, struggling to sit up. Mrs. Hollyhock pushed her gently back onto the pillows.

"You look weak. Just stay where I put ya. You don't know what's good for ya at a time like this."

Sighing, Jessie lay back on the pillow and closed her eyes. A sharp cramp caught her off guard, and a little squeak of pain slipped through her lips before she could stop it.

"What is it, girl?" Mrs. Hollyhock peered anxiously in her face, as if she suspected Jessie of having some horrible ailment.

"Nothing much, really. Just a tiny pain."

As if summoned to duty, Mrs. Hollyhock began eyeballing Jessie for symptoms. Leaning forward, she inspected her eyes, muttering speculatively.

"The whites ain't yeller, so it ain't the liver," she said, sounding relieved. "Roll your head to the side so I can have a look-see into your ear."

Jessie raised her eyebrows. "I'm *fine*, Mrs. Hollyhock. It's just my monthly. For some reason I seem to have a hard time with them."

"Well, why didn't you say so, child? I have a pouch full of herbs that'll make ya feel better right quick. I'll be back before you get the chance to miss me." Winking, she whisked out of the room in a flurry of flannel.

Reentering the main room, Mrs. Hollyhock nodded approvingly as Gabe and Virgil went back and forth to the wagon for the supplies. "Who's this strapping young man helpin' put things away?" she asked, looking from Gabe to Chase. "He your son, Mr. Logan?"

Before Chase had a chance to answer, she'd moved on to Sarah. "And to think I doubted the existence of wood pixies. Here sits one right 'fore my very eyes, as sure as I'm standing here."

Sarah looked up from her seat at the table. She was nibbling on some raisins Chase had bought in town. Covering her smile with her hand, she giggled when Mrs. Hollyhock tickled her tummy.

Chase had no choice but to introduce the children. "This is Gabe Garrison and Sarah. They're going to be living here with Jessie—I mean, Mrs. Strong."

Mrs. Hollyhock stared at him in surprise.

"Mrs. Strong. Has. Adopted them," he explained, haltingly, trying to make the strange situation sound normal.

Silent for a moment, Mrs. Hollyhock eyed all three. Then, breaking into a smile that bespoke of great secrets, she zeroed in on Gabe. "Would you mind puttin' on the kettle to boil? I have some herbs that'll have your new ma feelin' fine in no time a'tall. After that, get the pot off the wagon seat. It's your supper."

After Jessie had finished her tea and was fast asleep, Mrs. Hollyhock tiptoed from the bedroom and quietly shut the door. She put her pot on the stove to warm, and then called the family to order.

"Jessie will be fine in a day or two. Be sure she don't wear herself out doin' for you and the little one," she said, looking at Gabe. "It's a shock to become a widder at such a young age. She'll have some adjustin' to do." Virgil, now slumped in a chair by the fire, let out a long saw blade–sounding snore.

"She's asleep just now and probably won't wake till mornin'," Mrs. Hollyhock went on. "Help yourself to the vittles, and Gabe, be sure to feed the little one before she gets hungry and starts fussing. I don't want Jessie to worry about nothin' a'tall."

She turned her attention to Chase. "What be your plans, Mr. Logan?" she asked innocently. "You have a family to rush back to?"

Chase almost winced. Inside this cabin was the only family he'd ever known. It'd felt nice being a part of it, even for such a short time. His thoughts turned to Jessie, tucked in her warm, cozy bed, and his heart gave a thump.

"No family. Just me and my horse." Chase stared at the ground. He didn't want to see the effect his words were having on Gabe.

"Well then, will you be riding on tonight? You certainly can't stay here."

He glanced at Sarah, hoping the child wouldn't choose this moment to speak up and call him Da. "Since things have settled—"

"Because iffin' you're interested," Mrs. Hollyhock interrupted, "I have a room I let out above my mercantile. It's yours if you need it for a day or two, or however long you decide to stay." She straightened her skirt and continued. "My boy Tommy used to live up there. Did I tell you how much you resemble him? Why, at a glance I can almost believe it's him standing here. Such a fine man, my Tommy is."

Chase chanced a look at Gabe. Not being able to see the hopeful look on the boy's face would be like not feeling the sun on a spring day. And, truth be known, he wasn't ready to leave quite yet. Just a couple of days more...to make sure Jessie was feeling better.

"That's a kind offer, Mrs. Hollyhock. I'm much obliged. I can stay a day or two more."

Gabe squared his shoulders, then looked Chase square in the eyes. It felt like a silent challenge.

What? Apprehension cut through Chase.

"Besides, Mr. Logan," Gabe said matter-of-factly. "I'll bet your head still hurts where the bullet grazed your scalp."

"You've been hurt, Mr. Logan?" Mrs. Hollyhock hurried toward Chase. "Would ya like me to take a look at it, make sure it's healin' up proper? Ya wouldn't want no gangrene ta set in."

"No thanks, ma'am." Chase pulled back to a safe distance. "It's just a little sore."

"Mrs. Strong sure did a fine job of doctoring him up," the boy went on nonchalantly. "For a while we weren't sure if he'd even make it. He was as helpless as a frozen snake."

"Well, I'll be." The woman stood, looking startled. "I was under the distinct impression you'd jist rode in today."

Mrs. Hollyhock drummed her fingers slowly as she looked around the room. "When did ya say you arrived?"

Ruining a girl's reputation was not something to be taken lightly in these parts. Any parts, actually. Respectable women, widows included, were watched over and protected by the townspeople. Chase knew it would only take a word from the boy to send the old woman scurrying for a preacher. And by Gabe's expression, he knew it too.

A hush fell upon the room. At some point in the conversation, Virgil had awoken. He and Mrs. Hollyhock waited for Chase's answer.

"I didn't."

At that moment Jessie's offer came floating back to Chase like something from a dream.

You could stay if you wanted. Her sweet invitation flowed over him like warm honey, making him long for the goodness of her. Could he take a chance and put the past aside? Take a stab at something more solid than his horse and the next trail?

"I guess that's so," she said, darting a knowing look at Virgil. "Well, go on, enlighten us."

Hold up, he thought. Telling the whole truth now wouldn't give Jessie any say in a decision that would change her whole life.

On the other hand, lying even more sat about as well with him as sharing a den with a polecat. Deciding to give as little information as they'd accept and letting the cards fall as they may felt like the most honest thing to do.

"Been here a handful of days." Chase ran his fingers through his hair nervously. "Two days after I arrived, someone shot me, and Mrs. Strong saved my life. When I was able, I rode into town and you know the rest of the story."

It put him on edge to have to explain his actions, especially with Gabe sitting there knowing he was leaving out a major chunk of the story.

"Hummm." Mrs. Hollyhock stood rooted to the floor. The color came up in her face, and it looked as though her eyes would pop out of her face at any moment.

"My-my-my," she stuttered, all the while shaking her head. "Just what exactly did ya plan ta do, Mr. Logan?"

She was working herself up, no question about it. Her voice squawked like that of a plucked jaybird.

Virgil stared at her as if she'd just sprouted another head.

"Didja plan ta ride off after ya had a piece of the pie, a taste of the pudding, not carin' what happens to Jessie, possibly leavin' her with another mouth ta feed? And her bein' a married woman and all! You should be ashamed of yourself, cozying up to her and playin' off her sympathies!"

"Hold on just a minute!" Chase shot back. "That's not the way it happened at all. And she's not married, at least not anymore." Mrs. Hollyhock had it all wrong. But there was no stopping her now.

"Just what kind of chance will she have of findin' a decent husband after people find out she's been livin' out here with the likes of you?" With that, she sighed wearily and plopped down into a chair at the table.

"That Garth...now *he's* a fine man, iffin' I've ever seen one. He's always had an eye for the girl, ain't that right, Virgil?"

Virgil seemed surprised that she'd remembered he was even in the room.

"Reckon so," he mumbled.

"But now..." Her voice faded as she slumped in the chair. At the moment, all bent and defeated, she seemed no stronger than a feather in a gust of wind.

"Why, it's only a matter of time before the whole town knows, being as any young'uns I've ever known could never keep a secret. And me and Virgil"—she slowly shook her head—"we know what kind a life a ruint girl has. You've seen 'em entertainin' upstairs at the saloons, the likes of any man who will pay for it...one after another." She'd lowered her voice and turned her face to Chase so the children couldn't hear her last comments. "Just a *shame.*"

Chase's mind flashed back to times when he himself had taken his ease in the arms of a woman like that. No, he couldn't picture Jessie doing that. He was jolted back to the present by a half sob from the old woman.

"I can't bear to think of Jessie at the mercy of some drunken..."

She left that sentence unfinished and suddenly snapped to attention, drilling Chase with an ice-blue stare.

CHAPTER TWENTY-TWO

*W*hy—why, you was here when Garth brought Jessie back from town yesterday. Weren't ya? Oh, heavens!" Mrs. Hollyhock looked as if she was about to swoon. "I'm sure he must've known there was somethin' amiss."

The tremble in Mrs. Hollyhock's voice, the glare in her eyes... If he didn't think of something—and quick—he would find himself the groom at a shotgun wedding.

Seeing the frightened look on Sarah's face, Chase dismissed his resolve to keep his distance, and picked her up. "It's all right, honeybunch, everything is fine," he said, stroking her hair. Sarah put her fingers into her mouth and laid her head down on his shoulder, never taking her eyes off the imposing little woman.

Gabe had been conspicuously quiet through the whole discussion. Chase figured after the boy's useful details about Jessie doctoring him up, he might be feeling a little sheepish about facing him. Or maybe he was just waiting for the right moment to drive the finishing nails into his coffin. If he let slip how he'd spent the night in Jessie's bedroom, pretending to be Nathan...

"Virgil, ya better head back ta town before dark," Mrs. Hollyhock said. "I'm stayin' here ta make sure the snake don't crawl back to the henhouse while I'm gone, so to speak." She gave Chase a cold stare.

"And you, Mr. Logan, can just saddle up and head on out." As she said this, she seemed to be holding her breath.

Here was his chance. He could make thirty miles tonight if he pushed Cody hard. No one would be able to find him if he decided to get lost.

Just go, a part of him urged. But...he'd promised Jessie he wouldn't leave without saying good-bye.

This was one promise he wasn't going to break.

"I'm not leaving until I talk with Jessie." Chase had gone up against countless men in his life. He wasn't about to let this half-pint female, more wrinkled than last year's apple, throw him out like yesterday's slop.

"Iffin' your mind's made up, so be it, but you ain't wakin' her tonight. Get your gear and head out to the barn. You can sleep with the other animals, where ya belong."

Mrs. Hollyhock held out her arms for the little girl. Chase hesitated a moment, then reluctantly handed Sarah to the woman. Instantly, he missed the sweet feel of her, and the tenderness she brought to his heart. His arms felt empty.

Exiting the cabin, Chase glanced at Gabe, who shrugged his shoulders and gave him a bewildered look. But pretend as he may, the boy couldn't hide the smile that was curving the corners of his mouth.

As soon as the door closed behind Chase, Mrs. Hollyhock took on a whole new demeanor. Her scowl vanished, and she went about humming cheerfully, as if she'd just received an invitation to tea with the Queen of England. She sent Virgil off, telling him to rush someone to Clancy in the morning for the preacher.

"Bring him out as soon as you're able, and don't let the grass grow under your feet. Be quick about it."

After Virgil departed, Mrs. Hollyhock set three bowls on the table and dished up the venison stew that had been reheating. For several minutes, the room was quiet while everyone concentrated on the meal.

Gabe looked into his bowl. He was doing more pushing than eating, and feeling more than a little guilty about the trouble he'd started. "What about Mr. Logan?" he said finally. "Do you want me to take some supper out to him?"

"No, I'll do that myself," Mrs. Hollyhock replied. "You get this little gal ready for bed," she added, nodding at Sarah. "I'll be back in a jiffy."

Taking a large blue mixing bowl, she filled it to the brim with stew. She placed the bowl and four thick slices of the bread on an old tray she found behind the cupboard and headed out to the barn.

"Well, Sarah, she sure is a funny old woman," Gabe said, helping the girl on with her night rail. "One moment she wants to string him up, and the next she's fussing over him like he's the town mayor."

Chase was mending the chin strap of his bridle by rigging the worn leather together with a strip of hide. He hoped it would hold until he could buy a new one. Working with his hands helped him to sort things out. It kept him busy. One more knot and he'd be done. He was past frustration, worry. Anger enveloped him.

Mrs. Hollyhock's footsteps outside the barn door were easy to recognize. She walked with the same full-skirted shuffle that'd so reminded him of a chicken, but now it didn't seem quite so endearing.

"Mr. Logan, you still here?" she called. "Mr. Logan?"

He stood and opened the door. "Come in."

"Thanky. I brought you some supper just in case you hadn't run off with your tail 'tween your legs. Come get it, iffin' you're hungry."

That stung. She'd expected him to sneak off. Well, she had another think coming.

"Yeah, I'm still here." He hung the bridle over the pommel of his saddle and turned to her, annoyance burgeoning inside. "Believe it or not, I'll be here in the morning too." The gamey scent of the venison vied for his attention, but his stomach was knotted like an old rawhide rope. Food was the last thing on his mind.

She sat the cloth-covered tray on a dusty milking stool long forgotten in the corner, then wiped her hands on her apron.

He fought the urge to intimidate the old bird, to use his size to extract some of that "I know your kind" look from her eyes. Though it was tempting, Chase wasn't the kind to bully a woman—and a little old one, at that.

"Is that all you wanted, to bring me some supper?"

She took her time to answer. "Like I expressed before, I was a-wantin' ta see iffin' you was still here. And what your intentions were. I hope you understand I jist have Jessie's best interests at heart, since now she don't have no one ta look after her. And now she has the young'uns, too. I'm hoping you'll do the honorable thing and marry the girl." She clasped her hands behind her back and peered up at him. "Her destiny is in your hands, Mr. Logan," she finished dramatically.

Chase mentally counted to five, then took a breath. "I *intend* to sleep in this barn until tomorrow, and then talk with Jessie. I told you before, I won't leave until I do," he said evenly, barely containing his agitation. "I have something that belongs to her."

Standing her ground, Mrs. Hollyhock did her best to look him straight in the eye. "That so? Well…" She sniffed. "Good. The right thing would be ta marry her, make her yer wife. She needs you."

She headed for the barn door but stopped with her hand on the wrought-iron handle. "Now, as you ponder on that, try ta get some shut-eye. Tomorrow's promising to be a busy day."

She pushed open the squeaky door and was off before he could get another word out.

"I'll bet it is," Chase said to himself. He had a sinking sensation tomorrow was going to be a lot more to him than just busy. If he weren't careful, it'd be his wedding day too. Confound it, he wasn't one to get bullied into anything he didn't want to do. He should've given Jessie the bankroll days ago and been gone. As it was, things were getting pretty involved. He'd do it tomorrow morning and be on his way. She could marry up with the blacksmith and everything would be fine.

Chase unbuckled the left side of his saddlebag, the one he used only for important papers, money, and such, and reached inside. He rummaged around for a few seconds before several alarm bells went off in his head. Where was the pouch with the money? And the locket?

Turning the saddlebag upside down, he dumped its entire contents onto the ground and stared at the odds and ends. The pouch was gone. Nowhere to be seen. When he'd been shot, he'd also been robbed.

That money was Jessie's future. Now she'd need to find employment in that tiny town. What would she do with Sarah when she was working? Besides, that was if and only if someone would hire her after they found out she'd been living out here with him. She *was* caught between a rock and a hard place, and it was all his doing!

Of course he would repay her, but it would take some time to make a withdrawal of that size and get the money wired here. Besides, now all the good she thought of him would fly out the window when she realized he'd never intended to be kind, to be thoughtful. He'd only come back to return her rightful belongings. And he hadn't even done that yet.

CHAPTER TWENTY-THREE

*T*he sun peeked in through Jessie's bedroom curtains, bringing with it soft, yellow light and the possibilities of a day without the usual clouds and bitter cold wind. Jessie stretched and smiled, rolling to her side. She pillowed her cheek on her hands.

Thanks to Mrs. Hollyhock's special brew, she felt much better this morning. She hadn't slept so well in years. Maybe that was why she was feeling so giddy. Jessie rolled onto her back, restless, excited. She couldn't shake the feeling of anticipation, like something mystical hung in the air, teasing her with hope and happiness.

A light tap sounded, and Mrs. Hollyhock's raspy voice whispered through the door.

"Dearie, you awake?"

She sat up in bed and pulled the warm covers up to her chin, not wanting any of the delicious warmth to escape. "Yes. Come in."

"Ah, I'm seein' you feel much better this mornin'. You look like the cat that ate the cream."

"I do?" Jessie laughed. "I *feel* like the cat that ate the cream. And it's all thanks to you."

"It was nothin', child. It's an easy recipe I'll teach ya before I leave. I used to have some problems with my woman times, but it's been so long ago I can hardly remember. You know, there are *some* benefits of growing old," she said with a twinkle in her eye.

"I jist can't seem to recall any of the others. Now, bundle up and run outside to take care of your necessities, and get back here real quick. We got things that need discussing."

Jessie didn't argue. It was nice having someone else take charge. She wondered how Chase was taking this headstrong woman. No use worrying over it, though. Besides, he probably enjoyed her company too.

On her way back to the cabin, Jessie paused a moment. She turned her face to the sun, letting its warmth caress her skin and warm her. Yes, it was true; she could feel it in her bones. *Today was special.* Smiling and humming a tune, she hurried up the path.

At the barn she paused. Was Chase in there? She hadn't seen him since yesterday. And with a start, she realized she missed him. The attachment she felt amazed her, especially considering how short a time she'd known him. She shook her head. Did she dare go in and say good morning?

No, better not. Mrs. Hollyhock had something she wanted to talk about. Turning back to the cabin, she hurried on her way.

In her bedroom, Jessie pondered what Mrs. Hollyhock was being so secretive about. The woman had fed Sarah and Gabe, and then sent them out to collect firewood, telling Gabe to take some time before they were done. Whatever she had up her sleeve was important.

Mrs. Hollyhock handed Jessie a cup of tea and seated herself in the chair by the bedroom window. The sight of her there reminded Jessie of her time nursing Chase, which made her feel slightly breathless. After the danger of his dying had passed, those days had been the happiest of her life.

"What do you want to talk about that's such a secret?" Jessie asked, smiling.

"Jessie," Mrs. Hollyhock began. She'd switched to her don't-argue-with-me, I'm-in-charge voice, alerting Jessie to the seriousness of the topic. "I know Mr. Logan has been staying here for quite some time, and that you nursed him back to health after he was shot."

Jessie straightened. Slowly, she nodded. "Yes, that's true." She wasn't sure what direction this conversation was headed. In the relatively short time she'd known Mrs. Hollyhock, the old woman had wormed her way into Jessie's heart. She was the only grandmother she'd ever had.

"You know I'm only thinking of you when I say iffin' this gets out—that he's stayed here with you with Nathan gone and without no other chaperone—you will be ruint for sure." Pausing, Mrs. Hollyhock took a sip of her tea. Placing her teacup delicately back into her saucer, she waited for Jessie's response.

Jessie sat speechless on the edge of her bed.

"Virgil will be here this mornin' with the preacher from Clancy," Mrs. Hollyhock went on. "You and Mr. Logan will be getting hitched."

"What!" Jessie sprang to her feet. Even her wildest imaginings hadn't prepared her for what Mrs. Hollyhock had to say. "You can't be serious! Is this some sort of jocularity?"

Mrs. Hollyhock stood up in a puff of mothballs and mint. Fussing with Jessie, she attempted to compose her. "Calm down, child, you'll make yourself sick again. After you think on it, you'll see it's for the best."

Jessie's worst fears were being realized. Somehow Mrs. Hollyhock had found out about Chase and would force her to trap him into marriage.

She just couldn't do it. She wouldn't. Not after all he'd done for her. He'd come back to help her out of the goodness of his heart. All the time he'd spent trying to guarantee her and the children's safety. He'd almost been killed because of them. He could've washed his hands of the burden his friend's wife presented him, and rightly so. But he hadn't. And this is how she would repay him—saddling him to a wife and family he didn't want. Well, she wouldn't do it!

Besides, she'd already asked him to stay, and he'd made his feelings about that perfectly clear. No, he didn't want her.

But...having Chase to lean on and love...

"I won't!" she cried, her voice breaking. "You can't make me. I'm a grown woman, and you can't force me to marry him." Jessie's voice grew louder until she was practically shouting.

But...Chase my husband, father to my children...

"It was completely innocent, nothing happened." Even as she said it, Jessie's face heated. Unable to look Mrs. Hollyhock in the eyes, Jessie turned away.

"Even if I believed it, which I don't, nobody in town would. You'd be branded a loose woman, and soon all the no-accounts would be out here hounding you night and day. What kind of a life would that be? Most likely the district judge would come and take the children away from here too."

"I'll move away to where nobody knows me. Start fresh!" Jessie pleaded.

"Think, child. Can you be moving around with children to feed? Do you have money for that? No place to stay, no man to look out for ya? It's a hard world. You and the boy might make it, but the little one, she don't stand a chance."

Jessie's hopes were slipping away. It was true what the older woman said about Sarah—how could she have forgotten about her and Gabe? Well, there had to be a way. Surely Mrs. Hollyhock wouldn't force her into a marriage if she thought she didn't care for Chase.

"I don't even like him. He's a big bully, and"—she thought about Molly—"he probably already has a wife somewhere waiting for him to come home. Mrs. Hollyhock, *please*," Jessie sobbed. "Don't make me do this. I'll do anything else. Anything. I don't want to marry him."

Mrs. Hollyhock studied Jessie as the girl beseeched her. Her face remained stern, but her eyes sparkled with a knowing glint.

"Well, my sweetie"—Mrs. Hollyhock put her arm gently around her shoulder—"I jist don't believe what ya say about not likin' him. I can see it in your eyes every time I mention his name. But it's really your choice. Wed Mr. Logan and keep the children. Or start over, alone. The townspeople won't let you keep the girl. Don't you think she'd be branded for the rest of her life for the decision you're making right now? The boy is old enough to go his own way, make decisions for hisself."

Color drained from Jessie's face as the woman's words sank in. She was trapped! One way she betrayed Chase, and the other she would lose Sarah. It felt as if her heart were being torn in two.

Suddenly the room seemed small and airless. She was suffocating. Jumping off the bed, she threw open the door—and flew straight into the hard wall of Chase's chest. With an anguished sob, she buried her face in his protective embrace, drinking in the feel of him. Her arms snaked around his middle, holding tight. If only she could stay like this forever, never making the decision that would tear their lives apart.

Untangling Jessie's fingers, Chase peeled them from around his waist. He tried to ignore how good it felt to have her snuggled up to him. The next few minutes could change the direction not only of his life, but also Jessie's and the children's. He had to think with his head and not his heart.

Stepping around Jessie, Chase stared down into Mrs. Hollyhock's wrinkled face. He'd almost swear the woman was enjoying herself. But did that make sense? If she loved Jessie as much as she claimed, she wouldn't force her to marry someone she didn't even like…would she?

"I'd like to talk with Jessie. Alone." Chase drew up as tall as he could, embarrassed by his desire to intimidate this pint-sized slip of calico with nerves of steel. "Go outside with the young'uns. I don't want you listening through the door."

Like a banty rooster, she drew up too, making her all but eye level with his chest. He would have laughed, but truly, she was proving to be a formidable adversary.

"All rightie, Mr. Logan, but don't you try nothin'. Jist remember, I'm right outside. If I hear anything that sounds as if you're mistreating Jessie, I'll be back, packing my shotgun."

She said it as if she really believed she could thrash him. The woman was unbelievable.

Unsteadily, Jessie followed Chase back into the bedroom. He closed the door.

The silence stretched between them.

Jessie stepped over to the bed and pulled up the covers. She patted and fluffed until Chase cleared his throat.

"I've been circling this thing for hours. All night, in fact," Chase said with a sigh.

"I'm sorry, I had no idea…I can't believe this is happening now after you were so good to come back to help me. For nothing. For nothing at all. This is what you get in return for your kindness."

With a glance, Chase interrupted her. "I couldn't help but hear your conversation with Mrs. Hollyhock. You don't really like being forced into this sham any more than I do. But I don't want to see you lose Sarah either. And even more, I don't want Sarah to lose you. I've become fond of her, and the thought of her being motherless after just being reunited…it's not something I want haunting me."

"Chase, I can't let you do this," Jessie said in a tiny voice. "I'll work it out myself, somehow."

"Let me finish." Again Chase was struck by how young she was, and by all the hardships she'd already faced alone. "I think I have an answer that can work for both of us." He paused to think the idea through his head one more time.

"We'll go along with the old goat."

"Chase!"

"She is an old goat, and you know it. We'll get married today. After making you a respectable woman"—he paused again, this time a teasing half smile played on his lips—"and all the fuss in town dies down, I'll ride off somewhere to work, and the same thing that happened to Nathan can happen to me. I'll be...trampled to death. Or shot in poker game with a..." He waved his hand as if to clear that idea away. "Never mind. I'll think of something. It's the best possible solution, and the only one I can come up with at this time."

"How horrible." The color drained from her face.

"Well...*not really!* It'll just look it when I send a telegram describing my demise."

He waited for Jessie's approval. When she didn't say anything, he added, "You told Mrs. Hollyhock not ten minutes ago that you'd do *anything* to keep Sarah. Were you lying, Jessie?"

"No. But I just don't know about your plan. It all sounds so involved."

Chase knew she didn't like him much, after what he'd heard her tell Mrs. Hollyhock, but what choices did she have?

Because of my losing her money...

"I can ride off today, and they'll take Sarah and possibly send her back to New Mexico. Or maybe a family here in town might want her. An extra set of hands is always useful, come harvest."

Jessie winced.

"And Gabe?" he added. "Well, he's awfully attached to her; he'd probably go wherever she goes."

"A marriage in name only," Jessie whispered to herself. "And then we'd part ways? What if you find someone someday and really want to get married? Then what would you do?"

"Like I said before, I'm not the settling type. I'm happy coming and going when I please. But I could ask the same of you."

"Well, I'm not really sure, but right now I don't feel like I'd want to ever be tied to another man again. They're not around much, and when you need them, they're always away anyway. As long as I can take care of my family by baking and sewing, that would suit me just fine. But, still…"

Chase glanced to the ceiling trying to understand what was holding her back. "Jessie?"

She turned and held his gaze. "A wedding vow is sacred."

"Well then, if that's how you feel, I don't know what to say. Or do. What about Sarah?"

Jessie slowly took one of his hands and held it in her own. "I'm not saying I won't marry you today. I'm just saying I'll mean the vows that I say. I'll do my best to love you as my husband, till death do us part. But then, I can't speak for you."

Chase felt his face warming. *OK. We'll cross the other bridge when we get to it. She'll come to her senses. One obstacle at a time.*

"Well then, that settles it. You get ready for your wedding, and I'll go give Mrs. Hollyhock the news."

CHAPTER TWENTY-FOUR

*C*hase stopped when he saw Mrs. Hollyhock and Gabe out in the yard. Sarah, hampered by layers of clothing, scampered around, trying to capture maple leaves as the breeze tossed them about over the hard ground. Chase listened to the girl's giggles as she darted here and there.

Sarah was a darling little creature, all fluff and softness. Her chestnut curls hung loose and danced about as she played. A sudden gust of wind scattered the leaves at her feet and sent her tresses flying. She'd be a real beauty when she was grown.

Chase's instincts told him that he was making the right decision in marrying Jessie and giving the little girl a stable home for however long it might be. And possibly, if he was honest with himself, he was even a little excited. He couldn't bear the thought of her going back to the orphanage. Or worse yet, growing up on the streets, as he had.

When Sarah spotted Chase, her eyes lit with pleasure and she flew as fast as her little feet would take her.

"Da!"

"Mornin', Sarah," Chase said, picking her up. He inhaled her sweetness of little girl and sunshine. "How are you?"

"Paying wiff Gabe," she said, giggling and hiding her face in his shoulder.

Mrs. Hollyhock approached with a quizzical look on her face. "It's 'Da' already? Lordy, Mr. Logan, you work faster than a robin on an anthill." Her crooked finger tapped her lined cheek.

Since he was about to marry Jessie, Chase decided to make peace with the old busybody. Things would be strained enough without him rising to her bait every time she goaded him. Besides, he wanted her to know he'd made the decision because it was the right thing to do, and not because he was forced into it.

"Jessie and I decided it would be best for everyone concerned if we got married today. Just wanted you to be the first to know."

Sarah had no idea what was going on and proceeded to fluff her fingers through Chase's hair.

That wasn't the case for Gabe. The boy looked everywhere but at him. It took guts for Gabe to have stood up against him for Jessie's sake. But he had. Gabe had acted like more of a man than he had, and Chase respected him all the more for it.

"It looks like we're going to be having a wedding today," Chase said, directing his look at Gabe. "Why don't you get cleaned up and help Sarah too. Mrs. Hollyhock, I'm sure Jessie would appreciate your assistance about now."

"And where are you off to, Mr. Logan? Don't want the bridegroom getting cold feet. Skedaddling when we ain't a-lookin'.'"

"No, ma'am, we wouldn't want that." Chase winked at Mrs. Hollyhock. "I'm grabbing my soap and heading to the creek to get rid of this stubble on my face. Don't want to scratch my new bride."

Speechless, Mrs. Hollyhock watched as Chase jogged to the barn and disappeared inside. "I'm not so sure he ain't tryin' to pull the wool over my old eyes. Boy, you keep a watch on him for anything suspicious."

Virgil arrived back with the Reverend Hawthorn in tow. All the men gathered in the small cabin. Chase hadn't seen Jessie since their talk that morning. Sarah and Mrs. Hollyhock were holed up with her in her room, doing whatever it was females did together. Chase could hear murmuring and other small noises coming from inside, all of which were making him edgy.

His wedding! He'd never thought he'd see the day. Never felt there was a woman who'd take him on. But then, this was different—not like Jessie really had a choice in the matter. She would do anything for Sarah. Even marry him.

He ran his palms down his thighs for the fiftieth time.

"Forgive me," the preacher said. "But I'd like to wrap this up as quick as possible and get back to Clancy. We've had strange things going on lately. It's dreadful. A young girl was recently sullied and murdered, God rest her soul. Normally, our little town never sees any violence, none much to speak of, anyway."

Chase stepped to the bedroom door and knocked. "Jessie, it's time. The preacher's waiting."

"We'll be out shortly," Mrs. Hollyhock snapped back. "It ain't proper to be rushin' the bride, Mr. Logan. Jist keep your pants on."

Reverend Hawthorn coughed and rolled his eyes.

Chase gave the minister a knowing look.

Virgil stood quietly in the corner. He slipped his hand into the upper pocket of his clean white shirt and pulled out a pocket watch.

"What time is it?" Chase paced back and forth.

"Two forty-five."

"Women," Chase said under his breath. "All it takes is a couple of I do's. Not all this fuss." He was definitely losing his composure. The sooner they got this thing over with, the better.

Finally the bedroom door opened. First came Sarah, with a light tiptoeing march. She seemed to know something special was about to happen because she couldn't keep the grin from her face. She was wearing a pink dress, and her hair was swept up and fastened haphazardly somehow on the top of her head with wisps falling all around her face. She smiled prettily and her eyes twinkled.

With his first glimpse of Jessie, Chase was smitten all over again. Even though she kept her gaze down, she was glowing from head to toe. He recognized her green wool dress, but she had added her shawl, which was softly draped across her shoulders and tied loosely between her breasts.

Chase assumed Mrs. Hollyhock had helped fix Jessie's hair, for he'd never seen it like this before. It was partially swept up and fastened at the top with a clip and adorned with pine needles and some other type of lacy-looking leaves. The rest of her hair streamed down her back like liquid gold, catching the light as she nervously walked to his side.

Chase wished she would look at him. He desperately yearned to see her face, to look into her eyes. Did she feel as crazy inside as he did? If she did, he couldn't see it.

The Reverend Hawthorn lifted his little black Bible. Seeing Gabe waiting over by the door, Chase asked, "Would you stand up with me, Gabe? Jessie has Sarah here. That is, if you want to."

Gabe looked surprised and pleased. "Sure, Chase." His voice was unnaturally low and husky. He stepped forward, taking his place next to Chase.

"We all ready?" the preacher asked, glancing from face to face.

"As a cat in a creamery," Mrs. Hollyhock chirped from the back. "Git on with it."

Clearing his throat, the Reverend Hawthorn began. "Friends, we are gathered here today in the presence of God for the sacrament of marriage of Chase Logan and Jessica Marie Strong. Today the two will be joined in the sight of God and man."

Marie.

Chase took Jessie's ice-cold hands and wrapped them into his own.

"Do you, Chase, take this woman, Jessica, to be your lawfully wedded wife? Do you promise to take care of her, and keep her, and be true to her in sickness and in health, through good times and bad; do you promise to cherish and love her until death do you part?"

Jessie finally glanced up into his face, her heart shining in her eyes. Her expression, one he couldn't read, caused his heart to thump almost painfully in his chest. She was more beautiful today than she'd—the preacher cleared his throat.

"I do."

"Do you, Jessica, take this man, Chase, to be your lawfully wedded husband, to have and to hold, through good times and in bad, in sickness and in health; do you promise to honor and obey him until death do you part?"

Fascinatingly enough, the corners of her lips tipped up just the tiniest bit before she whispered, "I do."

"What God has joined together, let no man put asunder. In the eyes of God and the great territory of Wyoming, I now pronounce you husband and wife. You may kiss your bride, Mr. Logan."

Chase gathered her close and brushed her lips with a brief kiss.

"Congratulations," Reverend Hawthorn chortled, slapping Chase on the back. "May you be blessed with many happy years and a house full of young'uns."

Mrs. Hollyhock was instantly crushing Jessie in a hug, her spindly arms wrapped tightly around her. "Don't worry, Jessie girl. This was the best thing that could've happened to ya. He's a good man—you'll see, and thank me later. The minute I met him in the mercantile, I liked him. But gittin' the two of you to see things my way took some doin'."

Turning to Chase, Mrs. Hollyhock reached up on tiptoe and tweaked his cheek. Her smile was apologetic.

"Ah, heck." Reaching down, Chase picked her up. She kissed him soundly on the lips and they both laughed.

"Thankee, Mr. Logan. From the moment I saw you, you reminded me so much of my son, I jist knew you must have a good heart. Jessie will take real good care of it. I know she will."

Sniffing, the woman turned away, dabbing a hankie to her eyes.

"Well," said the reverend, "if we're all done here, I need to head back to Clancy."

"Thank you, Reverend," Chase said, gently pulling Jessie back to his side. He chanced a quick look at her and saw her eyes widen. "We appreciate you coming all the way out here. Can I give you something for your trouble?"

"If you're so inclined," the man said, clutching his Bible to his chest. "Times are hard, and I always have a widow or two who can use the extra the church can send her way."

Chase reached in his pocket and handed the man several silver coins. Reverend Hawthorn looked overwhelmed by Chase's generosity. "Oh, bless you. I'm sure the good Lord is smiling down on you today."

Shrugging into his overcoat, the reverend turned around. "I almost forgot about the wedding papers. Without them the wedding wouldn't be official."

The man extracted a quill and bottle of ink from his black leather bag. Dipping it, he handed the pen to Chase.

Chase slowly scratched out an X on the top line. Turning, he handed the pen to Jessie, seeing the surprise in her eyes. *Now she knows.* Her new husband can't even write his own name.

Jessie took the pen, dipped it, and quickly signed her name. She handed the pen back to the Reverend Hawthorn, and he filled in the date and location.

After Mrs. Hollyhock and Gabe signed as witnesses, the reverend carefully laid the paper down to dry.

"Children, gather your things and load up in the wagon. We'll be starting for town shortly," Mrs. Hollyhock said as she bustled about. "It was a beautiful weddin', jist beautiful." She looked as if she might start crying again.

"Where are you taking the children?" Jessie spoke up for the first time since becoming Mrs. Logan. Her voice had a ring of panic to it.

"Town, of course. A man and wife need a few days alone to get acquainted with each other. Ain't that right, Virgil?"

Virgil just shrugged and nodded.

"That won't be necessary," Chase spoke up for Jessie. "We're used to having them about."

"Nonsense! Now don't argue with me. I have plenty of room at my place. Besides, it will give this young man a chance to meet some of the other boys in town."

Seeing he wasn't going to change the woman's mind, Chase let it go. "Jessie, I'm going to saddle Cody and ride with the wagon to the edge of the bluff. Watch till they're at the edge of town. I'll be back within a half hour. Take care of everything that needs doing outside before we leave." Chase's tone left no room for argument. He pulled on his gloves and coat and headed out the door.

CHAPTER TWENTY-FIVE

*T*he wagon rolled away, bringing a sinking feeling to Jessie's stomach. She was tormented between worry for the children and unease with being alone with Chase.

Sarah was so young. And they were so recently reunited. She was just now settling in. Would she be scared without her? She'd looked happy as a clam squished between Mrs. Hollyhock and Gabe. What if she woke up with a nightmare tonight and nobody heard her cries?

You're being an old worrywart, she scolded herself. *Gabe has taken good care of her for a long time. He won't let her cry. He woke up night before last when she'd had the nightmare. They'll be just fine.*

Jessie went about doing anything to keep busy. When Chase returned, he'd be hungry. Neither of them had taken the time to eat a morning or noon meal. Fixing him something hot to eat was the least she could do. Besides, it was the best method she knew to settle down herself.

Quickly, she changed out of her good dress and slipped on her work dress and apron. Biscuits and gravy, with a slice of venison, would have to do after such an eventful day.

"I'm back, Jessie. Open the door."

Jessie almost dropped the pan of biscuits she was taking from the oven. Setting it down, she quickly ran her hands down the front of her apron. Her stomach flipped over and she feared she might be sick. Maybe she should have stayed in her good dress. This one was so old, and she'd worn it almost every day since Chase had arrived. Would he notice? At least her hair was still fixed the pretty way Mrs. Hollyhock had insisted she wear it. Not wanting to keep Chase waiting in the cold any longer, she hurried to the door.

Chase stepped in. "Thanks." He smacked his hands together a few times and glanced around. He looked anxious too.

Her nerves tingled with anticipation and a little fear. Unease coursed through her body, just like the first time she'd let him in, not that many days ago.

Shrugging out of his coat, he hung it by the door and took off his hat. "Sure smells good in here." He glanced over her to the stove.

"Sit down and I'll get some coffee. Everything is almost done."

Jessie hurried over and poured from her old metal pot. This was so strange and yet so similar to when Chase had first arrived. It was unbelievable that so much had happened so quickly.

Uncomfortable with the silence, Jessie searched for something to say. For the life of her, she couldn't think of a single thing. Finally she blurted out, "That sure didn't take long."

Embarrassed by the tenuous sound of her voice, Jessie turned back to her bubbling gravy. With her wooden spoon she attacked the lumps of flour with a vengeance, sending little puffs here and there.

Walking up behind her, Chase carefully picked up the coffee she'd poured but forgotten to give him. He silently returned to the table and sat down.

Her eyes squeezed shut in frustration. *I'm such a fool. He must think I'm a brainless goose for being so jumpy.* When he was so close, she felt as if she just might melt away right into her pan of gravy.

"I let Cody run. It's been so long since he's had a hard workout, I think he really enjoyed it. I know I did." Chase took a sip of his hot coffee and settled back into his chair. "Nothing like cold air to clear a man's head."

What was *that* supposed to mean? He needed to clear his head from the decision of marrying her? Or, how had he been so stupid as to let Mrs. Hollyhock force him into tying himself to some woman down on her luck? It could mean one in a hundred different things. Jessie felt irritated over each possibility.

The pan of gravy blurred in front of her eyes. She stiffened her back. "This is almost ready." She wished she were somewhere, anywhere—even back at the orphanage—other than here in this moment with him sitting there watching her.

With a clean dish towel, Jessie pried the fluffy, hot biscuits from the baking tin and piled them into a woven basket, and then placed them in the center of the table. She plopped three onto the middle of Chase's plate. Quickly she turned for the gravy pan.

"Whoa there, Jessie. This isn't a race."

She could almost feel his gaze on her backside from head to toe. What was he thinking? What did he expect?

"I know. But you must be starving. I just want to get you fed and this mess cleaned up. It's been a long day."

"About the longest day of my life, and it's not yet half over."

That was it! She couldn't keep her vexation in another moment. If she did she just might burst. "Well, Chase Logan, if you'd been a little smarter, a little wiser, you could have been miles away from here days ago," she said over her shoulder, still working on his supper.

Sputtering and the sound of Chase's cup slamming down on the table made her shutter.

"Just what are you insinuating? If you have something to say, spit it out."

Jessie whirled about, spoon in hand, hair flying. "I'm insinuating," she drawled out, mimicking him, "someone with a lick of
sense wouldn't have been roped into this stupid situation." He was
wiping his mouth on the back of his sleeve. "I just figured you
were brighter than that." She knew she should hold her tongue,
but darn the little devil inside just wouldn't keep quiet. "Guess I
was wrong."

Chase stood slowly, never taking his gaze from hers. She could
see the muscle in his jaw clench and release. She realized too late
she'd never really seen him angry before. She knew she was tread-
ing on thin ice, but hells bells, he'd asked for it. It felt good to
release some of her pent-up frustration. Once she got going, it was
darn hard to stop.

"Some men just can't help playing the hero. Rescuing the
damsel in distress."

Taking her apron in one hand and the old wooden spoon in
the other she made an eloquent bow.

Chase's eyes smoldered. "I wasn't the one married to a man
who went off and left me. Why was Nathan working halfway
across the territory? Couldn't he stand your sharp tongue? And
sassy mouth? If he'd been at home where he belonged, maybe he'd
be alive today."

His words hit their mark, and Jessie's anger faded quickly.
She hastily swung back to the stove and wrapped the dish towel
around the heated handle of the cast-iron fry pan. But when she
went to pick it up, it was still too hot. She let out a yelp of pain. The
pan crashed to the floor, slopping its contents all over.

Chase rushed forward, grabbed her injured hand, and plunged
it in the bucket of water on the sideboard. He pulled her body
close to his. "Shhh...don't cry," he murmured, still keeping her
burnt hand submerged. "The pain will ease up in a bit."

Jessie couldn't hold back any longer. All the hurt, fear, and
uncertainties of the past week came rolling down her face. Big
sobs racked her body.

"Jessie," there was a ring of alarm to his voice. "Let me have another look at your hand."

"It's all right," she said, burying her face into the strong wall of his chest. It felt so good, so safe. *So right.* "I'm just so sorry for pulling you into this stupid mess. I've ruined your life, and I feel awful about it."

"Is *that* why you're crying?" Chase chuckled as they rocked back and forth. His fingers were doing magical things to her back.

Jessie nodded, and then peeked at the gravy spattered all over the floor. She couldn't bring herself to look at him.

"Well, stop thinking. We'll work it out. I'm relieved it's just our marriage situation that's bothering you and not the burn on your hand. Now move over so I can try to save some of my supper fixings."

CHAPTER TWENTY-SIX

$\mathcal{T}$he wagon rolled slowly through town, creaking and groaning as it went. Sarah was huddled next to Gabe, wrapped snuggly in a warm blanket. The motion lulled the little girl, and she was sleeping soundly in Gabe's protective embrace.

"Whoa now," Virgil's whiney voice called out. The wagon eased to a stop in front of a store. Sarah stirred in Gabe's arms.

"Well, children, here we are. Jist climb on out and I'll show ya where you'll be a'staying."

Gabe untangled Sarah and slowly climbed off the wagon. A boy about his age watched them from the shadow of the livery barn door.

"That there's Jake. He's one of the local boys I was talking about. 'Bout your age, I guess. Run over and say hello, iffin' you want. I'll watch after the little one."

"No, I'll just stay here with Sarah." Gabe reached for the sleeping child. "I don't want her to wake up and be scared."

Mrs. Hollyhock shook her head. "Suit yourself. I was only hoping that you'd make yourself some friends while you're here. I ain't trying to tell ya what to do."

Gabe followed her into the store with Sarah in his arms like a sack of potatoes. Inside, he looked around for a place to lay her.

"Up the stairs and to the left is a room with a cot. You can put her there." When Gabe hesitated, the woman squawked, "Quit your balking. No one's gonna hurt her."

The room was small and sparsely furnished. Beautiful colored quilts sat about folded or hung on the wall, giving the room a cheery feeling. Gabe laid Sarah down and tucked the coverlet about her. "I'll be right downstairs," he murmured. Sarah rolled over, burrowing herself into the fluffy warmth of the covers.

Gabe hesitated at the top of the stairs. He was torn between his curiosity and his sense of duty. He wanted to see all the things for sale in the store, but how long would Sarah sleep? Deciding to look around for only a minute and then return, he headed down.

Voices stopped him midway.

"How is Jessie doing with the news, Violet?" a woman's voice inquired.

"Better now, poor dear. Things have a way of working out for the best."

Gabe couldn't see the women, being as he was still on the stairs, but their conversation was clear enough.

"What about that man, that Mr. Logan? Is he staying in town, or did he ride on yesterday after he took the supplies out?" There was an undercurrent of interest in her voice when the unknown woman said Chase's name. Gabe wondered what she wanted.

"I don't want to be gossipin' about my Jessie, but the news will be known soon enough," Mrs. Hollyhock said in a wispy voice. "Jessie is now Mrs. Logan."

A loud gasp echoed though the room. Gabe took one step back farther into the protection of the stairway.

"What! That's not fair! She's already had a husband, and now she up and marries Mr. Logan without giving anyone else a chance to get to know him. Why, she's only been a widow for a few days, for heaven's sake." With each word, her voice rose in intensity.

"Keep your voice down. I don't want to be upsetting the children."

Blood rushed to Gabe's face. How dare she talk like that about Jessie! Whoever she was, she wasn't fit to wipe Jessie's boots.

"Beth, don't carry on. You're jist upset about Tommy. He'll be back soon. I jist know he will. Then you and him can get married, jist like you planned."

"Oh, phooey!" The woman's voice oozed with disgust. "It's been too long. I think he must be dead. Or worse, he's run off to get away from this town and *you*. By now he's probably up and married someone else." She stomped around like an angry moose. "And now Jessie steals the—" She cut herself off with a sob and Gabe thought her tirade was over, but he was wrong. "That's so typical of Miss Sweet and Innocent," she went on. "She probably got him to feel sorry for her, and before he knew what she was about, snap, she caught him in her trap."

"You're being awfully mean-spirited talking that way about me, Beth. I want you to know your words have cut me to the quick." Mrs. Hollyhock's voice sounded shaky, hushed. Gabe felt sorry for her. "I want you to go on home and get some rest. You're overly tired. But I want you to remember, Jessie's never done nothin' to hurt you. You shouldn't talk about her like you jist did."

Strained silence floated up to Gabe's hiding spot. Then the swish of fabric and the rapid fire of Beth's boot heels rang out on the old plank floor, sounding like his Colt at target practice. At this point he was in no hurry to meet her.

"I'll see ya in the mornin', dear. Sleep well."

She didn't respond. The door closed with a bang, and the little bell above it rattled out in protest. Gabe proceeded cautiously down the stairs.

"I reckon you heard all that caterwauling?"

"Yeah."

"She's really a sweet girl. It's jist that she's worried over Tommy being gone. Tommy's my—" Mrs. Hollyhock straightened, went behind the counter and started straightening up.

"I didn't like what she said about Jessie trapping Chase. That's not the way it happened at all."

"You know it and I know it," Mrs. Hollyhock said, "but that don't mean we can stop other people from thinkin' it."

"I could stop her from sayin' it." Gabe straightened his shoulders. "My pa used to tell me not to let a bully push me or anyone else around. And that's what she is, a big, loud-mouth bully."

"Now don't you go gettin' ornery on me too. I have enough to worry about without throwing you into the mix."

CHAPTER TWENTY-SEVEN

*T*he bell sounded again, and Gabe was suddenly hopeful it was Beth coming back. He'd give her the tongue-lashing she deserved. It wasn't. The boy Mrs. Hollyhock had pointed out as Jake when they'd first arrived stepped through the door.

"Howdy, Granny." He smiled. "You got any chores for me?"

"Not today, Jake. It's gittin' late and your ma will want ya home. Come back in the mornin' and you can straighten out the back room. Looks like a cyclone hit it."

Gabe tried not to stare, but the boy's untamed hair and unkempt wildness made it look like he'd been through a cyclone. Fidgeting with a lantern globe gave him something to look at instead of Mrs. Hollyhock and her visitor. It slipped through his fingers and dropped onto the shelf, almost shattering it.

"It's not broke," Gabe said sheepishly.

Mrs. Hollyhock seemed not to notice he'd almost broken an expensive item.

"Gabe, this here's Jake. Jake, this here's Gabe. He's new in town. Maybe tomorra you could show Gabe around town?"

"I reckon I could, if I got time. Pops don't like me takin' too much time off."

"Before ya run off, let me pay ya for the work ya did for me last week." She went over to an old burlap sack and took out four brown potatoes. Setting them on the front counter, she reached behind for the coffee tin and scooped out a cup of beans. "I'm addin' a little sugar for the good job ya done."

"Thanks." Jake blushed.

Gabe figured he was embarrassed by the woman's praise. Jake looked Gabe over curiously, taking in every detail.

"How 'bout a quick game of checkers?" Jake asked, hitching his head.

Gabe looked to see a barrel set on end and a couple of three-legged stools. An old checkerboard with black and red playing pieces waited for someone to take interest.

"What about your ma, Jake?" Mrs. Hollyhock asked. "She'll be wantin' ya home soon. You don't need to go a-lookin' for trouble. It finds you easy enough on its own."

"Nah, she don't care. She's been busy with the cowhands from the Northbend Ranch. She won't miss me," he answered light-heartedly. "Come on, Gabe, let's play."

Gabe liked him. There was something about his scruffy looks and dirty clothes that had adventure written all over him.

"What's your color?" Jake asked.

"Black."

"Well, iffin' you're set on stayin'," Mrs. Hollyhock said, "how 'bout if I fix you boys a cup of cocoa? Got some fresh milk yesterday. Tommy used to pester me all the time for a cup of my special recipe."

"Yes'm," both boys sang in unison.

Mrs. Hollyhock busied herself with the cocoa making—a little of this, a pinch of that. She seemed busy, but Gabe noticed that she kept her eyes and ears focused on them.

Jake jumped one of Gabe's pieces. "Where you from?"

"Virginia, originally. My family had a farm and a nice parcel of land. Sold it when we decided to come west."

"Did ya come in a prairie schooner?"

Gabe nodded.

Shaking his head, Jake gave a long whistle. "I've always wanted to travel in one. That would sure be somethin'. Where's it now, if you don't mind me asking?"

"Don't have it anymore. I had to burn it when my ma and pa and sister died. People said it was infected with the cholera. They wouldn't let me keep it anymore." Gabe turned his attention out the window.

Jake fidgeted in his seat. "That's tough."

"Which one of you outlaws is winnin'?" Mrs. Hollyhock asked as she placed steaming hot cups of cocoa down carefully.

"Well, Granny, he's got me beat for now," Jake said with a nod toward Gabe. "But I'm just about to see what he might have to wager to make this game a little more interesting. Then we'll see what he's made of."

"No bettin' any of that hard-earned food, Jake," Mrs. Hollyhock scolded. "You know how mad your mama can get. She'll be expecting something for her supper tonight."

"Nah, I wouldn't do that."

"Shiftless white trash, that woman," Mrs. Hollyhock said under her breath as she walked away. "Using his earnin's for her own selfish needs. Pitiful."

"She really your grandma?" Gabe asked behind his hand. He couldn't believe Jake would dare talk to her the way he did if they were really related.

"Mrs. Hollyhock?" Jake laughed. "No, just friends. I reckon I've known her just about all my life. It just feels like she's my granny. Wouldn't mind if she was though. She's taken care of me lots when my own ma has thrown me out."

Gabe picked up his cup and blew on the hot, chocolaty milk. This was the first time he'd actually get to try some. The sweet aroma tickled his nose and made his mouth water.

"Be careful—it's hot," Mrs. Hollyhock warned.

With his first sip Gabe was in heaven. He held the mixture in his mouth experiencing the unique, rich, sweet taste. "This is *good*. I've never tasted anything like it before." He hoped Mrs. Hollyhock had thought about Sarah. She would sure love some too.

"Got ya." Jake jumped three of Gabe's black men with his red king. "That about does you in. Better luck next time."

Jake stood. He gulped down his hot drink and wiped his mouth with the back of his sleeve.

"Good as always, Granny. Thanks a bunch."

"Mercy sakes, Jake. I told you before, you need to be learning some manners. You ain't got no couth! You're getting older now— you're fifteen."

"Almost sixteen," he corrected.

"Well, someday you're gonna want to court some nice young lady, and her ma and pa won't let you within fifty feet of her because you act like a billy goat in a mud hole. You'll look back and wish you'd taken my words ta heart and done somethin' about it."

"I s'pect so. But, I'm happy right now the way I am. Besides, I ain't plannin' to stay here my whole life. I'm ridin' on soon as I save enough money," Jake announced with pride. He looked to Gabe for the boy's reaction.

"Don't you go sassin' me, young man. I helped raise you from a wee babe." She got a sad, searching expression every time she looked at Jake.

"You goin' by yourself?" Gabe asked, placing his cup on the counter and wiping his mouth like Jake had done.

"Reckon I am. Or maybe I'll interest someone else in a trip out west. I'm bettin' there's still lots of gold out there in the hills and rivers of California. Enough to make a man rich for the rest of his life." His eyes turned dreamy as he leaned back against the counter.

"Jake." Mrs. Hollyhock snapped him out of his reverie. "You'd better skedaddle home. It's gittin' late. Run along and we'll see ya in the mornin'."

Hefting his sack of goods, Jake thrust out his hand to Gabe. "With some luck Pops will let me off some tomorrow, and I'll come by."

"Sure."

Jake was out the door and down the road in the paling evening light.

"He sure is something," Gabe said with a shake of his head. "Making his own destiny and all."

"That he is. But you best remember he has *nothin'* here to hold him. Whatever he finds in California or wherever he ends up will be a sight better than what he has now," Mrs. Hollyhock said as her face scrunched up in a thoughtful look, pulling all the wrinkles together. "Now you..." she said, beaming, as she slid her skinny arm around his shoulders.

Gabe stiffened slightly.

"There's a different story entirely. You've got Jessie and Sarah and now Mr. Logan, and they all love and depend on you. I jist wish Jake could find a family like you've got to take him in, teach him how to be a good man."

Gabe slipped out from under her arm and walked to the stairs. It'd been some time since he'd put Sarah down. He wanted to run up and see if she was still asleep.

Quietly walking down the hall, Gabe peeked into the shadowy little room where he had left Sarah. He was alarmed when he saw her sitting silently on the edge of her bed, not making a sound.

"Sarah, honey, you're awake. Why didn't you call out for me?" Gabe crooned.

When Sarah saw him she threw her arms around his neck and hung on for dear life.

"I was right downstairs in the mercantile and thought you were asleep. Don't be scared anymore." Reassuringly he rubbed her back and rocked back and forth.

"Ma," Sarah whispered.

"You'll see Ma tomorrow, and until then you're going to have a real fun time here with Mrs. Hollyhock and me. You remember Mrs. Hollyhock, the nice lady who brought us here?"

Sarah nodded her head but didn't say anything.

"She has a cup of hot cocoa for you downstairs just waitin' for when you wake up. You ready for it?" Gabe asked, hoping he was right and the little girl wouldn't be disappointed. Again Sarah only nodded.

"Good, let's go find it."

CHAPTER TWENTY-EIGHT

*J*essie spent her wedding night alone in her bed. After supper she'd busied herself cleaning up and baking some bread. Chase had sat quietly by the fire, rubbing oil over his reins and bridle. The smell of leather filled the room.

Chase seemed perfectly comfortable with the silence between them. Sometimes an hour would slip by without a word spoken.

But for Jessie, now accustomed to Sarah and Gabe's shenanigans, the silence had grown long and burdensome. The stillness put her on edge, and she would sometimes refill Chase's coffee cup before it was empty just so she could hear him mumble out a thanks.

The evening had worn on like any other until Jessie, tired from the events of the day, crawled into bed and soon was fast asleep.

Rising before sunup, she quickly splashed cold water on her face and ran a comb through her tangled hair. Hastily, she braided it and threw it over her shoulder, dressed, then peeked out the door.

Chase was nowhere to be seen, but his bedroll was still laid out by the fireplace, rumpled and disarrayed. Relief filled her. After their argument yesterday she worried he might up and leave. She wouldn't blame him if he did. She cringed at the memory of her mocking him for his gallantry. She must be touched in the head!

She put the coffeepot on the hot stove next to a pot of warming water, thankful that Chase had started the fire. The warmth in the little cabin felt good, and she silently thanked God for sending someone as thoughtful as Chase.

Jessie practically ran to the outhouse and then down to the stream. She wanted to be back quickly to have a nice breakfast ready for Chase when he returned from wherever he'd gone.

By the time she made it back to the cabin, Jessie's skin tingled from the cold and exercise. She scrunched her toes and wiggled her fingers to get the blood flowing. No need to pinch her cheeks this morning.

Yanking open the door, she faltered, then stopped. Chase stood in front of the stove in only his pants, his chest glistening wet and soapy. His stomach muscles were stretched taut above the top of his belt. The cords in his neck stood out as he washed.

His hand stopped in midair. "Thought you'd be gone a little longer. I planned to be finished by the time you returned." He dipped the cloth back into the basin and wrung out the excess water. "I have to confess, it's mighty nice having warm water to wash with on a chilly mornin'." He quickly rinsed off, then reached for a towel. "There's plenty left for you."

"Thank you." Jessie turned around. The vision of his stomach, hard with ridges, was impressed on her mind. It reminded Jessie of something. It was almost like…

"Like…I could wash a shirt on it," she mumbled.

"What was that?"

"I said, I'll have your breakfast whipped up right away." Jessie whirled into action, banging pots and pans.

"There's no big rush, Jessie. Let's not forget what happened yesterday. Besides, my ears can't stand much more of your clamor." Taking the heavy cast iron skillet from her hands, he set it on the stove. "There, that's better."

Chase shrugged into his shirt. "I think today we should make some plans. The weather's been cooperating so far, but it's bound to snow soon. I want to fix this place up proper. Patch the barn. Fix the fence that's falling down out back." Chase pulled out a chair and sat.

"That's a fine idea."

Minutes later, Jessie set a plate full of fried potatoes, gravy, and sliced venison in front of Chase. She filled a mug of coffee for herself and Chase, then sat down beside him. She was much too keyed up to eat.

He scooped up a big bite and chewed. "What things would you like to see mended?" Chase asked after swallowing. His eyes closed briefly. "This sure is good, Jessie."

"Thank you. There're plenty more."

He nodded. "I'll start on the fence today. I figure the barn roof is a job that can wait until I have Gabe's help."

"You don't have to do all that."

Wiping his mouth, he looked at her. A faint light twinkled in their dark depths. "I know I don't. But, this place is not ready for winter. And the repairs shouldn't take too long with Gabe helping." He took a sip from his cup and looked at her again. He smiled.

Jessie couldn't help responding to his warmth with a smile of her own. It was amazing how his boyish grin made him look years younger. His freshly shaven face had a warm glow, and she ached to reach out and feel its texture. It would be so easy to forget he meant to leave someday.

A bit breathless, Jessie pulled her gaze away. "It sounds like you've given this quite some thought."

Chase pushed the empty plate away. "Just about all night."

"Fine then. I'll start thinking on what needs to get done. Is there anything else I can get you?"

"No, I'm full down to the hocks." He stood and stretched. "I'm going to check out the new horses and see if their equipment needs any repair." At the door he shrugged into his coat. "I'm going to work each horse and tune 'em up. I'll be around, not too far off. Just give a shout if you need anything. Then later we'll ride into town together and collect the young'uns."

"Chase..." Jessie said, stopping him as he opened the door to leave.

He looked at her expectantly.

"I've been thinking too."

His brows rose over his expressive eyes. She readied for a playful remark, but one never came.

"Yes?" he prompted.

Nervously, she bit her lip. It had seemed like a good idea when she was thinking about it last night in bed, but now that the time had come, she was doubtful.

"What's your idea?"

"Well," she began slowly. "You're doing all these things for me and the children, and…" She stopped.

Chase closed the door and waited patiently. "This doesn't have to be so hard, Jessie."

"OK, I'm just going to say it straight out like you always do. I'd like to do something for you in return for your kindness. I'd like to teach you to read and write, if you want me to."

His face clouded. She was afraid he'd storm out again and they would lose this wonderful friendship that was growing. She should've left well enough alone.

It felt like an eternity before he responded. "Actually, I'd like that very much. At least so as I can sign my own name." He chuckled softly, and her worry was chased away by the endearing look in his eyes.

She wanted to jump up and down. Run to him and throw herself into his arms. Instead, she said excitedly, "Chase, it's easy! With a little practice you'll be reading *everything*."

He scuffed a boot, looking uncertain. "Well, let's not jump ahead of ourselves."

"It's true. And," she added breathlessly, "I'm a really good teacher. I used to teach in the orphanage. You'll see. It'll be fun."

Jessie sat down to make a list. She was so filled with happiness, she could hardly get her thoughts together. First she'd list the things Chase had already mentioned. The barn roof. The fence. Hmmm, the chimney flue on top of the cabin had started to smoke now and then. Maybe that was something he could fix. The leaky roof and drafty walls. So many things. She hadn't realized how run-down the place had gotten. Lands, he could be here for years if he intended to repair everything that needed fixing. The thought made her giggle. She surely wouldn't complain.

Jessie bundled up and headed to the woodpile. She needed to refill the inside wood bin with a few logs for today. Gabe could do the rest when he returned. Chase was nowhere in sight.

The piercing screech of a blue jay broke the quiet stillness of the day. She glanced around. This is how it used to be not all that long ago. No Chase, no children. Just her and the elements surviving from day to day.

She turned and glanced over her shoulder as a sudden feeling of unease edged up her spine, making her spook. Then the distinct feeling of being watched raised the hair on the nape of her neck. When the sun disappeared behind a cloud she shivered. "Stop it! Quit being such a ninny," she scolded herself as she quickly gathered some logs.

Just as she came around the back corner of the woodpile, a hand reached out and gripped her arm. With a screech Jessie dropped the logs and went flying.

"Told you I'd be seein' you again, sugar pie." Lonnie pushed her back up against a tree, knocking the air from her lungs. Her head cracked against the trunk with force making stars dance before her eyes. Inhaling was painful as she tried to fight him off. Her futile struggles only made him laugh. Grasping her around the throat, he smiled, victory shining in his eyes.

"Ain't no woman ever hit me and got away with it," he snickered as he leered in her face. "I was gittin' mighty impatient waitin' for that cowboy to ride out."

Jessie opened her mouth to scream, but he smashed his hand savagely over her lips. A sob lodged in her throat, burning, hot.

Breathe! I need to breathe! She twisted her head to the opposite side. Sarah's doll was lying on the porch.

With renewed vigor, Jessie bucked against Lonnie, fighting ferociously. She wriggled one of her hands free and gouged her fingernails into his face, pulling down with all her might. Four bright red lines appeared from his forehead to his chin.

"Aaaahhh!" His painful scream seared through her head. If she didn't get away now he'd kill her for sure. He pressed his hand to his face, and then looked at his palm. Seeing the blood she'd drawn, his face contorted.

With all her might Jessie stomped her boot heel blindly trying to find his foot. He easily avoided her attack and they fell to the cold, solid ground. He took a hold of her bodice and ripped.

CHAPTER TWENTY-NINE

*T*he fabric of Jessie's dress gave way, and cold air and the rock-littered earth tortured her skin. She continued to fight, refusing to let him know how frightened she was.

A string of obscenities filled the air. Chase's enraged eyes were all that she could see as he seized Lonnie and threw him against a tree, causing needles to rain down on them both.

Chase pummeled Lonnie's face and torso. Lonnie brought his knee up, knocking the wind from Chase, which gave him an opportunity to dive away. Chase was on him instantly, and they rolled together, stopping a few feet away. Lonnie's hand found the handle of Jessie's ax. He gripped it quickly, but Chase pinned his hand, then wrestled the ax from Lonnie's grasp. He pressed the razor-sharp blade to Lonnie's throat.

Jessie gasped. "Chase! No!"

Growling like an animal, Chase flipped the ax over and struck Lonnie on the head with the blunt end, knocking him out cold.

Jessie fumbled with her torn dress, shaking uncontrollably.

"Jess, you're hurt," Chase blurted, as he rushed to her aid. "My God, your shoulder!"

"No, I'm all right."

"But…"

"Those are old scars. I'm OK, really."

The violence Jessie had experienced seeped into every pore of her body. Her lip and neck burned from Lonnie's punishment. She hurt all over. Her eyes filled until the tears ran unchecked.

Chase picked her up and wrapped her in his arms. "Shhh, it's all right," he crooned against her ear. He cradled her gently next to his chest, carrying her like a baby inside the cabin and gently placed her on the bed.

Chase took in her every detail. Ripped dress. Bloody lip. She'd have bruises from head to toe. Leaves and dirt clung to the back of her hair. *But* she was alive. And that was the *only* thing that mattered. His relief was enormous.

He covered her with a blanket and sat on the edge of the bed in silence. He couldn't imagine what had happened to disfigure her shoulder in such a way. His heart trembled.

"I'll be back," he whispered softly. "I need to take care of things outside." He brushed a strand of hair out of her eyes. "Will you be all right here for a few minutes?"

Jessie smiled, unaware her teeth were covered with blood. She nodded. "Thank you."

He couldn't respond. The emotions swirling around inside were too deep, too strong.

By the time Chase was back, Jessie had slipped out of her ruined dress and was wrapped in a warm blanket. He watched as she wiped blood from her face and neck with a damp cloth and then put on the kettle for tea. "Is he the man from the mercantile?" he asked.

"Yes."

"Lonnie." Chase paced back and forth in front of the fire like a caged animal. He remembered every vivid detail she had told him. "Have you ever seen him before that day?"

"No." Jessie's fingers went up to her neck, and she carefully touched the angry welts Lonnie had left behind.

"You said there were two men. Who was the other?" Chase asked, stifling his anger at the sight of abuse Lonnie had inflicted.

"It was his brother, I think. He called him Joe."

"Nathan didn't smoke, did he?"

Jessie turned at his odd question and looked at Chase.

He held up a half-smoked cigarette. "I found this behind the barn. It has been out there for a while. Could it have been Nathan's?"

Her eyes grew round, and she shook her head.

"I didn't think so. I'd bet this isn't the first time Lonnie and Joe have been out here, Jessie. No telling how long they have been sneaking around."

Jessie pulled out a chair and slowly sat down, her hands shaking as she cupped her tea.

"This changes everything," Chase said. She didn't realize it, but Jessie was in more danger now than ever before.

"What do you mean?"

With frustration he ran his fingers through his hair. "Don't you see? When we take Lonnie into town, he'll stand trial and probably hang. You saw what kind of man he is. Well, his brother can't be much better. He'll want revenge."

Jessie's eyes widened. "They'll hang him for hurting me?" She tried to get up, but Chase gently nudged her back into the chair.

"No, not for hurting you, although I'd like them to hang him for that. Remember, the reverend said a girl was raped and murdered over in Clancy a short while ago. I'd bet a month's pay those brothers were responsible. Skunks like them can't change stripes that fast." At the thought of Lonnie getting what he had coming to him, Chase calmed down considerably. "He'll get a trial, be found

167

guilty, and then he'll hang. Or at the very least he'll end up in the territorial prison down in Laramie."

Jessie took a sip from her teacup.

"I can't leave you and Sarah here. Gabe would try, but I'm not sure he'd be able to protect the two of you against vermin like Lonnie or Joe."

She started to protest, but he put up his hand to silence her. "I know you don't want to leave, but you have to think of Sarah. How'd she suffer in the hands of someone like that…especially someone like that bent on revenge."

"Where will we go?" A note of apprehension had crept into her voice.

"To Logan Meadows, I figure."

"Logan Meadows?" Jessie said in surprise. "Like Chase Logan?"

"Well, I'm from there, but it's not named after me. I named myself after the town."

"Oh."

"I was young. All I went by was Chase. When I was getting ready to ride out, I picked the name Logan. One, I was tired of not having a name like all the other men I rode with, and two, I didn't want to forget the name of the town where I banked my savings. I told you about the little place I own there, the one I've never settled on." He pushed down the gnawing of guilt that whispered the ranch was Molly's place. His and Molly's. "I figure it's as good a place as any, and it'll only take a couple of weeks to get there."

Excitement and trepidation coursed through Jessie at the same time. It was wonderful, the thought of a new home. But where would that leave Chase? It was his. Was he planning just to ride off once they were settled?

"It's your place though. We couldn't take it and leave you with nothing."

"Like I said, I've owned it for years. Never could settle on it. Once you see the place you may not want to stay. It's pretty small—run-down. Makes this place look like a palace."

Small and run-down or not, it sounded wonderful to Jessie. She couldn't help feeling hopeful.

"OK," Jessie said, sitting forward. She could feel her heart somersault at the thought of actually going someplace new...with Chase. "What should our plan be?"

"Today when we go into town to get Sarah and Gabe, we should check around for the things we'll need. A large, sturdy wagon, preferably one with a cover. Extra clothes and warm coats for the young'uns and you. We already have two extra horses. They can pull, Gabe will drive, and I'll ride shotgun."

Home. The thought of a fresh start on life was like a breath of spring air. It caressed her inside and out. Sighing, she envisioned calling her family into a Sunday afternoon supper from a freshly painted porch. A swing hung from a beam in the corner and a beautiful white picket fence circled the yard. Potatoes and gravy, and heaps of fresh corn from her garden adorned the table. Last but not least, a freshly baked apple pie waited in the kitchen window to be enjoyed.

"Jessie?" Chase's voice drew her out of her daydream.

"Yes?"

"Every time I see your swollen lip and the welts on your neck or even think about him touching you, hurting you..." He stopped and wiped his hand across his face.

Jessie set her cup on the table and reached up and stroked Chase's cheek. "I'm not certain about too many things these days except maybe this one," she said without a hint of coyness. "If you hadn't been here today, something terrible would have happened to me. I might even be dead right now. I'm very grateful to you."

He took her hand and kissed her palm. Then he gently set it back down on the table. "Ah, Jess, when I found you there, I thought you were dead. It scared me." He cleared his throat. "For the first time in my life, I feel like I'm doing something good. Helping you and little Sarah and even Gabe in your time of need. Maybe I can make up for all the times"—he took a deep breath—"I've let people down." With his finger, he gently traced her swollen lip and the angry red welts marring her delicate skin. "I'm sorry."

"You're the one who rescued me, remember?"

"I just wished I'd gotten there sooner. Before he had the chance to hurt you."

"I'm not made of glass. I'll be good as new by tomorrow. I just hope Sarah's not scared when she sees me today."

"I know. I've been thinkin' the same thing," Chase replied. "We'll have to level with Gabe. There's no pullin' the wool over his eyes, but the little one doesn't need to know." He glanced to the chest where she kept her things. "Do you have a blouse with a high neck, maybe some of that lacy stuff?"

Jessie thought for a moment. "One. I think it'll work."

"You feel up to getting dressed to go?

"Yes. The sooner the better. I miss Sarah and Gabe."

Chase chuckled. "It's only been one day. I think I'll call you Old Mother Hubbard."

"Chase Logan!" Jessie huffed. "I'm not old, and you know it."

"Really?" he replied, thrumming his fingers teasingly together. "Never did find out how old my wife is."

Jessie eyed him up and down as if trying to figure out if he was serious. "I'll be nineteen on my next birthday."

He let out a loud whistle. "I didn't figure you for being that old. That'll teach me to ask questions first, next time, before I make any important decisions."

The look on her face said he'd better retreat.

"I'll go get the horses saddled. You pack up some things and get ready. I'm sure Sarah is just as excited about seeing you as you are about getting to her." He turned to go. "Oh, and just in case you're wondering, I'm an ancient twenty-six."

CHAPTER THIRTY

*I*t took willpower not to stare at the picture Jessie made sitting atop the little chestnut mare they'd named Cricket. Even in her strange outfit, and with a bruised face, she was beautiful. Her oversized blue herringbone coat was so large on her he felt certain it must be a hand-me-down from Nathan. Lonnie, bound, gagged, and slung over the paint, was still out cold. Chase refused to let the unpleasant task of bringing him in ruin his wife's first ride on her new horse.

His wife.

That was a mind-boggling thought.

Even with her swollen lip, she was a delightful sight.

His legal wife.

There it was again, that dangerous thought. He'd better guard himself from thinking of her in those terms.

Her petticoat ruffles fluttered in the breeze, and she kept yanking at them to try to cover up her comely legs. He was thankful she didn't own a pair of trousers like some women. He was enjoying the unusual treat.

"How's she feel?" Chase asked, looking over at Jessie.

"Just fine. I haven't ridden much, but she seems to be gentle enough. I wonder if she knows how scared I am?"

"She knows," Chase said matter-of-factly. "Horses can sense those kinds of things. But she's a sweet mare and will take good care of you if you're kind to her."

"I'll try," she said sincerely. "But I don't know too much about horses. You'll have to watch me and make sure I don't do anything that will hurt her."

"Don't worry, Jessie," he said, trying to hide the smile he felt coming on. "I won't take my eyes off you."

Silent minutes slipped by, but Jessie didn't seem to notice. Chase decided to ask the question that'd been on his mind since the first time she'd opened her door.

"How'd you and Nathan get together?" At Jessie's startled look, he quickly added, "I mean, you two just seem like an odd match, him being so much older and all." Not wanting to lose the easy rapport they'd built, he shook his head. "Sorry, it's none of my business."

"No, that's all right. I think you've earned the right to ask some questions. After all, you did me the favor of marrying me."

Chase rode on patiently, not wanting to rush her, but curious all the same.

"I came out on an orphan train when I turned sixteen. That was the age you were sent away if you hadn't been taken in by a family. Mr. Hobbs looked for placement in homes in other towns. If that didn't happen, you were expected to find a job in one of the places you were traveling through."

Jessie nervously patted her mare's neck.

"I was taken in by a family of four who had a little farm. They lived a few miles out of town. At first it seemed like it would work out fine. I helped Mrs. Parks with the cooking and cleaning and watched after the two little ones too. When planting time rolled around, Mr. Parks had me help in the fields."

Chase smiled his encouragement. He knew it must be hard for her to share her story.

"Then Mrs. Parks got with child again." Jessie's face turned crimson, and she kept her eyes trained straight ahead. "The other two girls were still so little, and I just didn't see how she would bear up through harvest, expecting and all."

"Go on," he said more harshly than he'd meant to. He didn't like the direction this story was headed.

"The night Mrs. Parks told her husband she was going to have a baby, I heard arguing in their room. I went over to the girls and held them, because they could hear it too. We were all scared. I heard him hitting her and her crying. I went to their door and knocked, but it was locked. He shouted for me to mind my own business.

"The next day Mrs. Parks wasn't feeling well and stayed in bed. She came down with a fever. I did everything I knew how to do to cool her down, get her well. But she just kept getting hotter until she was burning alive."

Jessie was whispering, and Chase had to step Cody closer so he could hear.

"Mr. Parks wouldn't let me go for the doctor, even though I begged him. He knew I'd tell them what had happened."

Her face was etched with guilt and sadness. She looked up and scanned the top of the trees as if searching for the right words. The wind had picked up a bit, and it played with the wispy strays of her hair.

"She lost the baby, and the next day she died. There was no comforting the girls, and I was afraid that Mr. Parks would get angry and hurt them too."

Chase never could understand a man beating a woman or a child. It wasn't right, any way you circled it. A man who found pleasure by beating someone weaker than himself was a mule's ass. There'd been times when he found himself wanting to wipe the grin off the face of many a braggart who admitted to it. And he had, a time or two.

"After the funeral things calmed down. Mr. Parks went about his business like nothing happened. Like he hadn't killed her. But I was always scared he'd turn on Hannah and Heather. The little girls tried their very best to do some of the household chores so I could help more in the fields, but they were little, and not much was getting done.

"Then he started looking at me…differently."

Jessie shivered violently, and Chase knew it wasn't from the cold.

"It made my skin crawl, so I stayed as far away from him as possible."

Town was just up and over the next slope. Chase reined Cody to a halt, and Jessie looked at him questioningly.

"I want you to have as much time as you need. We're in no rush." He unwound his scarf and sidestepped Cody closer still to Cricket. Gently he wrapped the scarf around Jessie's neck. "Besides, I don't think I could get much done today if you didn't finish your story."

Nodding, she continued. "Soon he began to bump into me and touch me for no reason at all. I was young, but I knew what he was leading up to. One night after he'd had a good dose of his corn whiskey and was good and drunk, I took the girls and walked to town.

"There was a lady there who'd been nice to me, so I went to her house and told her what happened to Mrs. Parks and why I couldn't stay there any longer. She told the sheriff and said she'd make sure the girls didn't go back to him. I didn't want to leave the girls, but I was afraid to stay in the same town as Mr. Parks."

The horses stood side by side, each resting a hind foot as if they'd been stablemates for years. Chase reached over and took her hand in his. She didn't resist.

"Ah, Jess, I'm sorry you had to go through that. I'd like to come face-to-face with that Mr. Parks. We'd see then how he liked gittin' the life beat outa him."

"Don't talk like that, Chase. Two wrongs don't make a right."

"Maybe not, but it'd sure make me feel a whole lot better." Chase could feel his jaw tighten, but he forced himself to stay calm. "Go on," he said gently.

"That lady, Mrs. Blackstone, gave me a little money, just enough to make it to the next town. She gave me the name of her friend there who owned a laundry business. She said she'd give me a job. But when I got there, the woman had died. My money was gone. I had just enough for one small meal."

Here Jessie stopped. Chase felt there was something she didn't want to tell.

"Don't worry, Jessie. There's nothing you could tell me that would make me think less of you. I've lived on the streets all my life. You'd be shocked if you knew one-quarter of the things I've done to survive." He hoped he could make her understand. He'd never been very good with words, never wanted to be. But this was important.

She took a breath, and Chase braced himself. He figured he knew what it was she didn't want to say. Even though he said it wouldn't bother him, he didn't like to think of her having to sell herself to survive.

"A few days went by. I slept anywhere I could. After I went to every business in town looking for a job unsuccessfully, I found myself at the last place on the street. It was a saloon, the kind where men go to meet women."

Chase nodded at her innocent description of a whorehouse.

"I didn't want to go in. I stood in front for a long time just looking at the door. Finally a woman came out and asked me if I wanted to come inside. Have something to eat."

Chase was still holding her hand. He rubbed his thumb back and forth across her small fingers.

"I went. I was cold. I was hungry. I hadn't seen a smiling face for days. The woman was kind, and even though she was a wh— you know, she seemed to want to help me. After a hot meal and bath, she let me borrow some clean clothes while she put mine in a bucket of hot water to soak.

"Her name was Rosalind, but the man she worked for called her Sweet-Smelling Rose, which she hated. He was big and fat and sweaty. He said he had a room for me if I wanted to work for him. His last girl had run off and started a laundry business but had caught something and died. He said it served her right for leaving."

Jessie glanced up at Chase. "You sure you want me to finish?"

His stomach was tied up tighter than a ball of rattlers, and felt twice as deadly. He knew what was coming, but it was hard to believe. Jessie seemed so innocent, not the kind of girl you'd find entertaining men. "Go on."

"He said I could keep half of what I made. At the time that sounded like a fortune. I didn't think I had any other choice."

With a smirk and a shake of her head, Jessie continued sarcastically. "Said I could start that night, being it was Saturday and they were sure to be busy."

Chase slammed his hand down on his saddle horn, making Cody jump. Looking off into the distance, he avoided her gaze. He'd thought he could take this, listen so she could get it off her chest, but now he wasn't sure.

"That's enough. You don't want to hear the rest."

"No, go on. Finish it," Chase bit out.

"That night I met Nathan. He was my first customer. He'd had a lot to drink and picked me, being I was a new face."

Jessie looked at him apologetically. "I was very nervous, but Rosalind said not to worry, because Mr. Strong was nice, that he'd be gentle, me being young and all. She said he wasn't the kind who'd hurt me.

"We went upstairs, but as he started to undress"—she blushed—"he couldn't. Said I looked too much like his baby sister. She'd been ruined by some no-account. He didn't want the same to happen to me."

A little smile played on her lips at the memory. "When I told him I didn't have a choice, he said that the next day he'd take me over to the next town where a group of mail-order brides were meeting up with prospective husbands. He'd heard that there were a lot more men than women to go around. Then at least, if I found a husband, I wouldn't have to work in a saloon."

Jessie looked wilted. Drained. Chase assumed this was probably the first time she'd ever told this to anyone. She continued softly. "Of course, I jumped at the offer. At least I wouldn't be a prostitute, even if it was a scary thought to marry someone I didn't know.

"So, Nathan paid to stay with me the whole night, and then the next day I went with him over to the next town. There were seven women wanting to find husbands. Some were very young, and two were widows. A woman came in and asked if any of us had anything unusual to be disclosed to the men before they would agree to marry us."

Jessie looked away. She was quiet for several minutes. "I've been badly burned on my back. You saw only a tiny portion. It happened at the orphanage. I'm sorry. I should've told you sooner—before we were married."

"That doesn't matter to me, Jessie." Chase was taken aback, shocked that something so superficial could make her feel so terrible. "I'm sure it's not as bad as you think."

She looked him solidly in the eyes. "It is. Anyway, after seeing it, no one wanted a wife like that. I was left standing there all alone on the platform. That's when Nathan stepped forward. He'd never said he was looking for a wife, but I think he felt sorry for me. He was a little old, not the man I envisioned I'd marry, but he was clean and nice and had a kind face."

Jessie smiled.

With a semblance of pride, she announced, "I was only a shady lady for one day. We were married that night by a justice of the peace."

Chase was so relieved, he felt like he'd died and gone to heaven. She hadn't had to bed sweaty, drunken men. He was happy, elated, on top of the world. And, he was very thankful to Nathan for saving her life.

Reaching over, Chase slung his arm around Jessie and pulled her over close to his saddle. To keep her balance, her hands came up and clutched at his jacket, holding tight; her lips almost brushed his.

"I hope you don't mind, but I'm going to give my wife a little kiss. It won't mean anything except that I'm happy how your story ended, and grateful my good friend Nathan was there for you in your time of need. Is that agreeable with you, Mrs. Logan?"

She nodded.

"By the way," he whispered against her lips. "You didn't have to make me sweat that out quite so long."

He pulled her closer still, breathing in her light scent, the one that had filled his dreams since the first night he'd come to her cabin. Her hair tickled his face, and his smile faded. He brushed his lips feather-light against hers.

Jessie winced when his lips touched her split one, and he pulled back just far enough as to see into her eyes.

"I wish I'd gotten there sooner, before he had a chance to hurt you." His fingers traced down her temple to her chin. "Ah, sweetheart," he mouthed as he moved his face closer and pressed his cheek to hers.

Never had anyone affected him so. Not even Molly, whom he had loved with every fiber of his being. Even she now seemed to pale in comparison.

Jessie was…different. She pulled at the heartstrings he'd thought he didn't have. Made him yearn for so much more in his life. Not only physical closeness—yes, he admitted to himself that he was thinking about her more and more in that way—but plain old-fashioned goodness. Doing what was right. Sacrifice. There was something deep in her eyes he couldn't describe.

She innocently turned her face so he could have access to the other cheek, which he covered protectively with his own.

"Oh, Chase," she breathed, a warm puff of breath kissing his face. "That feels so wonderful."

Cricket put her muzzle next to Cody's and let out an ear-splitting squeal. She pinned her ears and jumped away from the gelding, almost spilling Jessie on the ground. Grabbing for the saddle horn, Jessie regained her balance and then reached for the reins.

"Chase!"

"You're fine. Just pull back. Easy now."

Jessie held up her hand, indicating she was fine. But she didn't say a word.

"Cat got your tongue?" he asked. A teasing light gleamed in his eyes as he stared at her.

She fidgeted.

"I guess so," Chase said, urging Cody on. "We best get to town."

CHAPTER THIRTY-ONE

At the mercantile, Mrs. Hollyhock eyed Jessie's injuries suspiciously, then turned on Chase ready to do battle.

"It's not what you think," Chase asserted, raising his hands in defense.

"You better start talkin'," the old matron barked. Her eyes conveyed the anger within. "And fast."

"It wasn't Chase," Jessie spoke up. "It was that man, Lonnie. The one who was in the store the other day."

Mrs. Hollyhock sucked in her breath and covered her mouth with her hand. "That no-good white trash? I was hoping he'd hightailed it outta here to some other town. Where is he now?"

"He's tied up outside. Is there a jail in town?" Chase asked.

At the sound of Jessie's voice, Sarah raced into the room and leaped into her adoptive mother's arms. She seemed too intent on playing with the buttons on Jessie's blouse to pay any attention to what was being said.

"No jail, just Martha Bindle's ice house." Mrs. Hollyhock fussed over Jessie's face as she talked. "That'll keep him until someone can take him over ta Clancy. It's over behind the livery. I'm going to steep a nice pot of rosehips to stave off any infection in Jessie's lip."

Mrs. Hollyhock bustled away to her stove.

"You'll be all right, then?" Chase asked. He seemed reluctant to leave her.

"I'll be fine. My goodness, Chase, I don't ever remember being babied so. You best hurry now. Gabe will be back soon and he'll wonder where you are."

Mrs. Hollyhock had informed them that Gabe was off somewhere with Jake. They'd left before noontime and were due back any moment. Jessie, knowing Jake, was glad that he and Gabe had struck up a friendship.

Chase backed away slowly. "I won't be long."

Jessie missed his presence the moment he walked out the door. Did all people feel like this when they were in love? No, they couldn't. No man was as wonderful as Chase. He was so handsome, he stole her breath away every time he looked her way. In fact, she'd been so overcome by his presence after they'd almost kissed on the way to town, she couldn't say a word. It was as though all the love in her heart had moved up and blocked her throat.

"So…?" Mrs. Hollyhock asked as she handed Jessie a cup of tea. Its aroma drifted about, mingling with the other fine smells in the store.

"What?" Jessie asked, knowing exactly what she was getting at.

"How did you and that new husband of yours make out last night?" Anticipation shone in her little eyes.

"Fine." Jessie didn't know what else to say.

"Jist fine? Did you consummate your vows?"

"Mrs. Hollyhock!" Jessie exclaimed. "I'd really rather not talk about this." Putting Sarah down, Jessie showed her the button box Mrs. Hollyhock had on a lower shelf, put there purposely to satisfy little hands.

"Nonsense, child. How else can younger women learn from the wealth of knowledge of the older ladies if we don't talk to each other about it? I assure you, everyone does."

"I've been married before. I know all there is to know," Jessie lied.

"This ain't quite the same thing. Nathan was an old man. Mr. Logan is young, healthy, and, might I add, quite the virile buck. If you treat him right, he'll be sure to be sure to make you happy." Mrs. Hollyhock was practically beaming. "Now don't start blushing on me, or I'll think you ain't never even had a lick of experience."

"I'm not blushing. It's just the hot tea you gave me. And I'm refusing to have this conversation," Jessie squeaked out. The thought of being in bed with Chase was enough to make her light-headed.

"Now be sure and be ready for him. Takin' a little time to freshen up before bed is a must. A little bird bath'll do ya fine. As healthy as Mr. Logan looks, I'm sure he'll want to consummate every night. At first, anyway."

Every night! Oh, lands. Is that what married couples did? "Mrs. Hollyhock, please, this really isn't necessary."

"It most certainly is necessary. I can tell by your hemmin' and hawin' you two weren't quite rolling in marital bliss last night, and I mean to correct that before another sun sets."

"It's my monthly, remember," Jessie added hurriedly. "Chase was quite the gentleman when he found out. And I'm sure when it's over, we'll be able to works things out on our own."

Mrs. Hollyhock eyed her disbelievingly as she made a poultice out of horsetail herbs. "Well, that shouldn't stop everything. At least I wouldn't suspect it'd put too much of a damper on a man like your husband."

"Chase was being considerate of my feelings. I can't fault him for that."

"I reckon not, Jessie. But if there's ever anything you'd need to be askin', don't be shy."

Mrs. Hollyhock handed Jessie the mushy mess she'd been working on. "I almost forgot. I have something for ya. I would've brought it out the other night, but I didn't know we was gonna have a weddin'."

She pulled a small box from under the counter. Handing it to Jessie, she smiled. "A weddin' present."

"Oh. Mrs. Hollyhock, I can't accept this," Jessie said, trying to hand it back. Emotion welled up within her, threatening to spill out.

"Of course you can. And will. Go on now, open it."

Jessie carefully unwrapped the gift as if it were made of spun gold. Not a rip or tear did she put in the serviceable brown paper. As she opened the lid she sucked in her breath. "It's beautiful." All she could see was soft golden lace, shimmering like heavenly rays of sun peeking over a clear mountain range.

"Take it out. See if it'll fit."

Fit? It sort of looked like a scarf. Jessie gently lifted the delicate garment, not wanting to damage it in any way. It was tiny. What exactly was it? She wasn't sure.

At her confused look Mrs. Hollyhock laughed. "It's one of them unmentionables they wear down at Sally's. I thought you and Mr. Logan might enjoy it. He jist looks like the sorta man that would."

Jessie looked aghast, and when she finally regained her speech, she said, "Mrs. Hollyhock, where did you find such a garment?"

"I order them every now and then from a seamstress over in Clancy. The girls at the saloon swear by them. They go through them like hotcakes." Mrs. Hollyhock couldn't keep the grin off her face. "Nothin' better to make a man feel manly than a little piece of lace on his woman."

Jessie eyed the soft glittering apparel doubtfully. She'd never have the nerve to wear something like this.

"I can see ya have some good ideas already for this here gift," Mrs. Hollyhock said with a knowing smile. "I hope you'll both enjoy it equally."

There were loud voices and footsteps outside on the wooden plank walk, and Jessie gently put the wedding present back into the box and closed the lid, then put the box with her coat.

Gabe and Jake came banging through the door at the same time, laughing and carrying on.

"Jessie!"

"Hello, Gabe. How are you getting along?"

"Well, thanks. Jake here has been showing me around. You know Jake?"

"Yes, I do. How are you, Jake?" Jessie tried to keep her face averted from the direction of the boys.

Jake's face flamed scarlet, and he shuffled nervously. "I'm fine, Mrs. Strong. I mean Mrs. Logan. I'm real sorry to hear about Mr. Strong dying—and congratulations on your weddin'."

Jake's awkwardness ironically put them all at ease, and everyone burst out laughing. Jake scratched his head for a moment, and then grinned himself.

"Thank you, Jake. That's very kind of you to say." Jessie sipped her lukewarm tea and gazed out the window. A flash of blue caught her eye.

Down the boardwalk came Chase, with his long ground-eating stride, and spurs jingling. Beth Fairington, hung on his arm as she tried to keep pace.

Chase looked cranky.

Beth's mouth was going a mile a minute. Chase looked far from being interested.

"Oh, my." Jessie tried to hide her smile. Beth Fairington was one person who tested her patience to the extreme. She was mean-spirited, and heaven only knew why Mrs. Hollyhock put up with her whining and griping all day long.

The two stopped at the door of the store and exchanged words. Jessie would have given ten dollars to be able to hear their conversation. It looked like Chase was trying get rid of her, but Beth was having none of it.

Beth reached up and straightened his collar.

Chase glared.

The door opened, and in stepped Beth. Chase followed.

"Violet, look who I ran into at the livery. It's Mr. Logan," Beth twittered.

The chilly air had turned her pale cheeks to large splotches of red.

"He's been escorting me all over town."

Chase looked pained but said nothing.

He scanned the room. Was he looking for her? A warm delicious feeling spread through Jessie's body.

Just when he was about to look in her direction, Sarah scampered up and shyly tugged on his pant leg. Jessie knew it must have taken every ounce of the little girl's courage to approach Chase with the strange lady in the room.

"Well, look at you, sunshine." The look on Chase's face changed from pain to pleasure. Bending down to eye level, he tickled Sarah under the chin. She smiled back timidly, twisting from side to side.

Beth looked unhappy about having to share Chase's attention with anyone, even a child.

The happiness shining from Chase's eyes was proof enough for Jessie that he loved Sarah as much as she did.

The boys had remained conspicuously quiet since Beth's arrival.

Beth edged closer to Chase and whispered loudly enough for Jessie and everyone else in the room to hear. "Mr. Logan, you should be more careful who your family associates with." She gestured toward Jake. "They're liable to pick up bad habits and who knows what else." She covered her nose and mouth with her hankie.

Jessie closed her eyes and breathed deeply, all the while counting to ten.

Jessie had known Jake since arriving in Valley Springs. He was always polite, helpful, and hardworking. Her heart bled for him now. She wanted to run forward and scratch Beth's eyes out for her cruel and untrue comment. But she knew she couldn't.

Setting her cup on the cracker barrel, she approached the little group.

"Oh, hello, Jessie." Beth looked taken aback to see her. "I didn't know you'd come to town."

"Good afternoon, Beth. I see you've met my husband and new family." It would be so easy to goad Beth now. Rub it in her face that she was a spinster and most likely would always be. Instead she warmly embraced her. "It's nice to see you."

Beth sputtered at Jessie's kindness. "Why, yes," Beth responded slowly, studying Jessie's face. Her neck.

A deliciously mean expression crossed the woman's face.

CHAPTER THIRTY-TWO

$\mathcal{O}$h, my, Jessie. What happened to your face?" She reached out as if to touch Jessie's cheek. "Mr. Logan has a temper, does he?" the woman cooed sweetly from behind her hankie.

The boys stepped forward for a closer look. Instantly, both looked upset. Confused.

"Beth!" A squawk of outrage came from Mrs. Hollyhock.

Chase stepped over and put his arm around Jessie. He pulled her close. "No, Miss Fairington, my new wife pleases me in every way. Now you…are another matter."

"Why…" She sputtered a moment. "I never!" Aghast, her mouth gaped wide open.

"Well, from the orneriness of you, I can see why." Chase's voice was even, cool.

"She'd better close that big ole mouth of hers, or she's liable to be catchin' some flies," Jake said. Gabe jabbed him sharply in the ribs. Both boys laughed.

Mrs. Hollyhock looked between the two as if she didn't know whose side to take. "Jake, you apologize to your elder. Right now."

He scuffed his foot. "Sorry."

Outnumbered, Beth turned. Ignoring everyone in the room, she spoke over her shoulder to Mrs. Hollyhock.

"I won't be working today, Violet. I have a headache. Have Virgil bring me some tea and toast."

"Yes, dear. Try to get some rest," Mrs. Hollyhock answered.

The moment the door banged behind Miss Fairington, Gabe rushed over to Jessie and studied her face. "What happened, Jessie?"

"A man came out to the cabin and assaulted Jessie this morning," Chase whispered. Jessie figured his low tone was on account of Sarah. "It was Lonnie."

"Lonnie," Jake echoed. "That's him. The man you was lookin' for the other day in the saloon."

"Where is he now? He didn't get away, did he?" Gabe asked.

"Because if he did…" Jake added.

"No, boys, Chase took care of him, praise God. He's locked up in the old ice house where he can't hurt anyone else," Jessie said, forcing a smile. "And he looks a whole lot worse than I do."

"Good," Jake and Gabe said in unison.

Chase turned to Jessie. "Have you told Mrs. Hollyhock yet?"

Mrs. Hollyhock perked up right away at the obvious mention of something she didn't know.

"No. I was waiting on you."

"What's this? Spit it out."

"We're leaving, Mrs. Hollyhock. Chase has a place about two weeks' ride west."

Mrs. Hollyhock stood in stunned silence. Jessie could see this was not what she'd been expecting. "A place? What kind of place?" she managed to get out.

"The house is small and old, but it's on some nice land. Lonnie has a brother out there somewhere. I don't want him hurting Jessie or the young'uns in revenge."

"How's it you didn't mention it before?" the woman asked suspiciously. She'd walked over to Jessie, taking a hold of her arm as if she could keep her from going.

"You didn't ask."

Jessie feared that the two would fall back into their old pattern of quibbling.

"Well, I jist don't think that's such a good idea. I thought you'd stay here." By the look on the woman's face, she was just coming to the realization that as Jessie's husband, Chase had full authority to take her anywhere he wanted.

"It's all right, Mrs. Hollyhock," Jessie said to quiet the shop-keeper's fears. "We'll be fine. And I'll write you every month."

"Ain't the same. You need someone ta look after ya, you and the young'uns."

Jessie gulped. This was harder than she'd figured. "We have Chase now—and Gabe," she added quickly. "Maybe you could come to visit sometime. This spring would be a beautiful time for a trip."

"When are ya going?"

Chase actually looked a little sad at the poor woman's heart-break. "As soon as I can round up everything we need. Two days, maybe three."

"Humph," Mrs. Hollyhock answered. "Never figured on this. Come on," she said, reaching her hand out. "You must have a list of things you need. I might as well start gathering."

The next three days were a whirlwind. Gathering things needed on the trail and for the new homestead were a priority in every-one's mind. Chase was lucky to find a covered wagon—not as large as a prairie schooner, but just the right size for a two-horse team. Chase thought it a good find, in good condition and big enough to sleep four. Not that he had any intention of sleeping inside. As long as there wasn't snow on the ground, he'd sleep underneath. Finally the day came when they were heading out.

"Does it make you sad, leaving this place?" Chase asked Jessie as they pulled out of the yard for the last time. Sarah was playing in back on one of the bedrolls, and Gabe was riding Cody. Chase wanted to drive the team first to make sure that they were dependable.

"Yes. And no," Jessie said somberly. "I'm excited to be going someplace new. Starting a new chapter in my life. This cabin has no ties on me, but…" She turned to get one more glimpse of the place before they rounded the bend. "I'm sorry that Nathan died. He did his best for me, and like you said, maybe if I'd been a better wife to him, he might still be alive today."

Chase took his eyes off the road to glance at Jessie. He hadn't realized his words spoken in anger had had such an impact on her. "I'm sorry about saying that. I'm sure if Nathan had wanted to be here, he would have been. Sometimes men have reasons for doing what they do none of us would understand."

"I reckon. Hope you're right." She shrugged. "I wonder who'll settle there next? Mr. Blackmon, the landlord, up and died last year, so we just stayed on not knowing who to pay. Maybe a family will move in, and they'll have to add on another room. But then, it really wasn't all that tiny."

"Yes, it was." Chase worked the brake as they descended a small hill. It squeaked loudly enough to make him wince. "Remind me to rub some grease on that tonight." He couldn't make this trip with that thing squeaking every moment, putting him on edge. Jessie was wearing her new coat and fur-lined gloves. He'd taken time to be sure everyone had warm clothing and a new pair of boots. The ones he'd forced Jessie to throw out were worn clear through. She looked pretty as a picture sitting there.

"Mrs. Hollyhock is taking this pretty hard," she said. "I hate to see her get so worked up at her age. I hope she'll be fine after we're gone." Jessie nestled deeper into her lap robe. The wind was cold, and each time she spoke a little puff of frost came out of her mouth.

"You warm enough?" he asked.

"Ummm. With my new coat and gloves, I hardly feel the cold." Jessie watched the team's heads as they bobbed up and down. "The horses must have cost you a fortune."

"What's money, if a man can't spend a little when he wants to?" His guilt over losing Jessie's money made him look away. Just as soon as he could, he'd get it back to her, with interest. But the locket was irreplaceable. He took a deep breath. "It's good to finally be back on the trail. Feels mighty nice."

"It was just so generous of you to buy us these new things. I can't help feeling overwhelmed."

A few moments of silence made him look over to see her studying him intently.

"Are you cold, Chase?"

He slapped the reins across the horses' backs, urging them forward. "'Course not."

Jessie scooted toward him a few inches and pulled the blanket over so he could put some on his own lap. "But when we get to town, what will the people think?"

"They'll think we're husband and wife. Plain and simple." *Hardly plain and never simple.*

This charade was taking on a life of its own. Mrs. Hollyhock was looking for any reason to keep Jessie in town and was watching them like a hawk. They'd had to act like love-struck newlyweds to keep her from catching on. Jessie seemed to be playing her part quite well. She was solicitous of his every need. Waiting on him hand and foot. And it seemed she truly enjoyed his closeness.

They rounded the bend into Valley Springs. As they passed the blacksmith shop, Garth walked out into the street to meet them.

"Whoa, now," Chase called to the team, pulling on the long reins. Garth didn't look pleased.

"Logan. Jessie." Garth tipped his hat to Jessie. Chase didn't miss the fact that he'd refused to call her Mrs. Logan.

"Shepard."

"I don't know how you did it, Logan, but marrying Jessie before we even knew Nathan was dead was underhanded. Makes a man wonder if maybe you had something to do with his death."

"What's done is done. Now step away. Wouldn't want to catch your foot under my wheel." Chase would welcome a confrontation. It still stuck in his craw how Garth had pushed his unwanted advances on Jessie the other day, friendly or not.

Garth grabbed one of the reins. "Just want you to know I plan to look into what happened to Nathan. If anything even hints at suspicious, I'll be on your trail."

Chase snapped the reins, making the wagon lurch forward. Garth had to jump out of the way or else get run over. "By the way, Shepard," Chase called out loudly, "the horses are working out mighty fine."

"Chase!"

"Will you miss him?" Chase asked angrily. "Maybe he'd be a better candidate for you and your brood."

"What makes you say that?" Jessie countered, her voice taking on a puzzled tone.

"We both know he's sweet on you." She knew. Women always knew when a man was sweet on them. They just liked to pretend they didn't.

Jessie laughed suddenly, the sound reminding him of bells.

"Why, Chase Logan," she said with amusement.

He glanced her way to see the reason for her delight.

"You're jealous."

"Jealous!" Chase barked. "Hardly."

"There's no other explanation for your statement," Jessie said in an overly innocent tone. "It's as plain as the nose on my face there's no love lost between you and Garth. Doesn't make any other sense."

"He accuses me of murdering my friend, and I'm not supposed to take offense." Chase pulled the wagon to a halt in front of Hollyhock's Mercantile. Wrapping the reins around the brake handle, he turned to face her. "That man has designs on you. You know it. Quit saying otherwise."

"Whatever you say," she replied sweetly as she turned for Sarah. "You going to stew there all day, or help us down?"

CHAPTER THIRTY-THREE

$\mathcal{I}$n the mercantile, Mrs. Hollyhock and Jessie were going through the herbal remedies the woman had packed to send along. The plants, neatly divided and wrapped in brown paper, were stored in a beautifully hand-carved box.

"Now, this one here is thyme. If you're having trouble sleeping, jist tie up a little in a cloth bag with some catnip and chamomile and put it under your pillow. Soon you'll be sawing logs with the best of 'em." Mrs. Hollyhock grinned, holding the herb under discussion.

Jessie looked doubtful. "I hope I can remember all this, Mrs. Hollyhock. It seems so complicated. What if I make a mistake? Can I harm someone?"

Chase, who was leaning against the counter, cleared his throat, his patience growing thin. He'd planned on saying goodbye and heading out. They'd been here nearly an hour.

Mrs. Hollyhock, ignoring Jessie's question, continued. "This here cylinder is lavender oil. It works wonders on restless and cranky babies, or adults, as the case may be," she said, rolling her eyes toward Chase. "On little ones use one drop—no more."

"One drop," Jessie echoed, as the woman placed the brown cylinder back in its place among the colorful array of herbs and bottles.

"Now, in the springtime, if the young'uns are looking a little peaked, boil up some tea from dandelion. It's chock full of good minerals and such. It's an overall good fortifier." She held up a sample for Jessie to examine. "Fresh is better, but dried will do. But mind you, too much will cause cramping and the flux, so be careful."

"That's it," Chase barked grumpily. "You know all you need to know, Jessie. Say your good-byes and let's go." He stomped over to the window and looked out. Garth was still watching their wagon from down the street.

Mrs. Hollyhock continued on as if she hadn't heard him. "Don't forget, Saint-John's-wort for sadness, ginger for nausea, and"—she pulled Jessie into her embrace—"skullcap for your monthlies." Her voice caught on the last word.

"Shhh...there, there, Mrs. Hollyhock. Please don't cry. If you do, I'll start and..." Jessie's voice trailed off quietly and ended with an emotional gulp.

"Oh, girl, I jist hope I did the right thing in marrying you off to Mr. Logan. I never dreamed he'd up and take ya away." The worry and fear that was etched on the pale wrinkled face pulled at Chase. "How am I supposed to take care of ya so far away?"

"We won't be too far." Jessie wiped a tear with the back of her hand. "Chase said you can write to us there, and we'll be sure to get the letter. Isn't that right, Chase?"

"That's right." He was watching the exchange. Jessie looked small and bruised and almost as fragile as the old woman. Her face was clouded with unshed tears. They'd best get going soon.

It seemed to take forever to get the wagon packed up, but finally they were rolling away. Jessie and Sarah waved good-bye to their friends. Mrs. Hollyhock stood on the boardwalk, a smile plastered on her face. Garth watched miserably from down the street, and Beth spied at them from the second-story window across the street.

"Wait!" the old woman yelled. She ran into the store and was back in an instant. She stood next to the wagon looking up at Jessie. "Here. I want you to take this."

"I can't take your Bible!"

"Yes, you can, girl. I want you to have it. Take it!" With determination she handed the book up to Jessie and backed up onto the boardwalk. "Take good care."

"One last stop and we're finally on our way," Chase said, trying to distract Jessie. Sarah was now sitting up front between them.

Jessie looked very sad. Questioningly, she glanced at Chase. "Where are we stopping?"

"The telegraph office. I want to wire a friend in Logan Meadows. Have him see to the condition of the house."

Chase could see Jessie was downhearted, but there was nothing he could do about it.

"Hey, Gabe, wait up." The sound of thundering hooves clamored down the street. Jake's big gray horse slid to a stop next to Chase.

"Can I ride along with ya to Logan Meadows?" He looked hopeful. His shaggy brown hair, fresh from washing, glistened in the sun. On the back of his saddle was his trail gear and bedroll. Strapped to his leg was an old Colt 45.

"Do you know how to use that?" Chase asked, motioning to the gun.

"Sure do. Learned to shoot when I was eight."

"OK, you're hired. I'll pay you when we arrive." Chase nodded, liking the fact they'd have the extra protection of another gun.

"Well, I'll be!" Jake let loose a deafening whoop. "Hey, Granny," he called out to Mrs. Hollyhock. "I'm on my way west. Say good-bye to my ma for me." He pulled out his gun, shooting off a couple of rounds in the air, spooking the wagon horses and making his own horse buck. It took Chase a moment to muscle them under control.

"Put that thing away," Chase ordered, cross with Jake's reckless shooting.

Sheepishly Jake holstered his firearm. Reining around, he jogged his horse up next to Gabe.

"He's already trouble," Chase said, gritting his teeth. "But the extra gun will make me feel a whole lot better."

"I'm glad you let him come along." Jessie pulled Sarah's fingers from her mouth. "He's never been given a chance to prove himself in this little town. Too many small-minded people. Now he can start fresh."

Stopping at the telegraph office, Chase jumped down off the wagon. "This'll just take a minute."

Inside he stepped up to the counter and tapped the silver bell. An older man came ambling out of the back room.

"Back so soon?" the man asked, a cheroot hanging from his mouth. The smoke curled up around his head like a halo.

"Need to send another wire. Actually two."

He lifted an old fountain pen and paper pad from a lower shelf.

Dipping the tip of the pen in a bottle of ink, the clerk looked at Chase expectantly.

"Coming home. Stop. Check house on Shady Creek. Stop. Clean up and have repairs made. Stop." Chase paused a moment, letting the clerk catch up.

"That all?" the clerk asked.

"No. Buy chickens and a cow. Stop. Should be there around Thanksgiving. Stop." Chase thought for a minute trying to figure the best way to tell Frank he was bringing Jessie.

The clerk stared at him.

"Bringing wife and young'uns." He'd have to explain later. On a whim he added, "Get a tom and fatten it up. Stop. Chase."

"Who's it go to?"

"Frank Lloyd, First National Bank of Logan Meadows."

The man made a few marks with the pen and scratched the top of his bald head. "That'll be a dollar fifty."

Chase pulled out three silver half-dollars and placed them on the countertop.

The clerk reached over to the telegraph. His finger moved quickly as the rhythmic tapping filled the room.

"All done."

"Much obliged." Chase had turned to leave when he remembered the ranch that was expecting him. There was no getting around it. "Send another to the Rocking Crown in Miles City, same place I wired before. Tell them I won't be coming this year." He tossed the man one more coin before leaving.

They were finally on their way. Jessie pulled out a tattered old book and began reading to Sarah. Each page was dog-eared and yellowing here and there, but Jessie held it as if it were a priceless jewel. As she read, her voice fell in rhythm with the wagon wheels, and Chase found himself listening and enjoying the story.

When she paused to turn the page, Chase took the opportunity to ask, "What's the name of the story you're reading?"

"*Little Women* by Louisa May Alcott. It's my all-time favorite book."

Chase nodded, and Jessie picked up reading where she'd left off. Sarah snuggled close in Jessie's lap. She nibbled on some dried pumpkin seeds Mrs. Hollyhock had tied up in a piece of bright yellow cloth.

"You can make somethin' outta the cloth when the pumpkin seeds are all gone," she'd said, kissing Sarah's cheek. Chase considered the old woman. He guessed she was good hearted—albeit meddlesome.

"How far will we go today?" Jessie asked, setting her book aside. Sarah had fallen asleep and her head rested in Jessie's lap.

"I'd like to make at least three or four hours. We need to start the animals off slow and work them up to longer days."

"And how long did you say we'd be on the trail?"

"I'm hoping two weeks at the very most. We should get to Logan Meadows around the end of the month."

Jessie's eyelids drooped as she listened. It was a strain packing for this move and leaving the people she loved. She looked tired. He was accustomed to picking up and going whenever it suited him, but Jessie was more of a homebody, fussing and fixing things, needing a place to call home. The old cabin she'd left behind was all the proof he needed.

And not one complaint. She'd worked alongside him long into the night getting everything they needed packed onto this wagon.

"Why don't you take Sarah and lay her down in the back? I'm sure she'll sleep better back there," Chase suggested.

Jessie glanced at him, and then down at the sleeping child. She rose slowly, getting her balance in the rocking wagon. She grasped the wooden bow that held up the canvas covering, steadying herself. As she clambered over the back of the seat, Chase reached out, placing his hand on her back.

"You'll get used to it soon."

"I hope so. I feel a little seasick. Is Sarah still asleep?"

"Yes."

Jessie lifted the sleeping child and laid her on a bedroll, covering her with one of the several quilts Mrs. Hollyhock had sent along.

"Just lay on down with her so she doesn't wake up," Chase called over his shoulder. "She's plumb tuckered out." When Jessie didn't argue, he smiled.

They ambled along at a leisurely pace. He would push the horses harder tomorrow. For now he was glad to be on the trail and moving.

What would Frank think when he got the telegram? He'd jump for joy, probably. He was always pestering Chase to come home, settle down, find a wife.

"*A wife of your own is just what you need, son.*" Chase could hear him now. It had been three years since his last visit to Logan Meadows. Plenty of time, if he'd been inclined, to marry and start a family.

Gabe and Cody seemed to be getting along fine, which was surprising. He usually was a pretty sensitive mount. "Traitor," Chase mumbled to himself.

He'd told the boys earlier to stay in sight of the wagon. "And keep that gun in its holster—unless it's a matter of life and death," he had pointedly told Jake.

The boys reined up in the bend in the road and waited for the wagon to catch up to them. They rode alongside as Chase kept moving.

"Where's Jessie?" Gabe asked.

"Keep your voice down," Chase scolded. "She and the tyke were exhausted from all the happenings. They're lying down in back."

Jake swung his horse around and peered into the interior of the wagon. "When we gonna make camp?"

"In an hour or so. You boys aren't tired already, are you?" Chase asked, tipping up his hat with his thumb. "When I was your age I could ride all day and all night too, if I had to."

"Heck no. We ain't tired," Jake shot back, rising to the bait. "Just wondering if we should water the horses down at that stream."

"No. They can trek longer than this on the trail. They have to learn to drink when we give them water and not just when they're thirsty." Chase looked down at Cody, checking him over as he walked along. His horse knew well the code of the trail, but the new horses might not. "This is their first lesson. They'll be good and thirsty by the time we make camp."

All four horses' heads came up like flags looking to the bend in the road.

"Someone's coming. Get alongside the wagon. Stay alert." Chase slid his Winchester out from under the wagon seat and opened his long coat from around his legs, giving him easy access to his guns.

CHAPTER THIRTY-FOUR

*A*round the corner plodded a horse. It looked better suited to pulling a plow than carrying a rider. As he neared, Chase could see the animal was very thin. It was matted with mud and was favoring the right front foot.

The man astride didn't look any better. He was covered in filth from his greasy hair to his worn-out boots. A shotgun rested across his lap and a jug of liquor hung from a cord tied around his saddle horn. His sneaky, snakelike eyes seemed to be taking in every detail, as if looking for something of value.

He reined up about twenty feet from the wagon. "Howdy."

Chase inclined his head but didn't say anything. This man was trouble. He could feel it in his bones. Intuition had saved his hide more than one time in his life. Who was he to argue?

"Got any vittles to spare?" the man asked.

"No."

"How far to town?" His eyes never stopped their perusal of the wagon. Chase had the feeling he knew the answer to his own question and was just trying to buy some time.

"'Bout half a day's ride." He was hoping Jessie, if she was awake, had the good sense to stay hidden in the back. A woman was always at risk on the trail. She was only as safe as her protector.

"Your horse is lame," Chase called.

"Yeah. He's been gimping for a while. He ain't lame enough he can't carry me though. On second thought, it's nigh on nightfall. Mind if I make camp with you?"

Chase hated to see a horse abused. It only confirmed his suspicions and heightened his dislike for the man.

"We're not stopping. You best keep right on heading to town."

"Ain't too friendly, are you?" He eyed the boys.

Sarah picked that moment to cry out and Chase could hear Jessie whispering to her to go back to sleep.

The stranger's eyes widened with interest. He kicked his horse in the ribs and as he passed, he gave Chase a smile. The few teeth he had were tobacco stained and green.

"Get up," Chase called to the team, sending the wagon rolling along.

Chase looked from one boy to the other as they rode up close to the wagon. "I don't trust him. Jake, you ride in back for a while and keep a close watch. Gabe, you stay up front and keep your eyes and ears open." Chase dragged out Jessie's old shotgun from under the seat and unwrapped it. He handed it to Gabe, who promptly checked to see if it was loaded and then slid it into his heavy leather scabbard.

Chase looked around at the fading light. He'd have liked to make camp now, before it got completely dark, but he didn't dare. He needed to put some space between him and that no-account. He'd seen the type before. He'd just as soon back-shoot you as say hello.

A bit farther on, he finally rolled the wagon to a stop. After their long nap, Sarah was impossible to keep still a moment longer, so Jessie climbed out the back with her, carefully scanning the area.

Chase leaned over the front hoof of the paint, checking for stones. Gabe and Jake set about loosening their saddle cinches and hobbling the horses so they could be turned out to eat.

"There's Gabe," Sarah called, in a singsong voice, full of vim and vigor.

"That's right. Why don't we go over and say hello."

As Jessie and Sarah approached Gabe and Jake, the boys stopped what they were doing. Gabe reached down to pick Sarah up. "Here's my honey pie. How you doing? Did you like the wagon ride?" Gabe never gave Sarah a chance to answer one question before he went on to the next.

"How old is she?" Jake asked.

"We're not exactly sure, but we think around four. She sometimes seems younger, from her years in the orphanage," Jessie answered. "Will you watch her, Gabe, while I talk with Chase?"

"Sure."

With a bellyful of butterflies, Jessie walked over to where Chase was working by lamplight. She waited for him to finish what he was doing.

"Something you need?" Chase straightened, dropping the horse's hoof and turning his attention to her. He didn't seem as accommodating as he had earlier in the wagon. When she didn't answer right away, he snapped, "There's a lot to be done, Jessie. What is it you wanted?"

She wanted to ask him about the man they'd passed on the trail. Chase had told her before leaving he wanted her to be careful about who she revealed herself and Sarah to, so she'd stayed inside when she'd heard them talking. But there was something creepy about his voice. She hoped that she was imagining it, but he sounded like Lonnie's brother. But Chase was tired now, she could tell by his tone. She'd ask after dinner.

"Nothing," she decided, surprised by his coldness. "I'll start a fire and warm some of the food Mrs. Hollyhock sent along."

"Fine."

Jessie made her way back to the wagon, picking up sticks and fallen limbs as she went. She heard Chase call out, "Jake, Gabe, hunt up some wood. Work in a pair and don't go far. Jessie, you and Sarah stay in camp."

Jessie dug out the Dutch oven from the rear of the wagon. They'd been lucky that Squirmy Johnson had one he wanted to sell. Managing without it would have been difficult. The oven was extremely heavy, and she struggled to carry it to the place they would build a fire and plopped it down. She and Sarah gathered some rocks to place around the perimeter.

"That looks pretty good, doesn't it, Sarah?" she asked, as they fit the last rock into place.

The little girl nodded. A movement at the edge of the clearing brought Jessie up short.

"Sorry if I scared ya." Jake holstered his Colt. Gabe, who was carrying all the wood, followed him.

"Where do you want this?" Gabe asked.

"Right here will do."

With a grunt, Gabe let the wood fall, then brushed off the front of his clothes. Jake promptly stepped up and started building a fire. After he stacked the wood, he stood and went to the back of the wagon.

"Where do ya keep the locofocos?" Jake called.

"The what?" Jessie asked.

"The phosphorous matches. I sure hope you remembered to bring some. I ain't too good at startin' a fire Indian style."

"They're in the box on top. Be careful taking it down. It's packed quite heavy."

Jessie unwrapped the cold turkey and pickles from the storage bin. She placed them on a fold-down shelf that doubled as the back of the wagon.

She quickly whipped up a batch of biscuits from two double fistfuls of flour, a glob of shortening, and about half a cup of water. It was the one thing she could make with her eyes closed. When cooked in the Dutch oven, they came out more like dumplings than biscuits.

"Supper's ready," Jessie called, as she watched Chase circle the camp for what seemed like the fiftieth time. She was sure that he must have worn a path by now.

Gabe was first to jump up. Grabbing a blue-speckled tin plate, he began helping himself. "Do you want me to fix a plate for Sarah?"

"Yes, please, Gabe. What would I do without you?" Jessie gingerly lifted the hot biscuits out of the oven and placed them in a linen cloth. "Go on, Jake. Don't be shy."

Chase finally headed in from the perimeter of camp. He looked tired and hungry. His hat was pulled low to shade his eyes, and dark stubble covered the lower half of his face. She should tell him now about the man. She should. Perhaps she'd wait until he'd eaten. Something hot in his belly might improve his mood.

Jake and Gabe were already eating by the time Chase sat down, so Jessie offered a silent blessing.

"Any sign of him?" Gabe asked, over a mouthful of turkey.

Never taking his attention away from his plate, Chase shook his head. "No. But if he were to come back, he wouldn't be leaving any sign. He's clever."

A shiver crept up Jessie's spine. Clever, just like Lonnie. She'd never even known he was at the cabin until he attacked her.

Sarah took a slurp of her water and edged over to Jake. She'd been watching him all night, and Jessie figured she'd taken a shine to him. Jake stiffened when she placed her wet hand on his knee.

Jake looked to Gabe. "What's she want?"

"Don't know. Why don't ya ask her?"

An owl hooted somewhere, and Sarah edged closer. Straightening up, Jake asked, "What do ya want, Sarah?" His voice was so shaky that Gabe burst out laughing.

"Big, bad Jake. Adventurer, mountain man." Slapping his knee, Gabe kept it up. "Cowhand, gambler. Soon-to-be miner. Tell me, Jake, what haven't you done?" Gabe shook his head, his eyes sparkling. "You're scared of a little girl. Now I've seen everything."

"Am not," Jake shot back angrily. "Who'd be afraid of a puny little thing like her?"

"Finish up, everyone," Chase said, "and head to bed. I want to get an early start in the morning."

Jessie noticed that even as Chase ate, he was ready. His gun was within easy access, and he sat casually, with the fire to his back. Watching.

Jessie couldn't help the feelings that welled up inside her. Here was a man thrown into a situation he'd never asked for. Who'd been forced to marry her, a stranger. And yet he cared enough not to abandon her or the children, seeing to it that nothing happened to them. A warm sensation flowed through her, making her long to go and sit with him by the fire. Curl up into his lap like the kitten she'd once had back in the orphanage.

"Come on, Sarah, let's get you ready for bed. We're going to have to bundle you up good so Mr. Frost can't nip your nose." Jessie scooped up the child.

"Gabe and Jake, grab your bedrolls and bring them out here by the fire. We'll alternate night watch." Chase stretched out his long legs and crossed them at the ankles. "Gabe first, Jake, then me. Keep the fire to your back. And keep it burning."

"Yes, sir," Jake replied. Gabe nodded.

Jessie gathered the supper plates and put them in a bucket of water to wash in the morning. Quickly storing the food and filling the coffeepot, she climbed into the wagon behind Sarah.

Chase stuck his head in. "We'll only have coffee when we break camp. Around midmorning we'll stop and have a bite to eat." His gaze, unreadable, followed her every move as she laid out the beds and gathered up more blankets.

"Will you be warm enough out there by the fire?" She searched his face for some sign of softness, a little bit of the caring that he'd displayed back at the cabin. She missed the man who'd so tenderly brushed her cheek with his own. Who had listened patiently, his heart in his eyes, to the story she'd never told anyone.

All she saw now was a man chiseled by the elements. Brutally honest and granite hard. Was she finally seeing the real Chase Logan, the man who was still alive today only because of his wits, instincts, and quick gun?

Chase didn't answer her question but riveted her with his gaze. "Don't leave the wagon for anything. Understand?" The muscle in his jaw clenched. "I don't want to scare you, but wolves and mountain lions live here."

"Yes."

Sarah scooted behind the crate packed with the few knick-knacks that Jessie owned. She seemed to sense a difference in Chase and didn't quite know what to make of it.

"Fine, then. I'll be under the wagon. Knock on the floor if you hear anything unusual."

CHAPTER THIRTY-FIVE

*T*he first night came and went without incident and was followed by five more farther along the trail. As they climbed in elevation, the weather worsened considerably, with big black storm clouds hanging low over the mountaintops. The frigid wind was relentless, whipping about, stinging faces, eyes, and hands with bits of ice.

Jessie tried to keep Sarah's poor little lips and hands from cracking and bleeding by rubbing castor oil on them, but the harsh elements were too much for her simple efforts. After a particularly unforgiving day, Sarah's lip cracked so badly, blood trickled down her chin. When Chase saw her, he angrily ordered her to stay in the back of the wagon out of the ferocious wind.

Each time Jessie tried to tell Chase that she thought she'd recognized the stranger's voice, he'd been standoffish and cold. He was building a wall between them, keeping her at a distance. Maybe she was making too much out of it, and it wasn't Lonnie's brother. Perhaps the stranger just had the same accent. From the wagon she really hadn't heard him all that well. And at Hollyhock's, he'd said very few words. If it was Joe, he'd have been back by now.

Chase was worried; Jessie could tell. Getting caught in a blizzard, especially with a small child, would be very bad. It would also make it impossible to proceed farther or return to Valley Springs, if that's what Chase thought was best. Constantly checking and rechecking the sky, she watched as he pushed them harder and faster, testing the animals.

And still he remained aloof. Secretly she'd hoped maybe he was becoming attached to her and the children. Maybe he'd want to stay once they were settled. But, with a heavy heart, she knew different. Everything he did or said was to the contrary.

She missed the closeness they'd shared in the cabin. Chase's boyish charm. She knew Sarah missed his warm smile that they hadn't seen in over a week.

"He's probably anxious to be free of this responsibility," she mumbled to herself.

Sarah, who'd been uncommonly cranky for the better part of the day, came down with some sort of stomach ailment. She cried, and not even Gabe could quiet her. Jessie feared that it might be something serious.

Carefully picking her way through Mrs. Hollyhock's herbal remedies, she wished the old woman were there. They all looked so much alike. She finally identified the tangy smell of catnip and brewed up one teaspoon in a cup of water, as Mrs. Hollyhock had instructed. Soon after drinking the mixture, Sarah was fast asleep.

"Whoa." Chase, now riding Cody, reined up in front of a river that was twice the width of the street in town they'd left. It wasn't particularly swift, but there were pockets where the water swirled black and forbidding in a mystical way. The gelding promptly dropped his head and took in big draughts of water. The wagon pulled up alongside, followed by Jake. All the animals drank greedily.

Chase frowned. The clouded sky churned above them, heavy with the snow to come. They'd never beat this storm. The blizzard would hit tonight—he could taste it in the air. Their luck had just run out.

"We need to find some shelter, some protection from the storm. When we get on the other side, watch for an overhang, a rock wall, or, if we're lucky, a cave."

Chase circled his horse around to face Jessie. Her haunting blue eyes were searching his face again. For what, he didn't know. Irritation flashed through him. What in the hell did she think she would find? He was who he was and nothing more.

"It'll snow soon. If it gets bad, Gabe may have to walk up in front with the horses, help them see the path. You may have to drive. Think you're ready for that?"

Jessie nodded. She'd quit talking to him much since he'd put up his defensive wall. But he'd had to. Sitting next to her in that wagon, the seat barely big enough for the two of them, had been gut-wrenching. It took everything he had not to pull her into his arms, to show her what he was really feeling. He had to keep reminding himself that he was her husband in name only.

"Fine, let's move out. Jake, you stay on this side until the wagon is on the opposite bank, just in case. Take the wagon through the shallow part of the river," Chase said to Gabe, pointing to a narrow but swift spot in the swirling torrent. Out of the corner of his eye he saw disappointment on Jessie's face. "I'll go first. If there are any big holes, I want to find them, not you."

She doesn't know why I'm rejecting her, Chase thought. She doesn't know that every time I'm around her, it's hard for me to keep my hands from bringing her close.

Cody sidestepped once when Chase nudged him, and then took a reluctant leap into the icy water. Chase sucked in his breath as his legs went numb. Cody fought the current as he swam, then climbed the bank on the opposite shore. He shook his head, and then the rest of his body, ridding himself and his rider of the frigid water clinging to them.

"Bring 'em across, nice and easy." Chase raised his arm, beckoning to Gabe. The wagon rolled down the small incline to the riverbank. When the horse's hooves sank up to their fetlocks in the sandy water, they struggled nervously in their harnesses.

Fear gripped Chase. Maybe he should be the one to bring them across. Driving a wagon could be tricky, let alone crossing a swollen river. Could Gabe handle it?

He felt stronger about being ready on Cody. In case something happened, there needed to be a pickup horse on both banks.

"Talk to them, Gabe. Use your voice to calm them," Chase yelled to be heard over the rushing water. "Easy now, easy."

Jessie sat next to Gabe. One hand clung to the bow of the wagon, and the other reached over the wagon seat and gripped Sarah, who crouched behind. Chase could see Jessie's mouth moving, talking to the horses or Sarah, he presumed, but he couldn't hear what she was saying.

The wagon groaned loudly as a surge of water buffeted its side. "Chase," Jessie called to him, a ring of panic in her voice.

Then, as if that weren't enough, a wagon wheel sunk in a hole up to the axle. The wagon careened sideways. Gabe slapped the reins over the horses' backs, demanding more power from them. They responded, pulling the wagon back around swiftly toward their destination.

Spurring Cody back out to the middle of the river, he rode up to Jessie's side of the wagon.

"You're doing fine." He smiled his encouragement. Her reaction was a mixture of hurt and confusion. "The hardest part is almost over. You'll be out before"—he looked at Sarah's scared face—"you can say 'Pop goes the weasel.'"

Sarah peered at him over the wooden seat and tried to respond with a smile of her own but her quivering body said something different.

Jessie's smile was tight. "He's right, Sarah. This is kind of fun."

"Come on now, let's get this wagon across and find shelter," Chase said with confidence. "My bones are aching."

"My thoughts exactly," Gabe added. "We're all cold and damp."

Once out of the river, they waited for Jake to cross and then proceeded along slowly. Gabe was up front now leading the horses, moving at a snail's pace. They'd switched at the riverbank, putting Jessie in the driver's seat.

Just as Chase had predicted, the sky had opened up and the snow came down hard and fast, making it impossible for animals or humans to see.

Jessie wrapped the stiff reins around her gloved hands to keep them from slipping. Pain shot up her arms and down her back. Driving a team had always looked like so much fun to her. She'd no idea of the strength it actually took. Bone weary and almost overcome with exhaustion, Jessie peered through the sheet of white trying to see Gabe.

"Don't think about the cold," she encouraged herself. "Soon you'll be settled in a beautiful little home to call your own." She shouldn't speculate about the future but the temptation was just too great. The thought of a snug bed with heaping blankets, and a cheerful, snapping fire in the hearth was the only thing that kept her from losing heart. Besides, Chase, Gabe, and Jake were out there somewhere. If they could withstand the elements, so could she.

Chase suddenly appeared out of the swirling wall of white. His scarf was wrapped around his mouth, his hat pulled low. He rode up next to the wagon seat.

"Everything all right here?" he shouted.

"Yes."

"I've found a grove of trees up ahead. Not too far. It's not much protection, but we'll have to make do. Follow me and keep the horses as steady as possible."

Jessie nodded. It took too much energy to answer in the howling wind.

Sarah peeked her head up over the seat behind where Jessie was driving, startling her.

"Sarah, honey. What is it? Get back inside out of the wind."

"Scared," Sarah said. She reached out and took hold of Jessie's coat. "Bad man."

CHAPTER THIRTY-SIX

*J*essie was shocked. She'd thought that Sarah didn't know about Lonnie and what he'd done back in Valley Springs. Did the little girl understand more than she let on?

"Don't be scared. By now the mean man is back in Clancy. He can't get you." Even as she said the words, a sliver of fear sliced through her. Would she ever feel safe again?

"Out," Sarah said, pointing to the swirling snow. She popped her two fingers into her mouth. Up until now, the habit of finger sucking had almost been forgotten.

"No, no, he's not out there. Just roll up in your blanket and stay warm. We'll be making camp soon, and I'll fix you something to eat, all right?"

She smiled at Sarah, wanting to put her at ease. She wished she felt better herself. The white wall of snow was eerie. The only sound was the screaming of the wind and the thunk of her own heart. Jessie hunkered down and gripped the reins, feeling totally alone. Anyone could be lurking five feet away and she'd never know it.

"Here, turn here." She heard Chase's voice call out through the storm. "Try to drive them between the two tallest trees."

Jessie heaved on the right rein, turning the horses into the spot Chase had directed. Pulling up, she winced as pain sliced through her hands. Even her heavy leather gloves were no match for a white Wyoming norther.

Chase was there again, this time on foot. He craned his neck to see her. "Stay inside and I'll unhitch. Bundle up and keep Sarah warm. The boys will be in shortly."

Jessie prepared to step over the wagon seat when she heard him call her name. She turned back in question.

"You did a fine job driving the team."

For one instant, Jessie saw the spark. It was there, lingering in the depths of his eyes. That fragile thread connecting them. Just as quickly, it vanished, leaving Jessie colder than she'd ever felt.

Finding the matches, Jessie debated whether to light the lantern in such a wind. The possibilities of starting a fire in the wagon were great. But the darkness put her on edge. She was being silly, but after the seed Sarah had planted, she had the frightful feeling of being watched.

"I think it'll be all right if we light this," she said to Sarah. "We'll have to watch it very closely not to knock it over." With a scratch Jessie lit the match. Cupping it in her hand, she carefully guided it to the lamp wick and lowered the glass encasing the small flame. "There, that's better."

The lantern cast a hopeful golden glow about the cold, dreary wagon. Jessie patted her lap, and Sarah gladly climbed up, snuggling in. The north wind screamed, and a sudden blast of cold wind sent the wagon rocking. The little flame danced as Sarah huddled closer. "Don't be scared, sweetie. Chase and the boys will be in here soon."

The sound of Sarah's growling stomach interrupted her.

"Oh, listen to your tummy. It's trying to tell me something. I'll fix supper as soon as the men get here."

With a squeal, Sarah jumped up and wrapped herself around Jessie's neck and head.

"Sorry, little one." It was Chase, looming just outside the back of the wagon. The only way Jessie knew it was him was by the sound of his voice. He was completely invisible in the blanket of snow. In the next instant, Gabe and Jake climbed in through the front, bringing the snow and wind whipping inside. Gabe jerked the canvas closed.

Jessie eyed the slush with dismay. It was impossible to keep anything dry. After days of trying, she was almost ready to give up. Still, it was a relief to have the men back.

"What's to eat?" Gabe asked. "I'm starved and froze to the bone."

Chase climbed in. He looked around. "This will be cramped with all five of us inside. But we'll get by."

Jessie looked from one frozen face to another. She couldn't bear to tell them the meat was gone and all they'd be eating was cold leftovers.

Jake slowly peeled off his sodden gloves and inspected his fingers. They were stiff and red. He stuck them inside his mouth and breathed hard. Even though he didn't say anything, she could tell they were hurting.

She glanced at Chase. Was he worried? Was this storm life threatening? If it was, he didn't let on.

His poor face was raw and red from the cold. Snow and ice clung to his whiskers and covered his expressive eyebrows in white. Jessie restrained the urge to reach over and wipe them off. Instead, she pulled out one of her kitchen cloths and handed it to him. "For your face."

"You boys get on over into the corner and give Jessie a little working room to set out the food," he said, using the proffered gift. He handed it to the boys when he was finished.

Jessie went through the supplies, taking out anything that would make up a meal. Thank heavens Mrs. Hollyhock had insisted Jessie take extra canned goods and anything else that wouldn't spoil. She'd even stuck in a couple dozen hard-boiled eggs. Keeping the food fresh hadn't been a problem in the cold weather.

"We've got plenty for supper," she said cheerfully. "Biscuits from today's noontime meal," she said, giving one a squeeze. "Not too hard." She held out the cloth and passed them around.

Chase took one and set another on Sarah's plate.

"Look what I've been saving," Jessie said excitedly, trying to raise everyone's spirits. She held up a basket, full of Mrs. Hollyhock's hard-boiled eggs. "With a little salt these are delicious."

The boys groaned.

"I can't wait to hit town. I'm gonna buy me the biggest, rawest steak this side of the Rockies," Jake said. "Heard they have some so big, three men can't finish it off. Sure would love to have one now, hot and juicy."

"Yeah, wouldn't we all?" Gabe chimed in.

Chase took two eggs and passed the basket to Jake. "Well, we don't, so we'll just make do with what we have. Won't be that much longer before we reach Logan Meadows. Eat the eggs. They're filling."

Jessie handed a jar of pickles to Chase, and he quickly snapped open the lid with his knife. Jessie nodded her thanks.

"Are they sweet, Jessie?" Jake asked. "They're my favorite."

"Yes, sir, they are. Take as many as you like."

Chase handed the jar over to Jake and watched as the youth dug in. Then he reached out to hand Sarah an egg, but the little girl shook her head.

"Come on, honey," he insisted. "You need food to keep your insides warm."

Sarah shook her head and clung to Jessie's back. She held her biscuit in her hands, which were shaking from the cold. Every now and then she would take a nibble.

Jessie rummaged for a can of beans and again handed them to Chase to open. She met his questioning gaze. "She's jumpy. The storm has her scared."

"Don't be scared, Sarah," Gabe said around a mouthful of food. "It's just a storm. We won't let anything happen to you." Extending his arm, he reached for her. Sarah clung tighter to Jessie and whimpered.

CHAPTER THIRTY-SEVEN

*T*he wind howled and launched another blast of snow against the wagon's side, rocking it back and forth. Chase had been in much worse storms than this one. As long as the passes didn't close up, they'd be fine.

He noticed that Sarah's gaze kept darting around the wagon, but it always ended up behind him, staring at the back opening. The thing was securely fastened, and Chase wondered what had her so spooked.

"Just the wind, Sarah," he said, trying to put the girl at ease. "That old norther is throwing a fit. It's scary now, but when you wake up the forest will be a real pretty sight." The boys exchanged glances and kept eating. They were too old to fall for that story, but Sarah smiled in appreciation.

"Chase is right, sweetie," Jessie soothed. "Here, eat this apple and you can give the core to Cody in the morning."

"Scared of man." Sarah looked to Chase.

"What's she talking about?"

"She thinks she saw someone out in the storm. She's been scared ever since."

He'd been careful to study their back trail, but since the bad weather had closed in around them, he'd used all his energies getting them to shelter. "You boys see anything out of the ordinary?"

"Through this wall of snow? I couldn't even see to wipe my nose." Gabe smiled at Sarah and winked.

"Naw. Too thick," Jake added.

"There's nothin' out there, honey," Chase said to comfort her. "But if it'll make you feel better, I'll take one more look around before we go to bed."

Sarah eased out of her protective corner behind Jessie and approached. Remorse filled him at her reluctance. He'd done a real good job of not only putting distance between him and Jessie, but him and Sarah as well. Space, he figured, would make it easier for her when he left.

Chase stretched his arms out to her. "Climb on up here and warm me up. Feels like a month of Sundays since I was warm." Sarah climbed up the best she could, an apple in one hand and her biscuit in the other. She settled in the crook of his arm. He guarded himself against her sweetness.

The boys took the opportunity to scoot closer to the lantern. Both held their hands up to the light, but the little flame didn't throw much heat.

"You're dreaming, boys," Chase said, his eyebrows arched in amusement. He was feeling mighty good with Sarah nestled in his lap. She tipped her head back to look at him. Her hand stole up slowly, and she touched his whiskers with her biscuit. "Scratchy. Not like Ma." The sweet scent of apple tickled his senses.

"You're right about that, little one. Your ma's as soft as a peach," Chase said, glancing over at Jessie. The boys looked at each other and grinned.

In the lamplight Jessie's cheeks turned the color of a rose petal.

He chided himself. This certainly wasn't the way to put distance between the two of them. But to tell the truth, he was sick and tired of trying to do the right thing. Right now he didn't care.

"Has everyone had enough?" Jessie asked as she organizing the food to put away.

"You didn't eat." Chase looked pointedly at her.

"I'm not hungry."

"Hogwash. If you're worried about food, don't be. We're not that far from Logan Meadows. Go on. Eat." His tone said he wouldn't take no for an answer.

"Fine."

Everyone, including Sarah, caught the irritation in Jessie's voice.

"Is there something special you'd like me to eat?" she asked dryly. "A pickle perhaps?" She fished her two fingers around the jar until she pulled one out. "How's this?"

"Looks good to me."

"Would you like one?"

"No, thanks. The eggs and biscuits filled me up just fine." Chase looked down at Sarah. "Can't say as when I ever enjoyed a meal so."

Sarah giggled, getting into the spirit of things. Both boys grimaced. Jessie's face flamed.

At once, Chase realized that Jessie was taking the lack of food personally. And she acted as if it were her fault they couldn't have a fire. Maybe he shouldn't tease her so. "Have a biscuit and egg too. This cold will sap more out of you than you think. You need to keep up your strength."

"Mercy sakes alive, Chase. You'd think I was two years old." The annoyance in her voice rang loud and clear. "I know what and when I need to eat."

"Maybe you do. Maybe you don't. I'm just trying to make sure you don't get sick before we reach town. Then Sarah here"—he tickled her tummy, drawing a laugh from her—"would have to drive the wagon."

Jessie ate as she tidied up. A bite of biscuit or egg, and a look. Every now and then he would swear she was making a face. Jessie's rancor amused him.

Jake pulled out a scratched, old harmonica and began to play some chords. The music was fast and jaunty, and soon Jessie's mouth curled up in the corners, to Chase's relief. Good. A little entertainment was just the medicine to take their minds off the bitter cold.

"Anyone know the words to this one?" Jake asked, and then started puffing away again.

"Sure do." Gabe joined in, singing and clapping his hands.

I came to town the other night,
I heard the noise, then saw the fight,
The watchman was a runnin' 'round,
Cryin' Old Dan Tucker's come to town.

Sarah scrambled off his lap and twirled in circles even in the cramped space. Her little braids swung out from her head, and merriment danced in her eyes. Jessie must have felt his gaze because she looked up and their gazes locked. His slow smile silently asked for her forgiveness for his teasing. The tip of her head and the smile in her eyes was all he needed to see. Is this what real husbands and wives felt? To know what the other is thinking with just a glance?

Gabe started the second verse.

Old Dan Tucker's back in town,
Swingin' the ladies all around;
First to the right and then to the left,
And then to the gal that he loves best.

As the last strains floated through the wagon, Sarah collapsed onto Jessie's lap. Her tiny cheeks were bright pink, and she struggled to catch her breath.

"Why, Sarah, I didn't know you were such a fancy dancer," Jessie laughed, as she smoothed the child's hair from her eyes. The silky strands stuck to her moist forehead.

"Chase, this one's for you. Sing along if you know the words." When Jake played off the introduction Sarah jumped to her feet and resumed her fast-paced twirls.

Chase grinned boyishly from ear to ear when he recognized the tune and joined Jake.

Monday was my wedding day,
Tuesday I was hitched,
Wednesday night I tried for a kiss,
And out the window I got pitched.

His tenor resounded from front to back, surprising even himself, and certainly Jessie by the look on her face. It felt good to sing and laugh. Without a doubt, this was a night to remember.

CHAPTER THIRTY-EIGHT

A blush crept up Jessie's face, but she kept her gaze glued to Sarah, who was still spinning in her mad caper. Even when Chase finished singing, Jessie refused to look at him.

Gabe and Jake chuckled at the newlyweds, seeming to thoroughly enjoy Jessie's embarrassment. They'd been serious for far too long. The impromptu party was a welcome relief.

Gabe broke the silence. "Hope that didn't embarrass you too much, Jessie. It was all done in good spirit."

"No, I liked it. I've always loved music," she said honestly. "Please, sing another. Sarah is having so much fun."

Chase smiled. He was glad she liked it too. A horse nickered outside, and Chase held up his hand for silence. Even little Sarah stopped, straining to hear if anything sounded unusual.

"I hate to end this little party, but tomorrow will come far too early," he said. "I want to make as much distance as we can in the deep snow." He pulled on his gloves and wound his scarf around his neck, then wedged his hat on securely. "I'm going to take one last look around. Check the horses. You all get bedded down as soon as possible." With a knowing look to the boys, he checked to see that their weapons were within easy reach.

By the time Chase made it back inside, everyone except Gabe was asleep. His back was braced on the wagon boards, his pistol lying across his lap. The lantern burned low, barely throwing enough light to see anything at all.

"Everything OK out there?" Gabe whispered, sleepy-eyed. "You were gone an awfully long time."

"Seems so. I wanted to check out what Sarah said. But it was next to impossible to see anything. We're going to have a heck of a time tomorrow in this snowfall."

"How much farther we got?"

"Hard to tell with this weather. Three days, possibly more." Chase slowly maneuvered around in the small space, being as quiet as possible. His large frame made it pretty tough. He barely missed knocking over the cups and plates stacked on a crate. "I'm getting a little worried about the stock. Don't know how much more they'll take without some decent food in their bellies."

"Can we clear some snow and let them forage tomorrow?"

"Can't risk the time. We need to get as far as we can while they still have strength to pull." Chase eyed the sleeping group. They were his responsibility, at least until this trip was over.

Where was he supposed to bed down? The wagon bed looked like a sea of blanket-covered bodies. "We still have a small supply of oats. That'll just have to do for a while."

Gabe motioned with his head to a spot between the back of the wagon and Jessie's and Sarah's feet. "Jessie put your bedroll over there. Can you squeeze in?"

"Sure. This wagon is cramped, but at least that makes it somewhat warm. I've spent too many stormy nights wondering whether I'd wake up in the morning or just drift off, peaceful-like."

Chase hunkered down, pulling the blanket Jessie had laid out for him up around his shoulders. Instead of lying down he leaned up against the wagon side. He made sure his gun was within easy reach, but plenty clear of Sarah.

"I'll take over the watch now, Gabe. You better get some shut-eye."

Gabe yawned and stretched his long legs in his bedroll. "Be sure to wake Jake in a couple of hours. You need your sleep, too."

"You can bet on it."

The night stretched on and the wind let up. Chase sat as if forged out of rock, listening to nothing but quiet. Once in a while one of the sleepers would turn over or pull a blanket. Other than that, the silence permeated every inch of their little haven.

There was a rustle, and Chase heard Sarah cry out.

"Shhh, honey, go back to sleep," Jessie murmured in hushed tones.

"Cold," Sarah cried. She thrashed about as Jessie tried to calm her. "Wet."

Jessie slid her hand down into the blankets. "Yes, you are and so is your blanket. Shhh, don't cry, it's all right."

Jessie fumbled around in the darkness trying to find something dry for Sarah to put on. The scratching of a match brought her attention to Chase.

"Did we wake you?" Jessie asked worriedly.

Her silken hair flowed down around her shoulders like an angel and her eyes were soft with sleep. She looked mighty inviting to a cold, uncomfortable cowboy.

"No. I'm just keeping watch." He leaned over to the lantern and lit the wick, turned it low for a bare minimum of light.

"Sarah's wet her blanket. I need to find her some dry clothes." Jessie reached over and rubbed Sarah's back. Sarah, hiding her face in Jessie's pillow, seemed to be taking it hard that she'd made a mess.

"Not surprising, with this cold," he said, trying to make Sarah feel better. Kneeling, he reached over Jake and grabbed the duffel bag containing Sarah's things. Extending his arm, he handed it to Jessie.

"Thank you." Jessie rummaged through, pulling out a warm pair of long johns. They looked larger than Sarah's size but would certainly keep the child warm through the night. "Mrs. Hollyhock stuck these in, bless her heart. Come here, Sarah, and change."

Sarah stayed face down in Jessie's pillow.

With a look at Chase, Jessie pulled gently on Sarah's arm. "Come on, honey, don't be shy."

She didn't budge.

Chase shrugged.

A knowing smile brightened Jessie's face. "Turn your head, Chase. It's you she's worried about."

It was only a moment before muffled sounds and whispers made his heart warm.

"There, we're all done. You can turn back around." Jessie scooted Sarah under her blanket and kissed her good night for the second time that evening.

Long minutes passed, but Chase didn't want to blow out the lantern just yet. "She asleep?"

"I think so."

"Neither of you will get much rest sharing that blanket. She's been restless all night. Why don't you crawl on over here?" Chase opened his blanket in invitation.

Chase's voice rumbled low, spreading like honey through Jessie's veins. The lamp cast its golden glow on Chase, illuminating the angles of his face, sending Jessie's heart skittering.

She hesitated. He'd been so distant the last few days. Why did he want her close now?

"It's all right," he encouraged. "We can warm each other up."

Like a bee to nectar, Jessie couldn't resist. As she carefully picked her way over to him, he leaned over and blew out the lantern. At once they were cast into darkness.

"Here I am," he said softly. "Crawl on in."

She slid into his arms, and he wrapped his big coat around her. His body was hard next to hers. And warm.

"Mmmm, you're warm," he whispered, cuddling her closer. His face was next to hers. So close that his cheek gently nudged hers, his whiskers tickling. "Comfortable?" he asked, as he pulled her in even tighter, forcing her to wrap her arms around his body.

"Yes," she barely got out. She was awash in feelings. Breathless. She rubbed her cheek against his, and imagined she could feel the beat of his heart against her breast. She turned slightly and his lips touched hers. All coherent thought fled. Her world spun crazily, tilted. All she could think about was his warm mouth, his gentle kiss. Chase. And how he made her feel.

Chase eased down to the bed of the wagon, taking Jessie with him and cradled her in his arms. Moving close, he concentrated on Jessie's lips, as his thumbs traced her eyes, her face.

"Chase?" Jessie breathed heavily.

"Shhh, don't talk." He was afraid she'd start asking questions. Questions he wouldn't be able to answer.

There was movement from the far side of the wagon.

"Chase, you awake?" Jake called quietly.

"Yeah," he whispered back, pulling Jessie protectively closer, acutely aware of her presence. He was sure Jake couldn't see her curled in his bedroll.

"What time is it?"

"Hard to tell without the stars. Somewhere around two, I'd guess."

"OK, it's my watch. Don't worry about anything; I've got sharp hearing. Get some shut-eye."

"Thanks, Jake," he said low. "I'll do that. Good night." He placed his lips next to Jessie's ear, gently kissing as he whispered, "Good night, sweetheart."

CHAPTER THIRTY-NINE

*J*essie was hopeful. She reminded herself over and over not to read anything into Chase's new demeanor. He seemed very different these past three days. Happier. Maybe it was because they'd made such good time after the storm. They'd been lucky it hadn't slowed them down too much.

Jessie was again overwhelmed with yearnings for Chase. First he'd been forced into a marriage he never wanted. Then he'd spent so much time and money on her and the young'uns, making sure they had all the things they needed to keep them warm. When they reached their destination, she'd have to be brave and remember that he'd probably sacrifice his freedom to stay with her if she asked. He was so honorable. She had to make it easy for him to ride on, if that was what he wanted.

The wheels of the wagon crunched along the well-worn path. The snow covering the road had melted and refrozen, creating a fine crystal base—beautiful but dangerous. The sun, which hadn't made an appearance for several days, now shone brightly, its rays shimmering off the endless expanse of white.

"I can hardly believe we're almost there," Jessie exclaimed to Gabe, who sat silently beside her, driving the wagon. The boy nodded, causing a thick lock of his chestnut hair to fall in his eyes. The golden sunlight kissed it, reminding Jessie of a beautifully polished piece of expensive furniture. She'd give him a trim when they got settled in. Chase and Jake needed one, too.

Today.

Today they should reach Logan Meadows.

Every time she thought about it, her stomach tightened up. What was Chase planning? What was he thinking every time she caught him watching her with his dark, contemplative eyes? He'd never said, but she felt it had something to do with Molly. Did she still live in his heart?

If he hadn't changed his mind and was still planning on leaving, she wanted as many memories with him as she could get. He was her husband, she reminded herself. She'd never love anyone after Chase. Would it be so wrong to be with him before he left? They *were* husband and wife.

When had she realized that she loved him? It seemed as if she'd always known deep down. She just hadn't known what to call it—what *love* really was.

"Today should be the day," Gabe answered back. He'd been deep in thought and seemed somewhat melancholy.

"Something bothering you?"

Gabe sat there, elbows braced on his knees, not paying much attention to the horses. After so many days on the trail, they practically drove themselves. "It's nothin'."

Jessie followed his troubled gaze. It fell on Chase riding one hundred feet in front. "It's Chase?" she kept up in motherly fashion. She was not that many years older than Gabe, but she felt a maternal protective yearning for him.

"I just don't understand him. Or you, either. Something ain't right, and you're not saying what it is." Gabe turned and pinned her with his gaze. "We are going to where Chase has a ranch, ain't we?"

"Yes, we are."

"Then what's the big secret? Why haven't you two been making plans and such?" Gabe turned his gaze back to the trail. He slowly shook his head. "I remember when my family was coming out from Virginia. Every night was full of talk. What we'd do when we arrived. What crop we'd plant first. Who had to milk the cow."

Jessie was speechless. She hadn't realized she and Chase were giving out such disconcerting signs. Her heart ached.

"You're nice enough to each other," Gabe continued, "but that's as far as it goes. Almost as if that's all you have planned. Gettin' to Logan Meadows."

What should she tell him? She didn't even know herself.

"Quit treating me like a baby, Jessie. I'm old enough to know, so tell me what's going on." His voice had changed from sad to irritated.

"You're right," she finally said. "Things are different with Chase and me. He's planning to set us up in the homestead he has—that was the truth—but then he's planning on leaving."

"Forever?"

"Yes."

"Why?" Gabe choked out. "He can't go. You're married." Gabe looked at her as if that's what he'd been thinking all along.

Jessie squared her shoulders. "Don't look at me like that, Gabe. He's doing his best for us. We can't expect him to change his whole life just because a friend dies and leaves behind a wife. My goodness. Think of all he's done already."

"Yeah." His voice was hoarse as he answered. He didn't look at her again.

"I'll be grateful to him forever," Jessie said, laying her hand on Gabe's shoulder. "And you should be too. He's done far more for us than anyone else would have even considered."

Chase waved his arm, and Jake rode up to where he waited. "Town's just around that corner," he said, excited and nervous all at the same time. "Ride on back and tell Jessie."

"Will do. What's that place there?" Jake pointed to an old log building that had been a boarding house when last he'd ridden out.

"The Red Rooster Inn. Oldest landmark in town." Chase watched Jake lope back to the wagon. So much had changed in the last few days. What was he supposed to do now? His head said leave quickly while he still had the chance, but his heart whispered to take hold of the happiness he'd found in Nathan's misfortune and never let go.

Indecision gnawed at his belly. Could he be what Jessie needed? Take care of her and grow old together? Could he spend the rest of his life sinking roots in the same place, day after day?

He knew what he wanted, what he yearned for. But the fear of letting Jessie and Sarah down kept him in doubt. He pulled off his hat and ran his gloved hand through his hair. He'd better get to thinking; time had just about run out.

Chase waited for the wagon to catch up, and then they all rode into town together. Amazingly enough, the town of Logan Meadows looked just the same as when he left, three years before.

Up ahead, almost at the end of the short block on the right, was the Bright Nugget Saloon. As they approached, a young woman dressed in red stepped out of the swinging café doors. When she caught sight of them she waved. She looked vaguely familiar, so Chase waved back. He didn't want to appear unfriendly.

Chase was relieved Jessie's attention was still on the El Dorado Hotel. If he remembered correctly, it was a fine establishment with a good restaurant inside. The Silky Hen? Maybe he'd treat them all to a supper out soon. They had certainly earned it.

"Oh, look, Chase," Jessie called, pointing across the street. A small building nestled among several larger ones gleamed with a new coat of white paint. "It's a bakery! I can smell the fritters right now."

Chase smiled. He was enjoying watching Jessie's reaction to the town. He could feel her excitement.

"Pull the wagon up here, Gabe, in front of the appraiser's office. The bank's right next door." Chase dismounted and tied Cody to the hitching post. "I'll be right back."

Chase entered the dim interior of the bank and let his eyes adjust. He was nervous. After glancing about and not finding Frank, he approached the teller window and rang the silver bell.

"May I help you?" a young dandy asked. He set aside the ledger he'd been working on and looked at Chase expectantly.

"Frank Lloyd in?"

"No, but he'll be back directly. Just stepped out for a moment." The teller cleared his throat. "Is there something I can help you with?"

"No," Chase answered abruptly, his nerves getting the best of him.

"Who should I say is here to see him?"

"Chase Logan."

CHAPTER FORTY

*F*ine, fine, Mr. Logan. You can wait in Mr. Lloyd's office." The excited teller escorted Chase into Frank's office, and he took the proffered seat next to the plate-glass window. If Frank didn't show up soon, he'd wait out at the wagon with everyone else.

Drumming his fingers atop the highly polished desk, he studied the neatly arranged articles. He'd really wanted a word in private with Frank before he introduced Jessie and the kids.

Footsteps rang out across the worn wooden planks. Frank always walked like he had an urgent task to complete. Chase heard the teller informing him of his visitor. Within moments Frank burst through the door.

"Chase, my boy! It's wonderful to see you." He grabbed Chase in a bear hug and pounded him on the back. "I was just starting to get worried." He gave Chase a wink. "That must be your darling wife out in the wagon. I spotted her from down the street." Frank leaned back so he could get a good look into Chase's face. He must have liked what he saw, because he grinned, the proudest smile Chase could remember.

"You look good, my boy. I see that marriage agrees with you."

"It's good to see you, Frank."

"Is that all you have to say?" Frank asked, again peering out the window at the wagon. "You ride in here after all these years, with a wife and three young'uns hanging about, and all you can say is 'It's good to see you'?"

"It's not quite what you think. I need to explain a few details," Chase admitted casually. He hated putting a damper on the man's happiness.

"That can wait." Frank waved him off. "First, I want to meet your wife. What's her name?"

"Jessie."

"Fine. Let's go meet Jessie and the rest of your family, and then we can catch up with all the news. I've so much to tell you. I don't really know where to begin."

Chase could hardly keep up with the man as he practically ran to the wagon. "This is Jessie," Chase said as he lifted her down from the wagon. "Jessie, this is Frank Lloyd, the friend I've been telling you about."

Jessie smiled. "Pleased to meet you, Mr. Lloyd."

"Believe me, Mrs. Logan, the pleasure is all mine. I'm just so happy Chase has finally found a sweet little lady to tame his wild ways." He cleared his throat. "I mean, to marry up with him." He turned his eyes to Sarah, who waited patiently on the wagon seat. "And this is…?"

"Sarah," Chase finished for him. Chase lifted the little girl down. Frank reached for the child, but she clung to Chase's neck with ferocity.

"She's shy." The emptiness inside his chest was filled with the wonderful feel of her charm.

Frank nodded his approval.

"There on the gray is Jake, and this here hombre is Gabe."

"Pleased to meet you, boys. How was your trip?"

"Fine, sir," Gabe answered. Jake just nodded.

"Well, you're finally here," Frank said, pleasure radiating from his face. "I've just about worn myself ragged since I got your telegram. I hope I fixed up the place to your liking." He looked expectantly at Jessie.

"I'm sure you did a fine job." Jessie gave Frank a brilliant smile. "Chase, can we take Sarah over to the bakery? She's never had very many sweets, and I'm sure she would just love one."

"Never had a doughnut!" Frank burst out. "Why, that's a sin. Follow me. It's my treat."

They all crammed into the tiny white building together. It was well kept and clean inside, with two little tables by the front window. The sweetness of the air tickled their noses, and the smell of frying batter made Jake's stomach rumble loudly. They all laughed.

"You ever had a doughnut, Jake?" Frank asked.

"Yes, sir. Mrs. Hollyhock would make 'em twice a year. Once on Christmas and once on my birthday. I love 'em. I'd say they're my favorite food."

"I bet you do. They're my favorite too." Looking across the counter, Frank smiled at the young woman frying a new batch of the dough. Her hair was piled on the top of her head, and she had a smear of flour across one cheek. "Lettie, this is a celebration. We'll have three dozen of your finest."

The woman smiled at his teasing. "Mr. Lloyd, you *know* I only have one kind. Would you like them frosted?"

Frank looked around at the expectant faces. "Absolutely."

The group devoured the donuts. They were mighty good after the harrowing trip they'd just completed.

Frank was watching Jessie intently. He was going to be madder than a wet rooster when Chase told him the truth. He'd tried to tell him in his office, but Frank hadn't wanted to listen then.

"Mrs. Logan," Frank said, wiping his hands on a napkin. "I have a niece just about your age. A nice young woman and I'll be happy to introduce the two of you. Her name is Hannah Hoskins." He nodded happily. "What are your plans for tonight, Chase? Are you riding out or staying in town?"

"I think everyone would like to get this move over with. We'll be heading out after we pick up some supplies at the mercantile."

"No need, I've taken care of everything. Hopefully you're stocked for a good long time."

"I can't thank you enough, Frank," Chase said sincerely. He glanced over at Jessie as she brushed some frosting from Sarah's mouth.

"You've thanked me already by just coming home."

Jessie watched the exchange as the two men talked. Mr. Lloyd seemed very fond of Chase, practically drinking in the very sight of him. She could tell Chase was delighted to be home too but for some reason seemed to be holding back.

Mr. Lloyd turned, and Jessie was embarrassed to be caught staring. "Well, would you like to venture out to your new home?" he asked.

New home. That had such a lovely ring to it. A permanent ring to it. She looked to Chase. He smiled and nodded. The seed of hope that had sprouted in her heart the other night took firm hold.

"Let's go, then," Chase called to the boys. "Are you coming, Frank?"

"Wouldn't miss it for the world."

The group turned around and headed back the way they came but turned right at the end of the street, in the opposite direction from which they'd entered.

"Oh, Gabe, isn't it wonderful?" Jessie said, as her gaze darted here and there. She pointed up a knoll where she'd spotted a small white church, with a well-tended graveyard.

"It sure is, Jessie." Gabe nodded. "It's about the grandest town I've ever set eyes on."

Chase and Frank rode a little ways in front of the wagon, catching up on old times. "Did you have any trouble finding any of the things I wired you about, Frank?" Chase turned, glancing back at the wagon.

"The milk cow took some doing, but I finally located one a day's ride out. Sent Humphries to get it."

"Hope Humphries didn't mind going all that way."

Frank chuckled and shook his head. "Don't worry, you paid him well enough."

Chase's eyebrows lifted in question. "Oh?"

"Yeah. You don't want to be stingy, do you?"

Chase was thoughtful. Frank was always the one harping on saving and not throwing money away foolishly. "No, wouldn't want to be stingy." Something strange was going on here that Frank wasn't saying.

When they came to a fork in the road, Chase followed the well-worn direction to the west. It was the route the stage traveled, and it also led to the house on Shady Creek.

"Chase, my boy," Frank called, as he veered off to the east. "Let's go this way. I have something I want to show you."

Chase bristled. "We're all tired, Frank. We've been on the trail for a long time." He was in no mood for sightseeing and was sure the others felt the same. "Tomorrow." He sat his horse stubbornly on the westbound road.

"No, it can't wait," Frank responded from the east. The wagon stopped in the fork, waiting for the decision. "Come on, it'll only take a few minutes, and then I promise we'll get your little family home and tucked away."

"How long will it take?" Chase wanted to be sure it was close. Frank sometimes had a way of getting carried away.

Frank grimaced, and then looked hopefully to Chase. "About fifteen minutes?"

"That's a half hour, round trip, Frank. You know how many days we've been on the trail?"

Frank tipped his hat up with his thumb. "I promise. It'll definitely be worth it."

He hated to give in, yet the man had done so much for him— not just this homecoming, but throughout the years. What was thirty minutes more?

"You won't tell me what this is all about? I just have to take your word on it?"

"That's right."

"All right. I guess you haven't steered me wrong yet."

Ten minutes rolled by. They came to another fork. Here the road continued east, but another swung to the north leading to the Broken Horn Ranch. The ranch was a beauty that Chase had seen a time or two.

"We're turning here."

"What?" Chase reined in his temper. This was too much. "Now why would we want to visit Hollister at the Broken Horn? Jessie can pay a social call some other time, when she's rested. You didn't drag us all this way just to go visiting, did you?"

"I guess you know me too well. No, I wouldn't bring you on a wild goose chase. I brought you home."

CHAPTER FORTY-ONE

*W*hat?" Chase was astounded. "Say that again."

"You've added some acreage since the last time you left. You're the new owner of the Broken Horn Ranch. It was too good of a deal to pass up."

Chase sat in pure disbelief. Jessie, Gabe, and Jake looked from one to the other trying to figure out what was going on.

"It's true. I've been waiting for a year and a half for you to drag that mangy hide of yours home. I never know where to reach you since, by the time you wired your pay, you were off to who-knows-where. You know, you could've waited for a reply just once."

"Quit your bellyaching and give me the details."

"Hollister lost his money on a couple of bad bets. He'd been gambling for years, but this time he couldn't dig himself out of the hole he'd created. He couldn't make his mortgage, so the bank got the place by default. I tried to help him all I could. I held the ranch for a year while he tried to scrape together the money to buy it back. He finally gave up and left town." He shook his head, clearly upset over the other man's loss. "You're the only one in town who could afford to buy the Broken Horn lock, stock, and barrel. Besides, it was logical, since your land runs up against it to the west."

It was too much to take in. It had to be someone's idea of a bad joke.

"My biggest fear was you'd up and get yourself killed before I had a chance to tell you. That's why I've been jumping for joy since the day I got your telegram." The man fairly beamed. "Come on, you're going home. And, Chase..." Frank had a smug I-told-you-so look on his face. "Didn't I tell you bank dividends have a magical way of adding up?"

"Many a time," Chase said, still shaking his head. "More times than I can remember."

The land was beautiful. Rolling pastures went on forever. They were still covered in a blanket of snow, but come spring, they would be as green and pretty as an Irish emerald. There were two barns: one for the horses, which had been Hollister's pride and joy, and another for barnyard animals and equipment.

But the house, even in its run-down condition, is what seemed to impress Jessie the most. She gazed at the beautiful chinked log cabin, built to last a lifetime...or two. The rooms were large and spacious, and there were three real bedrooms.

"Sorry it's so barren, Mrs. Logan," Frank said, sweeping his arm across the empty expanse of the room. "Most of the big pieces of furniture Hollister sold bit by bit to support his gambling. It's a true shame, because some of the pieces had been in his family for generations. It was a good thing old Sherm Hollister wasn't around to see how irresponsible his son turned out to be."

"It's so beautiful." Jessie walked around the room, her hand touching a Tiffany lamp that stood on a corner table.

"Mrs. Logan, look at this," Frank said, swinging open a door off the kitchen. Jessie peeked in. "It's a built-in soaking tub. Let's warm some water and you can have a bath tonight."

Jessie gasped, making Mr. Lloyd's face go white. He looked to Chase.

"She's just all wore out. The trip and now this is too much of a shock for her. Come on, Jessie, lie down a minute and catch your breath."

"No. What about Sarah?" She looked around. "I need to—"

"Gabe and Jake are showing her the cow in the barn. Come on." Tears shimmered in her eyes, ready to spill over. He led her to one of the bedrooms and was thankful to see a bed, nicely made up with a colorful quilt.

"Here." Chase patted the spot next to him. "Sit next to me and we'll talk."

She nodded and took a deep breath, struggling with her emotions. Was she as confused as he was?

"It's gonna be fine, Jess. We'll work this out. Come morning, you'll wonder what you were so worked up about."

"No." The strength in her voice surprised Chase. "If I stay and stick with our plan, you'll leave. This is your dream, Chase. A chance of a lifetime. I know you could build this into a fine horse ranch. I'm leaving tonight. Not even unloading the wagon."

"Are you touched in the head, woman?" Chase's voice rang out. "You're worn out. Sarah's worn out. The animals couldn't take another step if you begged them. You just get that foolish notion out of your head this minute."

She was breathless as she continued. "The other house; the one on Shady Creek. We'll go there until I've had a chance to think this through."

The need to comfort Jessie stole over Chase like a cool breeze in the hot summer sun. Her darned pride was almost as strong as his was.

"We'll see. But for right now I want you to lie back just for a moment while I talk with Frank. Will you do that one thing for me? And then we'll finish this discussion." Chase gave her a little push and Jessie sank into the soft feather bed.

"Sarah?" she quietly asked.

"I'll watch her."

Chase found Frank having a smoke on the porch. He looked worried as he gazed out across the open expanse of endless snow. Chase pulled a stool over next to him. Frank offered a cigar.

"No, thanks." Chase gazed out over the land too. "Quite a view, isn't it?"

"Yes, it is. Chase, do you like it? I hope you're not angry that I took the liberty with your money. It was just such a good deal. And land is always your best bet for investment."

"Angry? That's absurd. No, it's a dream come true. Who wouldn't love this place?"

"Mrs. Logan, perhaps?" He dropped his stub to the porch and ground it out with his heel.

"Jessie?" Chase said, surprised. "No, you're wrong. She loves it. She's just worried about other things, that's all."

"Anything I can help with?"

"No. But thanks. We'll work it out."

"I'm heading back to town. There're a few ranch hands living down at the bunkhouse. They've been keeping the place up since Hollister left. Just doing the bare essentials and watching for squatters."

"Thanks, Frank. I can never thank you enough. You're the only father I've ever known. You were the only one willing to take a chance on me. And now look at this. It's all because of you."

Frank's face went red. "Ah, Chase. Don't you know I'd do anything for you? Now, get some rest, son, and we'll talk in the morning. Good night."

CHAPTER FORTY-TWO

*C*hase awoke around midnight, sleep eluding him for the eighth night in a row. He told himself he just wasn't used to sleeping in a bed, especially one as big and comfortable as this one was. But he knew that wasn't the case. Rolling to his other side, he punched his pillow.

Jessie was obsessed with the notion of not taking this ranch from him. She insisted she and the children would go to the Shady Creek house until she found a place to relocate.

Was it really her way of saying she didn't want another man in her life?

"Stubborn woman," he muttered, rolling over yet again.

Exasperated, he climbed from the bed and grabbed his crumpled pants, hastily pulling them on. Not bothering with a shirt, he walked barefoot into the large living room. Cold or not, he needed some air.

Slipping his heavy coat over his shirtless body, he stepped out onto the front porch and leaned against the post. The stars shone brightly in the vastness of the night sky. Felt like forever since that first night when he'd sat out with Jessie, her on the porch and him on the wood bin. The night she'd asked him about the angels and talked about God.

What was eating him? His decision was made. Jessie would be fine without him, and with the ranch, she was sure to find someone else to take care of her. To love her.

Is that what he wanted? Life without Jessie and Sarah sounded so empty. The boys too. Leaving the ranch was nothing compared to never again having Jessie's smiling face light up a room.

Back in Valley Springs she'd wanted him to stay. She'd said her vows were true, before God; that she intended to be a real wife to him. But what about now? Vague doubts gnawed at his insides. Maybe she was anxious to end this chapter of her life and start another.

Sighing, he glanced back toward the house, and Jessie.

Mrs. Logan, he corrected himself.

She was in sleeping with Sarah. Probably all warm and cozy. Would he ever be able to forget the feel of her in his arms?

A horse nickered, drawing Chase's attention down to the corral. Several horses clustered to one side of the pen were milling about. As Chase examined the area in the golden light of the moon, the outline of a person emerged. Looking more closely, he recognized Jessie's willowy form. She was probably checking on Cricket, the mare she'd grown so fond of.

Tugging on his boots, he walked down to the corral. "What are you doing out here alone?" he called when he was within hearing distance. She jumped when she heard his voice and swung around to meet him.

"I just needed to get some air, Chase. Don't go getting mad."

Her hair was loose and blowing in the chilly night breeze. It glimmered in the moonlight, and Chase fought the urge to feel its softness.

"It's such a beautiful night. I had to come out for a walk."

Not as beautiful as the picture she made with the stars to her back. Chase noticed again how small she was, her head barely reaching to his chin. "Well, you shouldn't go alone."

She laid her hand on his arm. "I'm not alone now."

He shrugged, not wanting to let go of his anger. Things needed to be settled; they'd drawn out far too long already.

"Don't be angry. I…" She stopped.

He looked into her eyes.

"I can't bear it when you're mad." She spoke clearly, her words an arrow to his heart. "I'm afraid you'll ride off and never come back." She stepped closer.

He drew back, struggling inwardly. "What is it you want? I need to know what you're thinking."

"I want you to be happy," she said simply. "Only that. I don't want you to feel bound to me out of obligation to Nathan, or Sarah, or me." She inched closer, throwing his heart off balance. "You've done more for us than any six people could have." She looked up at him, her gaze touching his face, warming his skin.

He was a man. Flesh and blood. "If you must know, *you* make me happy, Jessie. Your smile, your touch, everything about you." There—it was out. But he needed to know how she felt. "But what about you? We've been walking this wide circle around each other. How do you feel about me? Exactly."

Jessie circled him in her arms, tilting her head to see his face. "I'm afraid," she whispered, "that what I say will trap you."

"You couldn't trap me. If I wanted to go, I'd be gone."

"I love you."

The words were whispered so sweetly, his heart thunked in his chest. Her face, awash in moonlight, mesmerized him. The arch of her brow, the curve of her lips. Everything about her was perfect.

"Jessie." He lowered his lips to hers.

Jessie melted. Could she be dreaming, or was this really happening? She'd told him what was in her heart, and he hadn't turned away. Happiness welled up in her, and she fought to keep it from spilling out. Could he possibly feel the same?

Chase scooped her up and, before she could protest, carried her into the barn. Up the ladder he climbed, holding her with one arm, as if she weighed less than nothing. Laying her gently in the sweet-smelling hay, he lowered his body to hers and pinned her with his weight.

"Chase?" Jessie whispered as he captured her mouth with his. The taste of him sent her senses spinning. Chase paused and in one movement stripped off his coat, revealing his bare chest. In the dark barn, Jessie could catch glimpses of it in the moonlight gliding through breaks in the slats.

He was so beautiful. Hard muscles rippled his body. Jessie's breath caught. Reaching up, she caressed his chest with one hand. Chase closed his eyes.

Thrilled at the pleasure she saw written on his face, she tipped her face up and kissed each eye, and then scattered more kisses down his strong jawline and under his throat. He pulled her closer. Chase's eyes, hungry now with passion and desire, gazed questioningly into her own. But she wasn't scared. This was Chase, whom she trusted and loved.

Chase moved with urgency. Working quickly down the buttons, he removed her coat and began to lift her night rail over her head, but stopped when she laid her hand on his heart.

"No?" he asked softly, his eyes searching her face.

She smiled at his seriousness.

"No...not that. My back. I want to show it to you first."

Jessie carefully extracted her arms from her night rail and crossing her arms, lifted up the back of the garment. For long moments she looked into his eyes before turning her back toward him.

Chase had a hard time not looking away. He steeled his emotions so his shock wouldn't show on his face or make his voice falter. How she'd suffered! Surviving had been a miracle. He reached out and traced one angry, burgundy blotch with his finger. She shivered. "How?"

"There was a fire in the nursery when Sarah was just a tiny baby. I went in after her, but I wasn't fast enough. A beam fell from the ceiling and knocked me down. Sarah rolled out of my arms and out of harm's way."

"Oh, sweetheart," Chase gulped out, shivering himself. How had she stood the pain? It must've been excruciating. "How old were you?" It came out in a whisper.

"Fourteen," she answered over her shoulder. Her profile, softly silhouetted by the moonlight, was somber.

"Where is the good in this, Jessie? It's tragic. You were so young." His voice broke, unable to go on.

She put her finger to his lips. "Shhh...there *is* a silver lining, Chase. Don't you see? These"—she traced a welt on her side—"made me strong. These made me able to survive anything life would throw my way. These brought me to you. For what I'm feeling right now, I'd do everything the same."

"Jessie...sweetheart, little darlin', I'm so, *so* sorry." His voice was hoarse, congested.

"It's OK," she whispered, comforting him. "It was long ago, and they don't hurt anymore." She finished pulling her night rail over her head and tossed it to the side. She lay back in the hay, a silent invitation.

CHAPTER FORTY-THREE

$\mathscr{H}$er eyes glistened in anticipation, her mouth soft, wanting. Chase believed now there was a God in heaven, for no one else could have created a creature so beautiful. She surpassed his every dream.

Jessie blushed at his intense scrutiny, but she held her ground. Suddenly, looking wasn't enough. He brought his lips to hers. Something inside him whispered to slow down, savor every second. But he couldn't. Her passion urged him on, until he could wait no more.

Her sudden cry of pain stopped him cold.

"Jessie?" Chase smoothed her hair back from her brow. Her eyes were squeezed shut and her breathing was shallow. His heart slammed in his chest. "I hurt you," he whispered against her silky skin.

"It's all right," she murmured. She reached up and touched his face. "The pain's almost gone."

Remorse filled him. If he'd known before, he'd have taken much more time, gone slowly. He'd have waited until they were in a big, soft bed, for goodness' sake. This explained Nathan's cavorting behavior the night he'd been killed. All this time he'd been judging Nathan unfairly for spending so many days away from his wife. He should have been thanking him instead.

"What is it?" she asked quietly.

He shook his head then kissed her lips gently. "Just a little something that must have been meant to be," he replied softly, as his gaze caught and held hers. Slowly, everything except Jessie faded into darkness.

Afterward, Jessie laid quietly in his arms, their hearts beating as one. Moments slipped by, and she didn't make a sound. He began to get worried. "Jessie?" With effort, Chase rolled his head so he could see her face. His chest filled with emotion. She loved him. She'd said so earlier. But still he could hardly believe it.

"I wish you'd told me you were…you know, a virgin," he said gently, brushing a strand of her hair from her forehead. "I'd… have done things differently. At least made sure we were on a bed. How is it possible you…?" Chase stopped, and then began again. "After a year of marriage…?"

She opened her eyes and looked at him. "Nathan was a good man. He thought of me as a girl needing help, not a wife."

Chase's eyes searched hers for regret, a hint of what she was thinking.

As if she knew what he was wondering about, she snuggled in closer. "I liked it just the way it was," she whispered. "I wouldn't have wanted it any different."

"That so?" Chase ran his finger down her side, and she giggled. "Talking pretty big, aren't you?"

Jessie raised her eyebrows.

He stopped his tickling.

She put her lips close to his ear. "Maybe we could go inside where it's a little warmer. That big, soft bed sounds really nice."

Days flew by. Thanksgiving arrived. Jessie had never hoped—or even dared to dream—that she could be this happy.

Frank joined them for dinner and brought a letter from Mrs. Hollyhock. She said she was doing fine. Beth had up and run off with some gambler in the middle of the night a few days after

Chase and Jessie left town. Mrs. Hollyhock wanted to come to Logan Meadows for a holiday. Wondered if Chase would mind if she stayed with them for a few weeks. Jessie was delighted. Chase not so much.

Sarah's eyes grew as round as moons when Chase lifted the turkey out of the oven, golden brown and smelling delicious. But when she'd learned it was her beloved Mr. Tom, she'd refused to eat a bite.

"Poor, poor Mr. Tom," she cried, running from the room. Chase, confounded, rode straightaway into town and brought back one of the kittens Jessie had seen in Miller's Mercantile the week before. She was a fluffy calico with a sweet personality. Sarah cuddled and kissed her and immediately named her Patches.

Between the two hired hands and the boys, Chase had almost all the help he needed to run the ranch smoothly. It would take a few years to build the herds back up to their previous count, but that didn't bother him. He liked a challenge.

Jessie watched him leave the house each morning and eagerly awaited his return for the noon meal. The boys had taken to sleeping and eating in the bunkhouse with the hired men, but always attended Sunday service with Jessie and Sarah and stayed up at the big house for supper. Chase was making huge strides in his reading and writing, and was able to read to Sarah from a level-one reader. He looked forward to it each and every evening.

The privacy was heavenly. After Sarah was put to bed, they spent many long hours together, learning what each loved the most. Mrs. Hollyhock's wedding gift was put to the test, to Chase's delight, and he vowed to buy Jessie a new one each year on their anniversary.

"I can't believe it's almost Christmas, sweetie," Jessie said, her heart trembling with happiness as she brushed Sarah's long, curly locks. "What present should we get for your pa?"

Tipping her head in thought, Sarah's eyes twinkled back at Jessie from her chamber-set mirror. Her little fingers played with the cup put there to hold her toothbrush.

"A kitty." Excitement at the prospect made her little body quiver.

Jessie laughed. "I don't know. I think one kitty per household is enough, don't you?" They both watched as Patches, tiny claws snagging, climbed quickly up the side of Sarah's quilt. "I'd like to have a few things left intact by the time she's grown. What else can you think of?"

"Umm..." A serious expression crossed the child's face.

"We could knit socks," Jessie went on. She could tell the idea didn't strike Sarah as quite as grand as a kitten.

"And we could make him some fudge." Sarah smiled at her idea, this one almost as good as a kitten.

"That's a nice idea," Jessie replied. "How about if we also make him a warm flannel shirt to match the socks we knit?" That was enough to make it sound exciting to the child, and she nodded enthusiastically. "We'll pick out a pretty color when we go into town tomorrow. That'll give us a whole week to finish it before Christmas."

"Pa will love Christmas," Sarah said purposely. Chase had been filling her head with story upon story of Saint Nicholas. He'd even promised her a real tree, in the house, with all the trimmings.

Jessie left Sarah playing on her bed with Patches. She went to the pantry and took out the fixings for supper. If she wasn't mistaken, she would have the most wonderful Christmas present to give Chase. Although it was too soon to be sure, Jessie was almost certain. Her heart ached with happiness thinking of the pleasure a baby would give him.

She should've started her monthly seven days ago. By Christmas, she'd be almost two weeks late. The sound of boots crossing the porch drew Jessie out of her reverie. The door opened, and Chase stepped in.

"You're home early!"

Crossing the room, Chase scooped her into his arms and carried her into the living room. Sitting down, he held her in his lap. "You complaining, Mrs. Logan?" he drawled, burying his face in the thick mass of her hair. He kissed her neck, sending delicious shivers curling down her spine.

"Never." She could barely get the word out. It amazed her how just the sight of him could intoxicate her so.

Sarah, hearing his voice, came scampering out of her room. She planted herself in front of them expectantly. "Hi, Da."

"Hi, dumpling," he said, giving Sarah a wink. "How's my best girl?"

"I'm fine. You wanna hold Patches?"

"I sure do. Can you find her for me?"

Off Sarah ran.

"You're wily as a fox, Chase Logan." Jessie laughed.

"With luck, Patches is tucked away somewhere real good." Chase nuzzled Jessie's neck.

A knock sounded on the door. "Shoot. Can't a man have a little privacy in his own home?" he grumbled. Then, louder: "Who's there?"

"Jake," came the reply.

"Come in."

Jake opened the door. His hat dangling in his hands, he glanced around the room and then spotted the pair on the chair together. "I'll come back later."

"No, no, it's all right. Come in," Jessie said, standing and straightening her clothes. Chase stood also. "What is it?"

Jake came farther into the room. "We found some sort of campsite past the north pasture, hidden in the trees. It seems abandoned now. We couldn't find anyone, but it didn't seem that old."

Chase went to the door and put his hat on. "You looked real good?"

"Yeah."

"Well, pass the word around to keep a sharp eye out. I don't like the sound of that."

Awakening the next morning, Jessie reached a hand behind her and felt for Chase's warm body. It had snowed long into the night, and Jessie relished the memories of clinging to him in the darkness. To her disappointment, she found his side of the bed empty and cold. She figured he was down at the barn, checking the mares that had been delivered two days ago. Well, she'd just get up and start a hearty breakfast for him. He'd no doubt be back shortly, wanting food and kisses.

Smiling, she wrapped herself in the warm, fluffy robe Chase had brought home from town. He'd gotten a matching one for Sarah, saying a little widow woman in town made them and needed the income. Pooh. He'd been spoiling them both rotten. She worried about him spending too much money.

Feeling cold air, Jessie stepped out of the bedroom to find the front door ajar. It was only slightly cracked, but it was so unlike Chase to go off and accidentally leave it open. Especially in this cold weather. Her smile faded as she hurried to close it.

Fear.

For the first time in so long, a bad feeling stole through her. She shook her head, telling herself she was being silly; not even Chase was perfect, even though she liked to think so.

With porridge on and biscuits in the oven, she set about tidying up. Sarah was a one-girl whirlwind. If she didn't keep up with the messes the child made, it wouldn't be long before they'd be up to their waists in clutter.

Doll, books, and buttons in hand, Jessie tiptoed into Sarah's room. Not wanting to wake her so early, she set the things carefully on the child's rocker and turned to leave. Again Jessie was hit with unease.

Turning back to Sarah's bed, she froze.

It was empty.

CHAPTER FORTY-FOUR

*S*arah?"

No answer.

"Sarah? Come out here right now! I'm in no mood for silly games."

There was still no reply, and Jessie's heart began to pound uncontrollably. *Calm down*, she told herself. *She has to be here. Think!*

"Sweetie, your porridge is done. Come to the table and you can put some honey on it."

Jessie waited. A noise. She wanted to hear Sarah coming out of hiding. Needed to see her running, jumping into her arms. But there was only silence. "I'm not playing, Sarah," Jessie whispered, barely able to get the words out. "I'm not playing…"

Scraping in the other room grabbed Jessie's attention. Her breath came out in a gush of relief, and she ran to the kitchen to find Patches nosing her milk dish hungrily. With a pitiful mew, the kitten rubbed against Jessie's leg.

She picked up the kitty for a moment and rubbed the soft fur against her cheek. Then panic enveloped her. Putting the cat down, she flung the door open and rushed outside. "Sarah!" she yelled.

Chase and Gabe heard her screams a good quarter mile away. Leaving the fence they'd been mending, Chase jumped on his horse and galloped all the way back to the ranch. The gelding leaped and surged through snowdrifts, his powerful legs straining with each effort.

Sliding to a stop, Chase vaulted from the saddle.

"Jessie!"

Around the front of the ranch house Jessie came, fighting her way through the snow. Her skirt was wet and her eyes wild with fear.

He grabbed her shoulders.

"Where's Sarah?"

"Gone."

"What do you mean?"

"She wasn't in her bed when I got up." Jessie's voice shook so hard she could barely get the words out. "The door was ajar. I've looked everywhere, Chase! She's gone!"

By this time, Gabe came rattling up in the wagon. "What is it? Where's Sarah?" His voice cracked with anguish.

"I don't know. It's as if she's just disappeared."

"Sarah!" Gabe's powerful voice rang out crisply, all boyishness gone. "Sarah?"

Chase turned Jessie toward the house. "Get back inside and get your old shotgun out. Stay there while Gabe and I search the area."

"I won't. I'm looking for Sarah too."

"No, you'll do as I say," Chase said sternly. "If I have to worry about you, I'll be distracted. I need to know you're safely locked away in the house. Besides, there's a chance Sarah just wandered off and will come back." He didn't believe it, but if it kept Jessie in the house, that's just what he'd meant to do. The child wasn't within hearing distance; he'd bet his life on it. "You don't want her finding the house empty, do you?"

"Of course not," Jessie cried. "I just want to find her. Bring her back, Chase. Please find our little girl."

"We will. We'll find her." He smoothed the damp hair from her face and kissed her forehead.

"Chase, over here," Gabe shouted from behind the smoke shack. With Jake draped across his back, Gabe staggered out from behind the building, his friend's weight almost enough to topple him.

Chase ran to help. "Let's get him inside."

Jessie held the door open while Chase and Gabe carried Jake's limp form into the house and laid him on their bed. Chase covered him with a blanket.

He felt for Jake's pulse. "He's alive," Chase said, also checking the knot on his head. "He was hit pretty darn hard, though. I'd say he's lucky to be breathing. You'll have to tend to him, Jessie. I've got to go after Sarah."

Jessie gasped. "You think someone's taken her?" She turned from wrapping Jake in another blanket.

Chase nodded grimly. "I'm afraid it's looking that way, what with this done to Jake. Gabe—" He turned abruptly to the boy. "Now that Jake's unconscious and I know what I'm looking for, you're going to stay here with Jessie."

"No!" Gabe shouted.

Chase all but lost his temper. "Listen to me. With the other hands in town, I need someone here in case whoever took Sarah decides to return."

Gabe's face was hot with defiance. Shaking his head, he fished in his pocket and pulled out something in his hand. "I found this in the snow lying next to Jake. Whoever hit him must have dropped it."

Jessie's eyes opened wide. "Let me see that," she said in a wobbly voice. She took the silver, heart-shaped locket from Gabe and turned it over. The name *Jessie* was there for everyone to see. She looked up at Chase in confusion.

"This is mine. I gave it to Nathan when we got married. He kept it with him always. What could this mean?"

Chase's mind went blank. In all his happiness of the last few weeks, he'd pushed away the detail of Jessie's stolen money and the locket. He'd tried to tell her several times, but he could never quite make it sound right. Besides, in light of their marriage and the new ranch and everything that'd happened, it all seemed irrelevant now. A forgotten piece of the past. One that could rip his happiness apart. His heart thumped in his chest and his guilt beckoned. Jessie must have seen his recognition.

"Chase?"

"It *is* your locket."

She looked from his face down to the heart in her hand and then back into his eyes. "How do you know?"

"Because I was supposed to give it to you when I delivered the news about Nathan. There was also his pay, six hundred and ninety-eight dollars. But with all the commotion over the adoption, and then…Well, I forgot to give it to you before I rode out."

He couldn't stand to watch as her understanding dawned. The love he'd grown so used to seeing, feeling, was replaced with suspicion and hurt.

Deflated, Jessie pulled a chair from the kitchen table and sat slowly, thinking. The tension was thick, smothering. Moments ticked by, and Patches jumped into her lap. Jessie buried her face in the cat's soft fur.

"*That's* why you came back," she whispered, still holding Patches to her face. Chase and Gabe stood as still as stone. Now, she turned and looked up at him. "To return my money. Not because you wanted to help me. Not out of the goodness in your heart as I so naively thought, but because you *owed* it to me. Isn't that right?"

CHAPTER FORTY-FIVE

*C*hase wanted to lie in the worst of ways. To make up some far-fetched story, fabricate his way out of this nightmare. But he couldn't. Not to Jessie.

"That's right."

Her eyes moved around the room slowly as she put the pieces of the puzzle together. "And," she began unhurriedly as she stood and walked over to the window and looked out, "when you came back, when you were acting like you were going to bed me, *that* was all to *punish me*—for the mix-up with Mr. Hobbs."

Despite the cold, Chase broke out in a sweat. "Yes."

She whirled around so he could see her face. It was no longer pensive and sad, but flushed and furious.

"And everything you've ever done since then has been a lie!"

"No, that's not true," he said in his defense. "Every time I'd decide to return it, I'd get sidetracked and forget. Then the day before our wedding I realized it had been stolen when I'd been shot."

Jessie gasped for breath as if she'd been sucker-punched. Her brows crashed down and her face scrunched in an expression of great sorrow, causing Chase a pain so deep in his heart it would last a lifetime. He took a step in her direction, but she held up her hand stopping him.

"Because," she continued, "you were going to return it to me that day and leave." Her voice was empty, but steely cold. "But when you found out it was gone, you felt *obligated* to marry me."

Her back was brutally straight, her nostrils flared, and if she'd had a gun, Chase was almost certain she'd have used it on him.

Gabe inched his way to the door. Chase stilled him with a look. "I will explain everything to you after I find Sarah. Right now, every second counts."

"You're right. Nothing else matters but that."

Her hollow voice pierced his soul. He tried to take her hands, but she jerked them away with such force, he was shocked. "I'll bring her back, Jessie. I promise."

Outside, by his horse, he gave the cinch a hard, tightening pull. He checked his saddlebags for extra cartridges and took the rifle Gabe offered. Jessie watched them from the porch. Her grief-stricken face pierced his heart. Swinging into the saddle like a man gone mad, he galloped off.

Chase rode through the trees as if pursued by demons, dodging snow-covered limbs that reached out seemingly to snatch him from the saddle. Frigid wind bit at his ears and stung his cheeks. With the freshly fallen snow, the trail he was looking for was easy to find and follow.

Only one horse.

He'd promised Jessie he'd bring Sarah back, and he would. Come hell or high water, nothing could keep him from finding his little girl. "Hang on, sweetheart," he said under his breath. "Pa's coming."

Pushing Cody as long as he safely could, he finally reined the gelding in so he could catch his breath. The horse's flanks were frothy and his chest heaved as he sucked in air. Great streams of white steam pumped from his nostrils.

The weight of his twin Colts pressed reassuringly on Chase's thighs. He scanned the area. It looked disturbed in several different directions.

"Either he doesn't know which way to go, or he's trying to confuse me."

Cody threw his head, snorting his impatience. Chase circled once, and then twice, looking for the trail.

Then he spotted it. A dark crimson blotch on the glistening white snow.

Blood!

Just one small drop. Then, as he approached, another. Trying not to think what it might mean, he pressed his spurs urgently into Cody's sides. Bounding through the lodge pines, Chase suddenly came upon a gigantic expanse of flat rocks. The trees surrounding it were dense and thick, and had protected the rocks from the snowfall. They were virtually bare and dry.

He dismounted and led Cody slowly over the large, smooth stones. Tracking on this would be difficult, as the horse he was following wasn't wearing shoes. Sarah's captor must have headed for these rocks purposely.

"What kind of man takes a little girl from her bed?" he said aloud in his frustration. Squatting, he ran his fingers across a scarring on top of the rock where the horse had slipped. But where did he go? He was losing time. Every moment, every tick of the clock took Sarah farther away.

Standing, Chase searched the hilltops. "Couldn't just disappear." Chase turned and looked behind at where he'd just come. Searching the area carefully was out of the question—it would take too much time.

Crushing fear. He gasped. He'd lost the trail. Which way had they gone? He gazed up into the expanse of the bright morning sky, thinking. He turned a full circle. Seconds turned into a minute. *What now? What the hell now?* Overwhelmed, he removed his hat, and then ground his thumb and knuckle into his stinging eyes.

Slowly, a warm calm descended over Chase. Something about the sun's reflection on the clouds drew his attention. He stared at them, just taking in the sight. Time slowed down, quiet enveloped him, his senses fairly hummed until he could feel each and every beat of his heart. Then he did something he'd never done in his life. He sank to his knees and closed his eyes.

"God?" He stopped at the desperate sound of his voice. "God, are you there? Jessie says you are. Well, I believe her. I need your help. Sarah needs you. Show me the way."

At that moment a breeze picked up and ruffled Chase's hair. It was cold and felt good against his face. Chase opened his eyes and staggered to his feet. Wedging his hat on, he picked up Cody's reins. Unexpectedly, a thought came to mind. He remembered hearing about a trick that the Indian scouts used when tracking. He mounted, giving Cody his head.

For several agonizing moments, Cody just stood there. Then, purposefully, the horse started off to the west, picking his way over the slippery, flat stones. Chase released his breath slowly, unaware he'd been holding it.

Time seemed to stand still. It was maddening not knowing whether they were even headed in the right direction.

Twenty minutes later, he saw an end to the rocks and the beginning of a snow bank picked up. Undisturbed snow surrounded him.

There was not a track in sight.

"Is this the way?" This was not what he'd been hoping for. As he sat trying to figure out what to do next, the sounds of running water caught his attention. To the left, at the edge of the outcropping of rocks, was a stream. He nudged his horse in. North. South was back toward the ranch. He didn't think the rider would double back at this point. Gut feelings and a prayer were all he had left.

A good five hundred yards up the stream, a trail exited the water. Next to the bank was a pile of fresh horse manure.

Chase proceeded carefully, knowing he couldn't be that far behind. Every few feet he'd stop and listen, straining to hear the slightest sound. Barreling in and getting himself killed wouldn't do Sarah any good.

Suddenly, Cody's head jerked up, and he looked to the left. Chase swung off, covering the horse's muzzle. When Cody lost interest, Chase looped one rein around a branch and left the gelding behind. He made his way carefully through the brush, silently drawing his gun from its holster. He forced all thought from his head. Out of habit, he checked the gun's chambers, knowing full well they were loaded.

"Quit your whinin', you little sniveler. You want to end up like this here horse?" a voice snarled out. "You best learn to behave yourself, 'cause you ain't never seeing your ma again."

Sarah's alive! A flash of relief ripped through Chase. He couldn't see her yet, but he could hear her soft cries.

"You better start running," Chase growled under his breath, his heart rate quickening as he barely controlled his urge to rush to Sarah. "Hold on, sweetheart." At that moment, Cody nickered.

Chase caught sight of his quarry in time to see the man snatch Sarah by the wrist and jump back, wedging spiderlike into a crevice between two rocks. The man's horse lay stretched on the ground, ridden to death.

"I know you're there," the man called. "Throw down your gun and show your stinkin' hide or I'll be a plugging this here purdy little girl child."

Staying out of sight, Chase edged around some trees, then dug through the snow for a rock. With a heave, he sent it sailing up and over to the right.

The boom of the man's shotgun echoed through the forest. Sarah screamed. Chase advanced and then dove behind some rocks, slipping closer to the pair.

"Shut your screaming mouth before I shut it for you." The sound of a slap filled the air. Then silence.

Chase's gut tightened. He gritted his teeth. "Touch her again, and you'll be begging to die when I get through with you!" Chase shouted, his heart beating wildly.

"Big words, big words."

Chase spotted a small ridge up behind their hiding place. If he could just get up there without being noticed, he might have a clear shot.

"Who are you, and what do you want with the child?" Chase hoped his question would keep the man talking while he made his way around and up.

"Don't you know? Didn't that sassy gal of yours tell you? I'm takin' this here girl in place of my kin, Lonnie. It's your fault he's dead."

"My fault! Your brother deserved to hang. He only got what he had coming," Chase said. "Anyway, he was alive the last time I saw him."

"Got gut shot trying to escape. That woman of yours is to blame. Lonnie used to watch her getting water from the stream. It was close to our claim. If she hadn't been sashaying around the store that day, Lonnie'd be alive today."

"So—it was you who shot me."

The man hawked and spit. "Not me. Lonnie."

Chase eased his way up the bluff and crawled on his belly through the snow.

"Poor Lonnie," the man continued. "Gut shot's a lousy way to go. And that's what I'll do to you—and leave you in the snow to die slow."

Chase could almost see him now. And Sarah too. A little farther and he'd have a clear shot. He inched behind a pine tree and peered around. There. It was the no-account they'd met on the road. Chase hunkered down, waiting for his chance.

CHAPTER FORTY-SIX

*W*here'd you sneak off to?"

Chase watched as he hauled Sarah up by her arm. Her eyes were wild with fear as she cowered back from his face.

Rage pounded through every inch of Chase's body. This was his Sarah, his sweet little girl. Memories of her curled up quietly on the foot of his bed that first morning shot through his heart. Her somber eyes, her shy, beguiling smile. The man gripping her now was buying himself a one-way ticket straight to hell.

Chase peered down the hill, never taking his eyes from the pair. The man seemed edgy and nervous, looking around for Chase. Frightened animals were dangerous, and so were panicky men. He needed Sarah out of there now, before Lonnie's brother did something rash. The man called out again.

"You, out there. Speak up, or I'll hurt her." The man squeezed her wrist, and Sarah whimpered. "Louder, I need him to hear." With that he grabbed Sarah by the back of her hair and gave it a good jerk.

Sweat broke out over Chase's body. If Sarah weren't in the way, he'd have drilled him already between his beady little snake eyes. Get this torture over with. He could hit him easily from this distance.

"Get down, Sarah," Chase whispered to himself. "Get down."

Without warning, the man lifted Sarah and darted out of his hiding place. He fought his way through the snow as he ran down the hillside, shotgun in one hand, Sarah in the other.

Where does he think he's going? Chase wondered. Without a horse, the man didn't stand a chance of getting away.

"Hold up," Chase yelled, shooting into the air.

The man dove to the ground, landing with a thud. Rolling onto his side, he slung his arm around Sarah and pulled her in front of him.

"Let her go!" Chase shouted. "Now!" Running behind the trees, he made his way closer to the pair.

"Can't do that." Unexpectedly, the man looked confused, as if he was just now realizing his predicament. Sarah's gaze was glued to the spot where she'd heard Chase's voice, her face frozen with fear.

"Gol' darn horse," the man sputtered. "If he hadn't up and died…" Suddenly he laughed loudly, crazily. "Just like the girl in Clancy. She weren't supposed to die neither…"

"Let her go," Chase demanded.

"Whoops—here she comes." The man shoved Sarah forward, at the same time swinging his shotgun up and firing in Chase's direction.

Sarah landed facedown in the snow and, to Chase's relief, stayed put. Chase returned fire, killing the man with one shot.

Chase bounded down the hill. He scooped Sarah up and held her tight against his heart. Relief, so acute it was nearly painful, flooded his senses.

Sarah, trembling uncontrollably, wrapped her arms around him and buried her face in his neck.

"I'd say you're glad to see me, pumpkin," he said finally when he composed himself, his voice husky. Turning his head, he gave her a kiss on her tear-stained cheek. "You're about as soft as a goose-down pillow."

Sarah's lips curled in a small smile, and she laid her cold hand lightly on his cheek, gazing into his eyes. "Da," she whispered.

Chase's throat closed. He ground his fingers into his burning eyes, wiping away the moisture. When he turned, he held her so she couldn't see the man lying a few feet away, his sightless eyes staring at the sky.

He gave a long whistle, and within moments Cody came loping through the trees, his reins trailing beside him. Setting Sarah in the saddle, he climbed up behind her. She was wet, shivering violently from the cold. He quickly unbuttoned his heavy coat, and then turned Sarah around and drew her close, folding her legs up and wrapping her arms around his trunk. Then he buttoned the coat up around her, so she could share his body heat.

Throughout the ride back, she was quiet and still, and it seemed he could feel her with every beat of his heart.

It was almost dark when Chase finally reached the ranch. Jessie came through the door. When she saw him, her face dropped, clouding with pain. It was clear she didn't see the child hidden beneath his coat.

"She's here," Chase called from twenty feet away. He patted his coat. Sarah had warmed up on the long ride home and had kept him toasty warm in the process.

Jessie bolted down the stairs and ran up to his horse, waiting for him to dismount. "Is she...?"

"She's all right. She's fine. She's asleep."

"Let me have her," Jessie said anxiously, reaching up.

"I'll take her inside," Chase replied, dismounting.

"Can you take care of Cody?" Chase asked Gabe, who'd followed Jessie out. "He'll need extra care." The boy nodded.

Jessie ran forward and opened the door.

Inside by the fire, Chase unbuttoned his coat and handed the sleeping child to Jessie, who cuddled her close in her arms. She kissed her warm, dewy cheek but Sarah didn't wake up. Jessie glanced into Chase's face. In her expression was something he'd never seen before, something he couldn't discern.

"How's Jake?" he asked, trying to sound all business, when inside he was as shaky as aspen leaves in the wind.

"He has a very bad headache, but other than that I think he will be fine in a day or two. Who took Sarah?"

"Lonnie's brother. After we turned Lonnie in, he tried to escape and was shot and killed in the process. Absurdly, because of us turning him in, his brother blamed us for his death, instead of Lonnie's own actions. In his sick way he was exchanging one person for the other."

"Is he...?" she slowly asked, her face guarded.

Chase nodded.

Jessie looked up, Sarah sleeping in her arms. He saw her heart in her eyes, but something else too. Regret, sadness, heartbreak...

"It's over, Chase." The words were spoken quietly, but rang through his head loud and long.

"I thought you might say that," he replied. "But I'm the one who's leaving—not you."

"I won't let you up and give me everything belonging to you," Jessie said, her eyes snapping.

"When?"

Jessie averted her eyes. "As soon as I can get a few things packed," she whispered. "Daybreak tomorrow."

Chase sat at the supper table, one hand holding a coffee mug, the other drumming restlessly. Awkward silence filled the room as Jessie heated water for Jake.

"Chase, you out there?" Jake called from the bedroom.

Chase stood, stretched his back, then went to see Jake.

"I let you down." Jake winced as he spoke. "When I saw that man behind the smokehouse, I went to see what he was up to, and whack, he hit me over the head."

Chase rolled the matchstick he held between his teeth. "Didn't let me down. I'm just glad you weren't hurt worse." He leaned over and looked at Jake's head. He gave a long whistle. "How's it feel?"

"Better now. But for a while I thought my head just might split directly down the middle." His hand came up and he gingerly inspected the injured area. "Jessie's willow-bark tea has helped considerably."

Jake's color was almost back to normal, but the huge lump on his forehead was taking on a purplish tint, its edges black and gray.

Chase glanced at Jessie, who was standing in the doorway. "You're getting pretty good at your doctoring; Mrs. Hollyhock would be proud. Will that willow tea help my aching back any?"

She looked tired as she moved about the kitchen. "Don't see why not." Her shoulders drooped, and he wished he could hold her, cuddle her. Heck, he desperately wanted to make love to her... restore her hope and feel the fire he knew burned deep inside.

She turned. His gaze held hers. She quickly lowered her lashes, but not before he saw the yearning, the glowing desire shining in her eyes.

His chest tightened with regret as her cheeks tinged with color. His emotions grew slowly and steadily into a thunderous storm of confused feelings. Yesterday he would have scooped her up and carried her off to their bedroom. How had things changed so fast? Daybreak was only a few short hours away.

CHAPTER FORTY-SEVEN

*T*he inky black of the eastern sky eased to gray as Chase sat sulking. Streaks of light, hair-thin lines of pink and white, criss-crossed the horizon. He'd been sitting in the same position on the cold front porch now for over two hours. His back muscles screamed for release, but he wouldn't give them any. A self-punishment of sorts, he thought.

Jessie had pulled out an hour ago, taking with her Sarah, Gabe, and, surprisingly, Jake too. She'd said that since she was unable to sleep, she may as well get started. It would be easier for Sarah to awaken in the wagon on their way to town than having to say good-bye to her pa.

Her pa!

Gabe and Jake had been stunned when Jessie had first told them that they'd be heading back to their old home soon. And then their disappointment had turned into something else. Bitterness.

Jake had said that he'd ride back, help them make the trip to Valley Springs, and then he was heading out to California, inviting Gabe to come along. Gabe had declined the offer, saying his place was with Jessie and Sarah. That he'd be the one looking after them from now on.

The boy would do a good job. He'd been doing a great job already. He'd proved that he could track, hunt, drive the wagon, and just about everything else they would need a man to do.

But what about Jessie?

She'd get over him and someday find another man to fall in love with. When she got settled, he'd send her that telegram he'd planned way back, when they were first discussing how they would end this marriage that had started out as a sham. Then he'd sell the ranch and head out to the West Coast himself. Maybe his destiny lay somewhere out there.

Sighing, he ran his hand across his tired face, feeling the thick growth of whiskers. He hadn't had a chance to shave for three days. First his mares had arrived early, and he'd spent all that day getting them to quiet down. The next morning Sarah had been abducted, and now this morning his wife and family had packed up and left. It wouldn't matter much if he never shaved again.

Without warning, his mind flashed back to Jessie running her hands over his freshly shaved cheeks, marveling over how soft they felt. Gently touching a nick he'd left in his chin. Drawing his face close. Kissing him. Taking his breath away with her tenderness.

Jessie!

Had he ever told her that he loved her? He'd kept that wonderful secret to himself.

One of the horses nickered from the corral. He knew he should get up. Tend to the animals, do chores. Still he didn't move.

The horse nickered again.

"All right, I'm coming." The new mares, which had brought him so much satisfaction before, now left him cold. They were well bred for working cattle and would do fine to build this ranch. Muscular hips and fine sloping shoulders. Small heads with intelligent eyes.

Chase laughed without humor, amused at how fast a dream could turn into a nightmare. They were merely horses, nothing more, animals that could easily be replaced.

He stroked one velvety muzzle and headed back to the house. Normally Jessie would be greeting him with a hot cup of coffee and a shy smile, one that couldn't hide the pleasure she'd been learning in his arms.

He went to the stove and filled his cup with the lukewarm sludge that had formed in the bottom of the pot. Taking a sip, he winced. Impatiently he set his cup on the table and paced over to the fire. The house was too quiet. It was too easy to hear his regrets taunting him, like specters in some ghoulish play.

This was absurd. He needed to get busy and stop feeling sorry for himself. He always knew deep in his heart that this would be the way things would end up. All he needed now was a diversion. He'd get cleaned up and ride into town, tell Frank to sell this place lock, stock, and barrel to the highest bidder. Then he'd be on his way.

Standing at the porcelain pitcher in their bedroom, Chase lathered his face with shaving soap. He swiped the sharp razor across his chin. The little shelf that hung next to the mirror called to him. He looked. Jessie must have forgotten her bottle of vanilla. Cursing himself for a fool, he pulled the stopper and breathed in the homey sweetness. His chest tightened.

Finishing up, he went over to where his clean shirt hung on a peg on the wall. As he pulled it over his shoulders, he glanced down. Poking out of the covers on his side of the bed was Sarah's doll, the one she'd been holding the morning she'd woken him from his laudanum-induced sleep. Tenderness filled his chest.

He picked it up and fingered where one of its button eyes had come off. Sarah had cried when it happened, saying her dolly couldn't see. But Jessie, cradling her, had promised to sew a new eye back on.

Chase stared at the one-eyed doll. Releasing his breath, he sat on the edge of the bed and cradled his head in the palms of his hands. Moments ticked by. A feeling of anticipation stole over him. Was it a coincidence that the doll was stuck in his side of the bed? Had Sarah placed it there? Or was it possibly more?

Maybe a sign?

Was he wrong about being responsible for the things that had happened in his past? His conscience screamed yes, he was responsible. Molly may still be alive today if not for him being gone. And yet his heart whispered no.

That one he'd have to work on.

He was being a blind fool. He held up the tattered doll and contemplated her. Time stopped. Minutes ticked by as he struggled for understanding.

Jessie directed Gabe to pull up in front of the Red Rooster Inn, the boarding house on the outskirts of town. The kind people of Logan Meadows would learn the truth about her and Chase soon enough, and she didn't think she could bear the sympathetic looks that were sure to come her way if she stayed at the popular place in the center of everything. Thanks to Frank Lloyd, the townspeople had welcomed them with open arms, and within days of their arrival she was receiving invitations to quilting parties and ladies' teas.

Her hand snaked down protectively to her abdomen. How could Chase have let them go so easily? He could barely even look at her when they'd left that morning. She couldn't believe the love she'd felt from him the past month was all a charade. But it was. And she had to move on. Her plan was to stay in town until they were ready to travel. Then, with the boys' help, she could make the trip back. Maybe since Beth was now gone, Mrs. Hollyhock would want some company and help in the store.

"Do you want me to get us a couple of rooms, Jessie?" Gabe wrapped the reins around the wagon brake.

"No. It's too early to wake them. We'll just wait in the wagon until we hear someone stirring inside. Besides, I don't want to wake Sarah just yet after the time she had yesterday."

She squared her shoulders. She was through feeling sorry for herself. She'd taken care of herself before. Certainly, she could do it again.

Not that the thought of being on her own again wasn't completely scary. Especially now with Sarah and the new baby. Had these kinds of circumstances forced her mother to abandon her for her own good? Had she done her best for as long as she could? Things weren't quite as black and white to Jessie any longer. Sympathy for her mother replaced her anger and disappointment. A seed of forgiveness blossomed and began to grow.

Chase took the steps of the Red Rooster Inn slowly, one at a time, and stopped just short of the door. Removing his hat, he rubbed the spot where he'd been wounded by Lonnie's bullet.

If he knew Jessie, her pride wasn't going to want to hear him out. He kept reminding himself he'd never told her that he loved her. He was ashamed of himself for that. Even after all this time. And all the nights they'd spent together.

How was she supposed to know what lay buried in his heart? Certainly, she'd know by his actions? Well, maybe not. He couldn't blame her if she didn't want to speak to him.

He was stalling. He knew it. Not giving himself any more time to think, he lifted his hand and rapped twice on the door. Expecting Dora Lee, the proprietress, to answer, Chase was stunned into silence when Mrs. Hollyhock stepped through the door. Her back was ramrod straight and ready for battle.

"Well, well, well," she eyed him coolly. "Jist what have we here?" Apparently, she hadn't missed him in the least.

"I want to talk to Jessie." Just the sight of her know-it-all gaze had him seeing red.

"She ain't here."

"Like hell she's not. The wagon is out front as plain as day."

The old woman, no taller that a child, pulled the door closed behind her, its click ringing loud with triumph. "She don't want to see you."

Chase counted to ten...and then to twenty. "Ask her."

"No. She's resting."

It was a standoff. Chase had the sinking feeling he wasn't going to get past this one-granny army without a fight. "Dora Lee," he called in a loud, commanding voice. "It's Chase Logan. I need to talk to you."

Mrs. Hollyhock's eyes lit with pleasure. She all but preened. "Ain't no use calling for Dora Lee. She's gone and sold the place ta me. Garth bought my old store in Valley Springs and kept my cousin Virgil on." She smiled sweetly. "Ain't ya gonna welcome me ta town?"

Frustrated, Chase crushed the brim of his hat in his hands. He lowered his voice. "Please."

"Mornin', Chase," Frank Lloyd said, riding up. He dismounted and tied his horse to the hitching post. "I see you've met our newest citizen of Logan Meadows."

Chase stared at his longtime friend. "Yes, I have." This was getting more interesting by the moment.

"After the papers were signed yesterday, Mrs. Hollyhock invited me over for a celebratory cup of coffee and a piece of her famous peach cobbler," Frank said. "I can hardly wait. By the way..." He looked at Chase inquisitively. "What are you doing here so early?"

It looked like he was going to have to bare his soul. That is, if he wanted Jessie back badly enough. And of course there was no question about that. He still felt as though he could throttle this busybody, but now maybe he wouldn't have to.

"I'm here to talk to Jessie."

Frank's eyebrows rose in question. "She's inside?"

Chase nodded. "*We*"—he gestured to Mrs. Hollyhock—"were just *discussing* the possibilities of me speaking with my *wife!*"

Mrs. Hollyhock clucked her tongue. She reached for Frank's arm but never left her position guarding the door. "Now don't go getting sassy. She's lying down. Resting. Her being in the family way and all."

Chase felt as if he'd been poleaxed. "What did you say?"

"Jessie has a bun in the oven. You know—she's caught." When he still didn't answer she grabbed her skirt and held it far out in front of her tiny body. "*Expecting?*"

Frank crushed him in his arms. "Congratulations, boy! I knew you had it in you."

Mrs. Hollyhock, as if knowing she couldn't hold him off any longer, stepped aside. He hurried through the door and looked around. Gabe and Jake sat quietly on the chesterfield, while Sarah played with some blocks on the floor. They'd been listening all along. Sarah smiled sweetly. Gabe pointed down the hall.

He was by Jessie's side in four long strides. Kneeling next to the bed on one knee, he took her hand and pressed it to his lips. "Why didn't you tell me?" he asked, his voice grave with emotion.

She blinked and looked away. "I was saving it for Christmas."

"Ah, Jessie." He reached out and took her into his arms. He cuddled her against his chest and stroked her hair.

"I love you," he whispered close to her ear. He nuzzled the nape of her neck, and the warmth of her skin tickled his senses. "I can't live without you." When she didn't answer right away, he thought maybe she hadn't heard what he'd said. "I love you so much, just the thought of never seeing you again...is too much to bear." His body jerked with emotion and he felt her hand caress his back. Reluctantly, he lifted himself to look into her face. "Say something, sweetheart. Please."

"I'm afraid, Chase. I don't want to trap you. And now that you know about the baby, you'll stay just for it." The regret in her voice tore at his insides.

He shook his head and tenderly kissed her forehead. "No, that's not true. I was already coming to bring you home. No matter what you said, I was determined to show you how much I love you. You belong with me. I never knew about the baby."

"Are you…sure?"

"He's sure as the manure he's traipsing across my clean floorboards." Mrs. Hollyhock's voice escalated as she gawked at the mess he'd brought in. She lifted her shotgun for all to see, but her eyes sparkled with unshed tears. "If he knows what's good fer him, he's sure."

Gabe, Jake, and Frank, who was holding little Sarah, burst out laughing. Against his will, Chase had to join in.

"See, honey?" He winked at Jessie, who radiated with happiness. "A man can't be any more sure than that."

EPILOGUE

*C*hristmas morning festivities were interrupted by a knock on the door. Jake jumped up from his seat by the fire, slowed not a bit by the lump on his head. The wound was healing slowly, but he'd announced repeatedly it would take more than a little knock on the head to stop him. The peppermint stick he'd found in his stocking was clenched between his teeth.

He opened the door.

"It's Mr. Lloyd," he called over his shoulder to Chase and Jessie. Gabe and Sarah were off in the kitchen warming some milk for hot cocoa.

Frank stepped in, shaking a dusting of newly fallen snow from his hat. "Sorry to barge in on Christmas Day."

Chase was at his side in a moment, taking his coat and squeezing his friend in a bear hug. "You're not barging in. You're family. You're always welcome here." Merriment reverberated from Chase's deep voice as Jessie stepped over into Chase's embrace. "And Merry Christmas," he added as he ran his hand lovingly down Jessie's arm.

Jessie's smile lit up her whole face. "Come in and sit down."

Frank moved slower than normal, and Chase wondered at the reason. Usually his friend was unstoppable, the center of attention. He looked uneasy.

"What is it, Frank?"

Frank ran a hand through his thick hair and gazed into the fire.

"I have some news. Good news. I thought you'd want it right away." His voice was serious, soft, and Jake withdrew slowly into the kitchen to give the adults their privacy.

Chase, already sitting again, leaned forward as if he could draw the information from his friend.

"Tell us, Frank. Out with it."

It didn't look like good news to Jessie. Her heart wedged itself up into her throat, and she felt like she might be sick. Automatically her hand dropped protectively to her bulging tummy as if to comfort the child growing inside. Whatever this news was, it wasn't good, and would most assuredly change her life. Laughter came from the kitchen, and the sweetness of the sound almost made her cry.

Chase nodded. "Frank?"

Frank cleared his throat. "It seems when Maude remodeled the mercantile years ago, she took sick and had to stay home for a few days. Since she wasn't there to ride herd over the carpenters, they did a shoddy job, not careful with important things. When they were moving the mail counter to the opposite side of the room, some letters fell into the open wall, and they were just discovered today. Maude had a snake in the store yesterday, and she ripped a few boards out to find the varmint."

His face was akin to the snow outside. He held out a letter. "From Molly."

Everything slowed down for Jessie. Like being in a dream, her arms and legs were instantly paralyzed, and she was rooted to her seat. Sucking in her breath took effort as she watched Chase ever so slowly reach out and take the dusty, bent envelope. He studied the letters spelling his name. Turning his head, he met her gaze. His eyes said it all.

Frank stood. "Let me know if there's anything I can do, or if I can help in any way." He went to the door and took his hat from the peg. "Merry Christmas."

Chase just looked at the envelope for several moments. His thumb brushed back and forth across the writing; and then he handed it to Jessie. She tried to read his dark, shuttered eyes, interpret his expression. His chest rose and fell, his hand shook. No words were needed. She slowly opened the post.

The paper was gray from lying in the dank wall. It smelled of mold and dirt. Remnants of what may have been a flower at one time fell out and dusted Jessie's lap. The writing inside was scribbled as if it had been written in great haste. It was dated September 8, 1871. "'My dearest Chase,'" Jessie read:

By the time you get this letter I will be a married woman. I hope someday you will forgive me for what I have done. Part of my heart will always belong only to you.

Please try to understand that when Hank came into town I knew we were destined to be together, forever. I ain't proud we robbed the bank. I'm feeling mighty bad 'bout that. And what the townspeople must think of me I can't even imagine. But wishing won't make it different.

Jessie glanced at Chase before turning the paper over. He held his head in his hands, staring at the floor. She continued.

I hurt mostly when I ponder what the scandal would do to you. I pray it weren't too bad. I have to hurry now because we're moving on and I've only got a few moments more to finish or this letter will never get in the United States mail.

We've been traveling by horseback and I'm dirty and smell about as good as my old henhouse. I'd give anything to stop for a spell and bathe.

Outlawing ain't as romantic as it sounds. But no regrets.

With deepest fondness,

Molly

Jessie finished reading and sat quietly. Chase was overwhelmed with emotion. All those years! The answer had been right under his nose all the time. And robbing the bank too. Not in his wildest dreams had he or anyone else ever suspected she was in on that job.

A tear ran down his cheek and dropped onto his boot.

"Chase?" Jessie's voice was soft. "What can I do to help?"

"There's nothing." He lifted his face and looked at her. She was a sight, and his heart swelled. "I just wonder if there'd been something I could've done different. So she wouldn't end up"—he paused—"an outlaw. I just can't believe it."

"Do you want to look for her?"

Chase thought about her words for a few seconds. "I wouldn't have any idea where to start. I don't know her married name or even the direction they were heading."

Sarah ran into the room then, breaking the gloomy spell. She snuggled between Chase and Jessie, a chocolate mustache under her nose and a stick of peppermint in her hand.

Chase scooped her onto his lap and buried his face into her neck, bringing forth a gentle giggle. He held her a long moment before he lifted his face to look into hers. "How's my best girl? Was the chocolate good?"

She nodded and hugged him back in her shy fashion.

Chase didn't let Sarah go but scooted closer to Jessie and encircled her into the embrace, then whispered into her ear, "You're right. God does bring something good out of every bad situation. It's certain I don't even have to look very hard to find mine."

Jessie cuddled closer. She looked into his eyes, sending a shiver of delight into his heart. "You're my silver lining too."

ACKNOWLEDGMENTS

There are many people I'm grateful to for their help and support in this endeavor...

My wonderful family, husband, Michael, and sons, Matthew and Adam, for giving me time and space throughout the years to stay holed up in my office for hours on end. Their unconditional love and faith are my inspiration.

My sisters, Shelly, Sherry, Jenny, and Mary, for their enthusiasm and unwavering conviction. They always believed—even when I didn't.

Authors Susan Crosby, Theresa Ragan, Robin Burcell, Susan Grant, and Elana Willey—greatest critique partners ever—for their generous insight and guidance.

My amazing editor, Lindsay Guzzardo, for loving Chase and Jessie's story and for bringing it to life at Montlake.

And, last but not least, St. Anthony...my special friend and purveyor of miracles.

ABOUT THE AUTHOR

Photo by The Family Gallery, 2007

 Caroline Fyffe was born in Waco, Texas, the first of many towns she would call home during her father's career with the US Air Force. A horse aficionado from an early age, she earned a Bachelor of Arts in communications from California State University-Chico before launching what would become a twenty-year career as an equine photographer. She began writing fiction to pass the time during long days in the show arena, channeling her love of horses and the Old West into a series of Western historicals. Her debut novel, *Where the Wind Blows*, won the Romance Writers of America's prestigious Golden Heart Award as well as the Wisconsin RWA's Write Touch Readers' Award. She and her husband have two grown sons and live in Kentucky.

40025565R00174

Made in the USA
Middletown, DE
01 February 2017